H

DUST TO DUST

KEN MCCLURE is the internationally bestselling author of medical thrillers such as *The Lazarus Strain*, *The Gulf Conspiracy*, *Hypocrites' Isle* and *White Death*. His books have been translated into over twenty languages and he has earned a reputation for meticulous research and the chilling accuracy of his predictions. McClure's work is informed by his background as an award-winning research scientist with the UK's Medical Research Council.

Other Titles by Ken McClure

DUST TO DUST

Ken McClure

Polygon

First published in Great Britain in 2010
by Polygon, an imprint of Birlinn Ltd
West Newington House
10 Newington Road
Edinburgh
EH9 1QS

www.birlinn.co.uk

ISBN: 978 1 84697 126 6

British Library Cataloguing-in-Publication Data
A catalogue record for this book is available
on request from the British Library

Typeset in Adobe Garamond by Palimpsest Book Production Limited,
Grangemouth, Stirlingshire
Printed and bound by Clays Ltd, St Ives plc

For dust thou art and
unto dust shalt thou return.

Genesis 3:19

ONE

'But this is crazy. Are you absolutely sure?'

'Yes, sir, I'm afraid there's no doubt. The test results were absolutely crystal clear.'

While clinics and consulting rooms in the public domain tend to look the part, with equipment and medical paraphernalia much in evidence and the smells of antisepsis lingering in the air, those in the private sector strive for the opposite. Sir Laurence Samson's consulting rooms in Harley Street were very much the model of English town-house furnishing at its best, giving well-heeled patients the assurance that money and privilege would help with medical care as it had in all other areas of their lives.

'Christ,' said the young man, sinking down into a leather armchair as if he'd suddenly lost the power of his legs. 'You've just sentenced me to death, Samson.'

Sir Laurence maintained an uneasy silence.

The young man rubbed his forehead, as if subconsciously trying to erase the terrifying implications of the news he had been given. 'How long have I got?'

Samson attempted a calming gesture with his hands. 'Let's not dwell on that, sir. These days, with appropriate drugs and careful monitoring, the onset of major symptoms can be delayed considerably.'

'But in the end . . . it's going to get me, right?'

'There is no cure, I'm afraid.'

The young man stared into the abyss for fully thirty seconds.

'Would you like a glass of water, sir?'

'Fuck water, Samson, I need a drink.'

Sir Laurence thought for a moment, as if wondering whether or not to comply, before getting to his feet and walking over to a writing bureau which he opened to reveal a drinks cabinet. He poured a generous measure of neat malt whisky into a crystal tumbler and handed it to the young man.

'You're not joining me?' asked the young man accusingly. 'Is this the start of the journey down that long and lonesome road? Your doctor no longer drinks with you?'

'I still have other patients to see, sir.'

'Of course you have, Samson,' the young man conceded. 'Christ, what's my father going to say? This could kill him.' He swirled the contents of his glass one way and then the other. 'Of all the . . . Jesus Christ, what rotten luck. You won't tell him, will you?'

'I'm duty bound, of course, to keep whatever passes between us confidential, sir. But, if I may offer an opinion, I'd advise you to confide in him as soon as possible. The repercussions for you and your family are . . . well, I need hardly point that out to you.'

'Fucking enormous,' said the young man with an air of resignation, taking a last gulp of the whisky in search of some escape from the accusing arrows flighting into him. 'What are the chances of you chaps coming up with a cure in the near future?'

'Not good, sir, I'm afraid. I attended a conference on the subject three months ago and the general consensus was that we are no nearer that today than we were at the outset.'

'Don't beat about the bush, will you?' murmured the young man.

'I'm sorry, sir, but I don't see the point of false optimism. There are those who might take a different view, but their motives usually have more to do with the attraction of research funding than anything else.'

'I suppose I should be thanking you for levelling with me, Samson, but I find myself desperately in need of something other than plain unvarnished truth right now,' said the young man, swallowing and sniffing – just the once – as he fought with his emotions.

Samson gave a sympathetic nod. 'We should start you on the drugs I mentioned as soon as possible.'

The young man nodded and put down his glass, declining the offer of another with a shake of the head. 'I'll be in touch soon.'

'And your father, sir?'

'I'll inform him . . . once I've had a bit of time to come to terms with it myself.'

FOUR DAYS LATER

Sir Laurence Samson had explained to a female patient that tests had shown that she would be unlikely to conceive in the normal way, and was starting on an explanation of the alternatives when the phone on his desk rang. He picked it up, snapping, 'I specifically asked not to be disturbed, Eve.'

'I really think you should take this one, Sir Laurence,' the receptionist said calmly.

'Very well,' said Samson, already regretting having snapped at the woman who had been with him for six years and wouldn't have dreamt of interrupting without good cause, but he was on edge; he had been for the past four days. He offered an apologetic smile to his patient, then stiffened when he heard the voice. 'Yes, sir, it is.' He silently took in what was being said, aware of his patient's gaze and trying not to betray any emotion. 'Very well, sir, I take it you'd like me to come there? . . . Fine. Tell the driver I'll be at the Harley Street address . . . I'll see you at eight this evening.'

8 P.M.

Samson felt nervous, which for a man so used to being in control was an unusual experience, but his surroundings would have been intimidating to most. He felt as if he'd been thrust on to a stage in a starring role without full knowledge of the script or any real desire to be in the performance. He'd even had to wipe his palm free of moisture by surreptitiously reaching into his trouser pocket and scrunching up a tissue before shaking hands with his unsmiling host when he entered.

The formalities were brief; Samson declined the offer of refreshment.

'I think we should cut to the chase, Sir Laurence. My son has told me everything. God, what a mess.'

'It is most unfortunate, sir, but I'm afraid viruses are no respecters of . . .' Samson was about say wealth and privilege but thought better of it and settled for 'persons'. The stare he received in reply was not filled with understanding.

'I'm glad he confided in you at this early stage, sir,' Samson continued. 'It couldn't have been easy for him given the circumstances, but I feel duty bound to remind you at the outset that, as my patient, I'm still not at liberty to . . .'

'Yes, well, let's not bother with all that Hippocratic oath stuff,' Samson's host interrupted with a dismissive wave of the hand. 'It sounds like a tired line from a film. I don't want to discuss any of the details of the condition. I just want my son cured.

4

I want him well again. I need him to free himself of this . . . thing and resume the course of his life.'

Samson swallowed, an act made more difficult by the fact his mouth had gone dry, but he was thrown by the unexpected lack of rationale in what his host had just said. He found himself stammering, 'I'm sorry, sir . . . while it's perfectly possible to achieve a considerable period of . . . remission, if I can put it that way, a cure is simply not possible . . . at this stage at least . . . although of course advances in medical science are being made every day . . .'

'I'm told that a cure has already been achieved.'

Samson felt that the stare he was being subjected to was some kind of examination and one he was bound to fail. When the silence became unbearable, he decided to blink first. 'I'm sorry, sir, I don't think I understand . . . I appear to be unaware of the advance you refer to . . .'

'Since receiving this bloody awful news, I've been making enquiries – discreet enquiries – and I've been told that a cure for the condition is no longer outside the realms of possibility. There is apparently a valid alternative to simply lying down and accepting one's fate.'

Alarm bells rang in Samson's head on hearing the word 'alternative'. He feared he was about to be drawn into the world of complementary medicine, something he had little time for, believing its so-called 'therapies' to be either bogus or, at best, variations on the placebo effect. 'Really, sir?'

'As pioneered in Berlin.'

'Berlin?' echoed Samson, before suddenly realising what his host was referring to. 'Ah,' he said, looking down at his shoes as if not entirely pleased with the direction the conversation was moving in. 'I think I do recall something about the unique case you're referring to, sir.'

Samson's host was clearly annoyed at Samson's perceptible lack of enthusiasm. 'What is it about you medical people?' he demanded. 'You're so bloody conservative when it comes to anything new. Well, what do you think? Was a cure achieved or wasn't it?'

'I'm not exactly au fait with all the details of the case, sir, although of course I did read the reports. I would, however, say that ... sometimes *unusual* medical procedures are carried out on patients who are believed to be beyond help.'

'Are you suggesting this patient was used as an experimental animal?'

Samson threw up his hands in horror. 'Far be it from me to criticise the decisions of European colleagues. As I understand it, it was a one-off, carried out on a patient who was already facing a poor prognosis for other reasons. It was a very risky course of action and could perhaps only be justified by another condition the patient was suffering from. It was a very long way from being a routine procedure; it's doubtful whether it ever could be.'

'My son is a very long way from being a routine case, Sir Laurence.'

'Indeed, sir.'

'The importance of his being able to father healthy children at some time in the future cannot be overstated.'

'Yes, sir.'

'Can it be done?'

Samson hesitated, clearly unhappy at being unable to dissuade his host from the course he was set on. 'It's theoretically possible, I suppose, if a perfect donor were to be found and everything else were to go like clockwork. The conditions, of course, would have to be ideal ... but I feel I must stress that the preparations for such a procedure would demand a very great deal of the patient. It has the potential to be a catastrophic undertaking . . .'

'And the alternatives to this potentially catastrophic undertaking, Sir Laurence?'

'Point taken, sir,' Samson conceded.

'Then set it up. I'm putting my son's health in your hands. I want him cured and I want it done in complete secrecy. No one must ever know of this.'

Samson shook his head and gathered himself for one last attempt at changing his host's mind. 'I said it was theoretically possible, sir,' he said. 'But the practical difficulties involved in setting up such an operation and keeping it a secret are just too . . .' Words failed him, and he lapsed into silence.

'I'm well aware you can't do this alone, Sir Laurence. I'm not a complete idiot. To that end I have approached a group of trusted friends, people in positions of power and influence. They will provide you with all the resources and help you need. You only have to ask. Well, what do you say?'

'I think I need time to think it over, sir.'

'Call me tomorrow.'

TWO

A gold carriage clock on the marble mantelpiece chimed the hour, the only thing to break the prolonged silence in the room apart from the almost imperceptible rumble of London traffic outside the double-glazed windows on a grey day in February.

'I thought we should all meet with Sir Laurence to discuss exactly what it is we have been asked to do and to make sure we all understand exactly what we are getting into,' said the owner of the Belgravia house. 'There will be no official sanction for what we're doing, no committees or advisory bodies to call upon, no spreading of the blame should things go wrong and no overt rewards if they don't. We will be and must remain the only people ever to know about this mission, apart, of course, from the man who has called upon our friendship and loyalty.'

The others in the room nodded their understanding.

'Can we be certain it will work?' asked a clearly nervous man, whose unease had caused him to break the pencil supplied with the pad in front of him. Like the others, he wore a dark suit, the uniform of the city, although the ties that some wore belied anonymity to varying extents. The question was put to a silver-haired man whose neckwear bore a snake and staff motif, proclaiming his link to the medical profession.

'No,' he replied. 'Sir Laurence and I agree: there can be no guarantees. The main element of the procedure is a risky business at the best of times – without taking into account the reason for it in this case – but, given the circumstances, it's almost certainly the only chance we have of . . . rescuing the situation.'

The man at the head of the table – a Cambridge graduate by his tie – gave a slight smile at the euphemism but added, 'And the only chance we have of preventing a monumental scandal.'

'Aren't we jumping the gun here?' said the nervous man. 'I mean, we seem to be going for broke before we've even considered the alternatives . . .'

'There aren't any,' said the Cambridge man, adopting an expression that seemed to suggest this was the reaction he'd been expecting from the nervous man. He looked down at the table as if willing the time to pass. Although bound in this instance by a common friendship, the two men had little time for each other, being poles apart in terms of personality and outlook. The Cambridge man was positive and self-confident to the point of arrogance while the nervous man was prone to analyse everything in great detail and was seen as caution personified.

'It would not be easy, of course,' continued the nervous man, 'but surely the risks involved in what you are proposing are just too great to contemplate? I think that, with decent PR and sensible management, the storm could be weathered. History suggests—'

'Times have changed', interrupted the Cambridge man, 'and so have people. This includes their perception of many things we might have taken for granted in the past. Had there been a feel-good factor abroad in the country at the moment, well, who knows, but the global recession, rising unemployment, sterling hovering on the brink – even the bloody weather's been conspiring against us this winter. Something like this coming on top of everything else could trigger a complete collapse of public confidence. It could be the final straw for many when they discover that everything they believed in, trusted or revered is turning to dust, especially when they are left with no jobs, no savings, no prospects and no belief in anything. Sociologists – not that I have any great truck with that lot – are already mooting the prospect of anger turning to anarchy in the none-too-distant future.'

'You say that no one would know apart from us,' said the nervous man. 'But surely others would have to be involved? I mean, it doesn't sound like something that could be carried out by a single doctor at a secret location.'

'A number of people will have to be involved along the way,' agreed the Cambridge man. 'But, as I understand it, there is nothing particularly unusual about the essential element of the procedure itself. Am I right, Sir Laurence?'

Laurence Samson nodded. 'It's not exactly routine but it is something that is carried out almost every day in some part of the country, albeit for other reasons. The difference in this case, of course, is the who and the why. Personnel screening for those engaged at the sharp end of things will have to be of the highest order.'

'James will see to that,' said the Cambridge man. He turned to the one man in the room wearing a plain tie. James Monk chose not to respond in any way, but sat coldly staring into the middle distance.

'James' job will be to ensure that absolute secrecy is maintained at all times. No one is going to end up *selling their story* – he suffused the phrase with contempt – 'or enlivening their otherwise forgettable memoirs with the details. This whole affair must be conducted in secret and remain a secret for all time. It is non-negotiable. Absolute silence from all concerned is a *sine qua non*.'

Laurence Samson looked at James Monk with suspicion in his eyes. 'I'm not at all sure how you can guarantee something like that,' he said, making it sound like an accusation.

Monk gave a slight shrug but didn't see fit to respond, and no one else seemed willing to elaborate. Samson was clearly uncomfortable with the information he was deducing – a clear case of there being some things it was better not to know but unfortunately knowing only too well what they were.

'We wouldn't expect you to be involved in . . . the mechanics of security, Sir Laurence,' said the Cambridge man, hoping to bring Samson back on board. 'We are here to assist you in any way we can in achieving our twin goals – a cure for our friend's son and to make sure that the whole affair remains a secret. You are solely concerned with the former.'

Samson nodded his understanding.

'What I would suggest', continued the Cambridge man, 'is that all of us simply concentrate on the role we each have to play.'

There were nods around the table.

'Good, then let's not concern ourselves too deeply with the duties of others. If we all play our individual parts, we must stand a good chance of pulling off something quite remarkable.'

'And if it should fail?' asked the nervous man.

'Let's not even consider that,' said the Cambridge man with ice in his voice.

'Hear hear,' said a couple of voices in unison, causing the nervous man to retreat into his shell.

'So, gentlemen, it's time for the big question. Are we all agreed that we should help our friend in his hour of need?' The Cambridge man looked around the room. 'Charles?'

A man wearing an Old Etonian tie nodded.

'Marcus? Christopher?'

11

Two more nods.

'Colonel?'

A man wearing a Guards regimental tie nodded. 'I'll certainly do my bit.'

'Malcolm?'

The nervous man nodded. 'I suppose so.'

'Doctor?'

The man wearing the caduceus tie said, 'Sir Laurence and I have identified the best practitioners in the country and given their details to James' people for screening after the initial approach.'

'And the initial approach?'

'The usual legal firm has agreed to manage things with its customary absolute discretion.'

'All candidates are currently under surveillance,' said Monk.

'Good,' said the Cambridge man. 'We don't want any of them swanning off to conferences on the other side of the world just when we need them most.'

THREE

'You were very restless last night,' Cassie Motram said when her husband appeared in the kitchen for breakfast. John Motram wrapped his dressing gown around him and manoeuvred himself up on to one of the new stools that Cassie had bought to accompany a recently installed breakfast bar. He was a little too short for this to be an entirely comfortable procedure and his irritation showed.

'I feel like I'm in an American film,' he complained. 'What in God's name was wrong with a table and chairs?'

'We're moving with the times,' Cassie insisted, dismissing his complaint. 'Now, as I was saying . . .'

'Bad dreams.'

'Mmm. You've been having a lot of these lately. What's on your mind?'

Her husband gave her a sideways glance, as if deciding whether or not to come clean, before saying, 'I don't think they're going to renew my research grant for the historical stuff.'

'They always have in the past. Why should this time be any different? Or are they using the credit crunch as an excuse like everyone else in this country?'

'It's not just that; the university's changing,' said John. 'Scholarship's becoming a thing of the past. The pursuit of knowledge is no longer good enough for the suits in the corridors of power: there has to be an "end product", something the bean counters

13

can patent, something they can sell. There has to be "economic justification" for what you do.'

'And researching fourteenth-century plagues doesn't fit the bill?'

'They couldn't have put it better themselves,' John agreed. 'Although, of course, they didn't, preferring instead to go all round the houses using that funny language they speak these days about "moving forward" and being "proactive in the need for networking" as we "embrace the twenty-first century". Where did they come up with all that junk?'

'These people are everywhere,' Cassie said sympathetically. 'A woman turned up at the WI the other day, giving a talk about detoxifying the system, as she put it. I asked her what toxins she would be removing and she got quite snippy, demanded to know if I was a qualified nutritionist. I said no, I was a bloody doctor and would she please answer the question, and of course she couldn't. Just what the hell is a qualified nutritionist when it's at home?'

'There's been some kind of fusion between science and fashion which means that pseudo-scientists are popping up everywhere, spouting their baloney.'

'Maybe we should go for a change of career.' Cassie accepted the milk jug.

'I may have to if any more grant money dries up. You know . . .' John paused for a moment while he struggled with the marmalade jar. 'I think I'm going to retrain as a celebrity nail technician.'

Cassie almost choked on her cornflakes. 'Where on earth did you come up with that one?' she gasped.

'I heard some woman on breakfast TV being introduced as that and I thought that's for me . . . John Motram, celebrity nail technician. To hell with higher education, let's do something really important and start polishing the fingernails of the rich and famous. How about you?'

'International hair colourist, I think,' said Cassie, after a moment's thought. 'Same source.'

'That's us sorted then,' said John. 'A new life awaits.'

'It's just a pity we're in our fifties,' said Cassie. 'And I have a full surgery waiting for me.'

'And I have a second-year class in medical microbiology to fill with awe if not shock,' said John. 'Such a pity. I was looking forward to jetting off to LA or wherever these people go at the weekend.'

The letter box clattered and the sound of mail hitting the floor caused Cassie to swing her legs round on her stool and pad off to the porch in her stockinged feet. She reappeared, head to one side as she shuffled her way through a bunch of envelopes, giving impromptu predictions of their contents. 'Bill . . . bill . . . junk . . . junk . . . postcard from Bill and Janet in Barcelona – we must go there: we've been talking about it for ages – and one for you from . . . the University of Oxford, Balliol College no less.'

'Really?' John accepted the letter and opened it untidily with his thumb, taking thirty seconds or so to read it before saying, 'Good Lord.'

'Well? Don't be so mysterious.'

'It's from the Master of Balliol. He wants to see me next week.'

'What about?'

'Doesn't say.' John handed the letter over.

'How odd. Will you go?'

'What's to lose?'

'Maybe he's heard you're thinking of a career change and offering you a chair in celebrity nail technology?'

'Could well be.' John nodded sagely. 'But I'll only accept if you're given a research fellowship in international hair colouring.'

'Deal,' said Cassie, slipping on her shoes. 'Meanwhile I have coughs to cure and bums to jab . . . Have a nice day, as we international hair colourists say.'

'You too. Maybe I'll have a think outside the box about all this . . .'

'Absolutely . . . Push the boundaries . . .'

Cassie left for the surgery and John cleared away the breakfast things, still feeling curious about the letter from Oxford. As a senior lecturer in cell biology at Newcastle University, he hadn't had much to with Oxbridge although he had visited both Oxford and Cambridge for various conferences and meetings over the years and liked them both. It had been almost inevitable that he would: he was a born academic and scholarship was so obviously cherished at both universities. It had been one of the regrets of his earlier life that he had been unable to take up a place at Cambridge after leaving school, but reading science at a university nearer home had made more sense at the time and enabled him to contribute to the family income through part-time work – a not insignificant consideration for the son of a mother who provided for her family by cleaning the homes of the well-off and a father who had been invalided out of mining thanks to the damage that thirty years underground had done to his lungs.

Although both his parents had been dead now for a long time, someone wheezing in the street could still trigger memories of the sound of his father's laboured breathing. His parents had lived to see him graduate with first class honours from Durham, although his father had died before he completed his PhD and never shared the pride his mother took in calling her son 'doctor'.

Not going up to Cambridge proved to be no drawback for Motram. His sheer ability had taken him through a couple of successful post-doctoral fellowships at prestigious American universities where he had established himself as a researcher of international repute in the mechanics of viral infection. His particular interest lay in the epidemiology of plagues of past times, although this generally had to take a back seat to the study of more modern problems for which it was easier to attract funding.

John had met Cassie shortly after getting a lectureship at the University of Newcastle, where she had been in her final year of a medical degree, and had decided very quickly that she was the girl for him – a choice not entirely applauded by Cassie's parents, who'd held higher social aspirations for their clever daughter. However, their love had survived the slings and arrows of outraged parents and they had married six months later.

The marriage had been successful from the outset, surviving the strain of the first few years of the demanding work that goes with being very new in their chosen professions, particularly for Cassie who, as a junior doctor in a busy hospital, seemed to be on call every hour of the day and night. Life had got easier with Cassie's move into general practice and John's growing academic reputation, which had made it easier for him to obtain research funding.

Two children had come along and the Motrams had been in a position to give them the best possible start in life. Their daughter, Chloe, was currently a translator with the European Commission in Brussels, and their son had followed his mother into medicine and was establishing a career in surgery. There were no grandchildren as yet but the possibility was a warming thought for both of them, and Cassie, who had an eye for décor, kept an eye out for possible changes to one of the upstairs rooms in their cottage which she felt might be 'nice for little people'.

FOUR

John Motram took his time on the walk through the streets of Oxford, savouring the undoubted charm of the place and letting its history seep into his bones. He smiled as he realised that his affection for its dreaming spires was not entirely born of academic regard; being an avid fan of Inspector Morse was certainly playing its part. He found himself keeping an eye out for a Mark Seven Jaguar.

Nothing disappointed him about the interior of Balliol College either. Everything just got better.

'The Master will see you now,' said a suitably deferential woman who looked as if she might have been a pillar of her church guild, sensibly dressed from her high collar with the cameo brooch to her polished brogues.

Motram was shown into a large office that couldn't fail to impress. Minimalist it was not; metal and plastic pointedly failed to make an appearance. Wood – old polished wood – reigned supreme, comfortable in the light that came in through a series of tall, leaded windows that also admitted the sound of chimes and bells, confirming Motram's arrival at the appointed hour of eleven a.m.

A tall, patrician man rose from behind his desk and smiled. 'Dr Motram, good of you to come. I'm Andrew Harvey, Master of Balliol. Please come and sit down. You must be wondering what all this is about.'

It wasn't a question, but Motram, who'd been thinking about little else for the past week, said, 'I think I'd be lying if I said I wasn't intrigued.'

'Quite so,' said Harvey. 'I'm afraid microbiology isn't exactly my field, but I understand that you are an expert on both the viruses of today and the epidemics of the past, shall we say?'

'That's a fair enough description.'

'What is it that intrigues you about past plagues, doctor?'

'Their cause. What many people don't realise is that microbiology is a very young science. Bacteria weren't discovered until the late 1800s and viruses even later, so the identification of the causes of the great epidemics of the past has been based largely on guesswork . . . or presumption.'

Harvey smiled at the acid emphasis Motram had put on the last word. 'I understand there is . . . something of a disagreement between you and your academic colleagues over the origin of the Black Death. Am I right?'

'You are.'

'Tell me about it.'

Motram frowned slightly. He didn't quite see where all this was leading, but he continued, 'There's a general assumption among the public and indeed some of my colleagues that the fourteenth-century pandemic generally called the Black Death, which wiped out a third of the population of Europe, was caused by an outbreak of bubonic plague.'

'I'm afraid I have to admit to being one of the public who subscribe to that view,' said Harvey. 'Wasn't it?'

'I don't think so.'

'Then what?'

'I'm convinced it was caused by a virus.'

Harvey looked slightly bemused and Motram smiled, recognising the problem. 'There is a very big difference between bacteria and viruses,' he said. 'They are completely different entities but, for some reason that escapes me, people appear reluctant to take this on board.'

'Ah, educating the public,' sighed Harvey, relaxing into his chair with a slightly amused expression on his face. 'Never an easy business. But in what way are they different, doctor?' He managed to endow the question with the unspoken rider, *And does it matter?*

'Bacteria can exist independently,' Motram explained. 'They are living entities in their own right. They have all they need to grow and divide provided they can find suitable nutriment. Viruses can only exist inside living cells. In fact, there is a long-standing argument over whether they should actually be regarded as living things at all.'

Harvey nodded. 'I see.'

'Another major and more practical difference is that you can treat bacterial infections with antibiotics: antibiotics are useless against viruses.'

'So what makes you think Black Death was caused by a virus and not plague – which presumably, in the light of what you've just said, is a bacterium?'

Motram nodded. 'A rod-shaped bacterium called *Yersinia pestis*, named after a Russian microbiologist called Yersin who worked with Louis Pasteur. It was originally called *Pasteurella pestis* after his boss, but in the end justice prevailed.'

Harvey gave a slightly pained smile that suggested *too much information* and Motram cut short the lecture. 'I suppose I began to wonder about ten years ago when I was studying the rate of spread of Black Death in Europe. It was all wrong for a bacterial infection like plague and it didn't show the seasonal differences you would expect.'

'Was the spread faster or slower than you expected?'

'Much faster. Plague is primarily a disease of rats. Human beings get it from fleas, but Black Death spread like wildfire, as if it were an airborne infection like flu.'

'Are you alone in your suspicions?'

'Not any more,' said Motram. 'Scientists have been working on a genetic mutation in human beings which confers resistance to certain virus infections. It's called Delta 32: basically it leads to the absence of a receptor on the surface of certain cells in the body, which denies viruses access to the cells they would normally infect.'

Harvey nodded, then said, 'I'm sorry, I must seem terribly dense but . . . where does the connection with Black Death come in?'

'Before Black Death swept over Europe, we estimate that the Delta 32 mutation was present in the general population at a frequency of about one in forty thousand.

'And after?' asked Harvey.

'About one in seven.'

Harvey let out his breath in a low, silent whistle. 'Now I see,' he said. 'So people without the mutation were much more susceptible to Black Death than those few at the time who had it.'

'Precisely. It was clearly an enormous advantage to have the Delta 32 mutation,' said Motram. 'What, of course, is absolutely crucial from my point of view is that the mutation stops *viruses* from entering cells, not bacteria. Bacteria don't need to enter cells. It makes absolutely no difference to them whether you have the Delta 32 mutation or not.'

'So there we have it,' said Harvey. 'Game, set and match to you, it would appear. Black Death was caused by a virus, not a bacterium.'

'I believe so.'

21

Harvey picked up on Motram's guarded response. 'So shouldn't that be an end to the argument?' he asked.

'I'm afraid not. The old guard still insist Black Death was caused by plague and see the new findings as academic stuff and nonsense – Disraeli's third kind of lie, if you like.'

'Statistics.' Harvey smiled.

'Even those who've moved to the virus camp are now falling out over which virus it might have been. Smallpox is one of the favourites and it's been shown that that could have exerted the selective pressure necessary for such a dramatic genetic shift in the population while plague certainly couldn't. There are others who propose it could have been due to a combination of infections, and there is of course one other intriguing possibility, that it could have been caused by a completely different virus altogether – something that existed then but is unknown to us today.'

'A killer from the past,' said Harvey, raising his eyebrows. 'Do pardon my ignorance, but isn't it possible to find out what caused it simply by . . . digging up the past, so to speak?'

'It's been tried on a number of occasions,' said Motram. 'But we're talking about seven hundred years ago. Mortal remains tend not to last that long.'

Harvey rested his elbows on his desk and formed a steeple with his fingertips as he appeared to gaze off into the middle distance. 'You know, I seem to remember reading something about a group of workers claiming to have recovered plague from Black Death victims . . . somewhere in Europe, I think.'

Motram nodded. 'France. They found plague bacilli in the dental pulp of an exhumed corpse. Trouble is, no one else has been able to reproduce their findings. Everyone else has drawn a blank.'

'So the French findings are . . . doubtful?'

'I wouldn't go that far,' said Motram. 'There seems little doubt that the body they examined was a plague victim, but without wholesale corroboration you can't really say that plague caused Black Death, only that plague caused the death of the body they were examining.'

Harvey nodded thoughtfully. 'So, it would help enormously if you were to come across a number of victims of Black Death preserved in good condition?'

'Indeed it would,' said Motram, 'but after seven hundred years the chances of that are—'

'That's really why I asked you here, Dr Motram.'

FIVE

The door opened and tea was brought in on a silver tray, leaving Motram to wonder if Harvey had a button behind his desk to press at an appropriate moment.

'Milk or lemon?'

'Neither,' replied Motram. 'Just as it comes please.'

'Good man. A decent Darjeeling needs no assistance.'

Motram accepted the china cup and saucer from the pourer – the woman who had shown him in – and reflected on how long it had been since he had held a cup and saucer in his hands. A mug in need of some interior scrubbing sat on his own desk up north.

'How much do you know about Balliol, doctor?'

'I understand it's probably the oldest college in Oxford.'

'So old that the foundation date is uncertain but generally taken as about 1263.'

Motram smiled. 'Even before Black Death.'

'Indeed, even before that,' Harvey agreed. 'Our co-founders were John Balliol, a wealthy man with estates in both France and England, and his wife Devorgilla, the daughter of a Scottish nobleman and a truly remarkable woman in her own right. Their offspring, also John Balliol, became King of Scotland, although a completely unremarkable one it has to be said and perhaps best forgotten. Devorgilla, however, is well remembered. Apart from co-founding this college and giving it its first seal, which we still have today, she endowed a new Cistercian abbey in Dumfries and Galloway – a daughter house of Dundrennan Abbey. It was to be called New Abbey but, for reasons some people find macabre, it ended up bearing the name of Sweetheart Abbey.'

Harvey paused to take a sip of his tea. Motram reflected that the man knew exactly the right place to pause in a story.

'When Devorgilla's husband died in 1269, she was beside herself with grief. She had his heart removed and embalmed so that she might carry it with her in an ivory and silver casket wherever she went.' Seeing the expression that appeared on Motram's face, Harvey said, 'I see you are experiencing the same mixture of admiration and revulsion that many feel on hearing this tale.'

Motram smiled and said, 'Sorry. Please, go on.'

'When she had the abbey built in his memory in 1273, the monks decided to call it *Dulce Cor* – sweet heart – instead of New Abbey as had been originally intended, and so it has remained for well over seven hundred years. She and her husband lie buried there today, the casket clutched to her chest.'

'Quite a story,' said Motram, giving no indication that he was wondering what on earth it had to do with him.

'Recently, the college has come into possession of something which adds a little more to the tale,' said Harvey. 'Some old papers rescued from a house in the Scottish Borders have shed light on the family responsible for the embalming of John Balliol's heart, the Le Clerks. Apparently, they were renowned for their expertise in the preservation of the dead and passed down their skills through generations of the family. When Black Death . . .' Harvey paused to enjoy the flicker of interest in Motram's eyes when he seemed to be coming to the point, 'affected England in 1346, the Scots were left largely untouched at first and, with ever an eye to the main chance, thought they saw an opportunity to invade. An army was raised and encamped in the forests around Selkirk awaiting the order to advance. It never came: Black Death arrived first. Men died in their hundreds in the woods of the Scottish Borders.'

'I can imagine,' said Motram, and he could. The image of Black Death breaking out in a hugely crowded military camp in the forest, turning it into a hell of squalor, filth and infection, filled his mind. Deserters would be running off in all directions but would only spread the infection rather than escape it. Bodies would pile up and be left to rot. The stench of filth and decomposition would fill the air, accompanying the moans of the sick, the groans of the dying . . .

'When news spread north to the cities, the families of some of the more noble Scottish participants were adamant they did not want their loved ones left to be rolled and tumbled into the communal pits and pyres of the forest. The Le Clerk family were tasked with preserving the bodies of those of noble birth they could find and transporting them up to Edinburgh and beyond for proper burial.

'This never happened: Black Death beat them to it. It had already spread north by the time the bodies had been preserved and was wreaking havoc throughout Scotland. The embalmed corpses remained in the Borders, where they were buried in a secret chamber at Dryburgh Abbey – the papers I mentioned earlier tell us where that chamber is. Sixteen Black Death victims, preserved by masters of the craft, lie waiting there. Are you interested, doctor?'

John Motram's face was wreathed in smiles. 'I feel as if Christmas has come early this year,' he said. 'What a fascinating story, and what an intriguing prospect . . . although . . .' The smile faded. 'There's a bit of a cloud on the horizon, I'm afraid. It seems my research funding in this area is not going to be renewed, and without it the cost of mounting an excavation would be prohibitive.'

Harvey leaned back in his chair as if master of all he surveyed and said, 'You know, I think we might be able to help there.'

'Really?'

'Have you heard of the Hotspur Foundation?'

Motram shook his head. 'I don't think so.'

'Neither had I until a few weeks ago, but we, among certain other academic institutions across the land, have been asked to recommend suitable candidates for funding – what the newspapers might call "top scientists" – in certain fields. You fall into one of the categories.'

'Bygone plagues?' said Motram with a look of incredulity.

'It's more your expertise in the mechanics of viral infection they're interested in,' said Harvey with a smile. 'Your broader area of expertise – but two birds with one stone and all that, eh, doctor? It's up to you how you spend the money.'

'Sounds too good to be true,' said Motram. 'Who's behind this foundation?'

'It's not clear,' replied Harvey, 'but that isn't unusual in these cases – probably a reclusive billionaire atoning for the past misdeeds which got him the fortune in the first place, I shouldn't wonder. He'll be bidding for a late entry pass through the gates of heaven – if you'll pardon my cynicism.'

Motram smiled. 'And what exactly would these people expect from me?' he asked.

'The only stipulation is that your expertise can be called upon without too much notice if and when the occasion arises during the next few months. Nothing more specific.'

'Pretty vague,' said Motram. 'Still, if this enables me to carry on with my work and lets me unlock the secrets lying in the Scottish Borders, I'm all for it.'

'Good. Then I can put your name forward?'

'Please do.' Motram hesitated, then asked, 'At the risk of sounding rude and perhaps even ungrateful, might I ask what you and the college are getting out of all this?'

Harvey smiled. 'Prestige, doctor – what we value most. After all, if you are successful, we would be instrumental in bringing about the resolution of an important academic argument, would we not?'

'Absolutely,' said Motram.

'Excellent,' exclaimed Harvey. 'Then I think we should put our collaboration on a more formal basis. I'll send off a letter to your university suggesting that we make you an honorary research fellow of the college for the duration of the investigation and put forward your credentials for funding from the Hotspur Foundation. Perhaps you'd care to join me for some lunch?'

Motram was entertained to the kind of lunch that had him thanking fate that he hadn't driven down to Oxford but had opted for the train instead. He wondered how people who lunched like that regularly could possibly function in the afternoon, although he had to admit that Harvey seemed perfectly alert. One thing was still intriguing him, so he asked, 'What made you decide to approach me?'

Harvey smiled. 'We didn't pick your name out of a hat, if that's what you're wondering,' he said. 'When the papers from the house in the Borders came into our possession, we did some research to find out who might best benefit from the new finding. Your reputation and expertise – not to mention the publicity given to the current academic argument – put you at the top of the list. I have to admit that the appearance of the Hotspur Foundation on the scene was something we hadn't anticipated, but why knock serendipity? Bringing all these factors together for mutual benefit is, well . . . what I do.'

'And very well too,' said Motram. 'I must say I'm intrigued by the Hotspur Foundation.'

'As I said, individual benefactors are by no means unusual, although I understand that in this case the funds are really quite substantial.'

'Perhaps those sorts of benefactors are not unusual in Oxford University.' Motram deliberately accentuated his northern accent. 'For us folk up north it's quite a different matter. How does it work? I mean, who makes the decisions? Who holds the purse strings?'

'In this instance, I understand it's a firm of London solicitors, although it would be naive to imagine that they actually make the decisions. They'll be charged with maintaining their client's anonymity while relaying their instructions and advice.'

'I seem to remember you saying that funding was being provided for researchers in "certain fields",' said Motram. 'Can you be more precise?'

Harvey nodded. 'Broadly speaking, within the compass of viral infection, immune response, transplantation technology and post-operative care.'

'Sexy science,' said Motram. 'No one ever puts up funding for research into arthritis, deafness or the stuff that makes life a misery for so many in later life. Unfortunately, old age is usually a case of never mind the quality, count the years.'

'Sadly true,' nodded Harvey. 'Death is seen as the great enemy.'

'And we'll all live for ever if only we can wipe out killer disease. It's a peculiar mindset.'

'Born out of fear,' said Harvey. 'Fear of the great unknown: it's the way it's always been. *The grave's a fine and private place, but none I think do there embrace.*'

'About sums it up,' said Motram.

Harvey replenished their glasses from a crystal decanter that had a Latin inscription on it which Motram kept trying to see in its entirety but fate kept denying him. 'Tell me more about your belief that Black Death was caused by a virus and not plague,' he said. 'I'm led to believe that you know more than perhaps anyone else about how viruses attack us. I read one of your papers as part of my homework on you and was most impressed. As I said, I'm not a scientist, but I came away knowing a lot more than I had before. That says much about your abilities as a teacher. You are more concerned with imparting knowledge than achieving self-promotion through complexity, a curse that afflicts so many.'

'Kind of you to say so.'

'One thing worries me, though . . .'

'What's that?'

'A short while ago you mentioned the possibility of Black Death's having been caused by a virus unknown to us today?'

'Just as a possibility,' said Motram.

'All the same, if that did turn out to be the case, wouldn't there be a chance of opening Pandora's box when it comes to breaching this vault in the Scottish Borders and bringing a killer back to life? I'd hate the college to be responsible for unleashing a new pandemic on the world.'

'I really don't think there's much chance of that,' said Motram. 'Viruses can't exist outside living tissue and these corpses have been lying there for seven centuries.'

'But in a preserved state, we hope,' Harvey reminded him.

'Most preservation methods involve an end to the living state,' said Motram. 'Once the host ceases to exist, so does the virus. I suppose it could be argued that one particular method of preservation involves *suspension* of the living state, but that would involves deep freezing. If this fourteenth-century family actually came up with a chest freezer that's been running at minus seventy degrees centigrade for the past seven hundred years without interruption, we could conceivably have a problem on our hands.'

'Fair enough.' Harvey, picked up the port decanter to refill Motram's glass. 'Mind you, we could be considering a virus we know nothing at all about.'

Motram grinned and said, 'Agreed. If it came from outer space, all bets are off.'

SIX

'It's come through,' announced John Motram, waving the letter he'd just opened in the air.

'That's nice, dear . . . what has?' Cassie was preoccupied with the morning paper.

'Permission in principle from Historic Scotland to investigate the site . . . subject to on-site evaluation and the presence of their inspector while work is in progress. Any further permissions will depend on his or her assessment of the situation on the ground.'

'Gosh, that was quick,' said Cassie, looking over her glasses. 'I thought these things were supposed to take ages.'

'This means we can start as soon as we determine the exact location of the tomb – maybe next week,' said John, with obvious pleasure and enthusiasm.

Cassie looked at him thoughtfully. 'Are you absolutely sure about this?' she asked.

'Of course I'm sure,' replied John, astonished. 'What d'you mean?'

'I mean . . . have you thought about the dangers that might be involved in opening up a tomb like that?'

'Cassie, I've been through all this with the chap at Oxford. It's been over seven hundred years. No bacterium or virus lasts that long. You're a doctor, you know that.'

'Mmm,' agreed Cassie, still sounding doubtful. 'But we're

talking about Black Death here ... and the Le Clerks were experts on preservation. Maybe they found ways of preserving bugs as well as bodies ...'

John could see that his wife was genuinely worried. 'That's another of the lines Harvey took. Look,' he said softly, 'I don't believe for one moment that there's any danger, but if it makes you feel better we'll be wearing coveralls and masks for the disinterment – actually to prevent us contaminating *them*, but it works both ways.'

'It does make me feel better,' said Cassie.

John continued opening his mail and Cassie returned to her paper until he interrupted again. 'Damnation.'

'Problems?'

'It's from the solicitors for the Hotspur Foundation – you know, the people who're funding the work in the Borders. They're calling in their part of the bargain. They want me in London for what they call "consultancy work".'

'What kind of consultancy work?'

'They don't say.'

'Where abouts?'

'A private hospital in west London, St Raphael's.'

'Will you go?'

'I don't have much choice. I agreed to their terms and conditions and they've been very generous with funding.'

'So the search for the tomb will have to be put on hold?'

Motram smiled. 'For a commercial break.'

Cassie left for work and John opened his briefcase to remove a bunch of papers which he spread out on the dining room table. His university had been so pleased about the collaboration with Balliol College, Oxford and the grant money coming in from the Hotspur Foundation that they had been more than helpful in agreeing to his taking time off to prepare for excavation. He had been excused all teaching duties for the remainder of the current term.

The papers that had come into Balliol's possession had revealed that the corpses taken from the Selkirk forests had been interred in an underground chamber in Dryburgh Abbey, near Melrose. This had meant seeking permission from Historic Scotland to carry out preliminary work on the site but a potentially bigger problem was that Dryburgh Abbey had been destroyed on several occasions down through the years and getting information about its layout in the fourteenth century had been proving problematical. The abbey had been burned by English troops in 1322, rebuilt but burned again in 1385. It had enjoyed a renaissance in the fifteenth century, only to be destroyed again in 1544.

Motram's task from the layouts in front of him was to identify, in the ruins of today, surviving parts of the original structure that could be used as reference points when interpreting the information given in the Balliol letter. To help him, Oxford academics had provided a translation of the Chaucerian English used in the text, and he was able to establish that the chapter house of the existing abbey – although surrounded by ruins – was in its original siting and, according to the collection of tourist pamphlets he had on the table, still retained elements of plaster and paintwork that dated back to the inception of the abbey.

There were a number of references in the Balliol letter to the chapter house, which encouraged Motram at first, but when it became apparent that the secret chamber might actually lie underneath it his spirits began to flag. It would be extremely unlikely – his academic translation of 'there wouldn't be a snowball's chance in hell' – that Historic Scotland would permit excavation work to go on inside perhaps the most precious part of the abbey.

But as he read further and made some relevant calculations it seemed that, although the entrance to the chamber might well be underneath the chapter house, the actual chamber itself stretched out to the east, outside the walls of the abbey. This meant that access to it might be achieved by digging east of the boundary wall – a much more acceptable proposal, he thought, for the authorities to sanction.

Motram examined some aerial photographs and identified what he thought might be the next problem. There were a number of very large mature trees in the grounds, which as he read further he learned were yews and cedars of Lebanon, very old and possibly planted by knights returning from the crusades.

Using the tip of his pen, he traced the likely location of the secret chamber to the east of the chapter house but found it impossible to judge how close to the roots of the trees it might come. His original thought had been to make an approach from the east end of the chamber – the end furthest from the abbey wall – but, if that was going to be a problem, he thought a compromise might be to gain access from the north or south sides where the ground would be clear but the digging would be closer to the abbey walls.

Some kind of on-site geosurvey would be necessary before shovels could break earth. If he could arrange this before his trip to London, he would be well satisfied with his progress. He repacked his briefcase and set off for the university, intending to seek advice from academic colleagues to see if they thought the survey work could be done in house.

By late afternoon he had concluded that specialist equipment would be required and that an outside contractor should be called in. He called Maxton Geo-Survey, a company recommended by his colleagues in the geology department, and arranged for them to be on site two days after he was due back from London. He then called Historic Scotland and told them what he'd arranged. After assuring them that no ground disturbance would be involved, they said that they would send someone to monitor proceedings.

'Good day?' asked Cassie when he got home.

'Very. It's been going like a dream. I'm pretty sure I know where the burial chamber is and I've arranged for a site survey to be done as soon as I get back from London.'

'I hope you've informed all the relevant authorities,' said Cassie.

'I've been in touch with Historic Scotland and one of their people will be standing by to come on site,' Motram assured her. 'If the geosurvey comes up trumps, we can open negotiations with the officer on site for a start date for the excavation. How was your day?'

'Pretty dull by comparison,' said Cassie. 'Not a single case of Black Death.'

SEVEN

John Motram smiled as he got out of the taxi and started to walk up the short, semicircular drive through well-tended gardens to the entrance of St Raphael's. The hospital was in the heart of London but seemed so peaceful that anyone might have been forgiven for thinking it was a country house. Reception too was a far cry from the noise and bustle of NHS facilities where imminent meltdown seemed to be a common theme. But then, there were no accident and emergency facilities in private hospitals, he reminded himself, no drunks, no knife wounds, no road traffic cases, no drug addicts, no bawling relatives, in fact nothing to interfere with the calm, ordered application of top-class medicine.

'Dr Motram, we've been expecting you,' said the receptionist, with a smile that would have put British Airways cabin crew to shame. It even seemed genuine. 'Kate will show you to the seminar room.'

As if by magic, another young woman, well coiffured and wearing the same pristine white uniform as the receptionist, materialised and smiled. 'Welcome to St Raphael's, doctor. If you'll just follow me.'

Motram was led along a corridor smelling of fresh flowers and furniture polish and shown into a bright, well-equipped seminar room where a number of people were waiting – four men and two women. Their dress suggested well-heeled professionals. When greetings had been exchanged, Motram asked, 'So who's the ringmaster?'

The others smiled and a tall man with a Mediterranean tan and a light grey suit to accentuate it, said, 'I think we all thought you were when you came in.'

'Does anyone know why we're here?' Motram asked.

'Not yet,' replied one of the women. 'I'm Sheila Barnes, by the way: I'm a radiologist.'

This was the cue for the rest to introduce themselves.

'Mark Limond, haematologist.'

'Susie Bruce, nursing director.'

'George Simpson, immunologist.'

'Jonathan Porter-Brown, transplant surgeon,' said the man with the tan.

'Tom Little, biochemist.'

Motram completed the introductions. 'John Motram, cell biologist.'

'John Motram the surface receptor man?' Little asked.

'I suppose,' said Motram modestly. 'That's my specialty.'

'I read your paper last month in the *Journal of Cell Biology*. Brilliant!'

The conversation was interrupted by the door opening and another well-dressed man entered, using his elbow on the door handle. He carried a briefcase in one hand and a pile of papers that seemed destined for independent flight under his other arm. 'So sorry I'm late,' he said. 'Bloody traffic. I'm Laurence Samson, by the way. Have you all met? . . . Good, but I'm sure you must all be wondering why you're here.' The comment received nothing other than blank looks in return. His audience were not for responding to the obvious: they were not TV quiz show material.

Samson accepted the fact graciously and moved on. 'You

are all recipients of support from the Hotspur Foundation. As such, you have agreed to contribute your expertise when called upon. Ladies and gentlemen, the call has come; that's why you're here. We need your participation in the treatment of a patient . . . a VIP patient . . . whom we will refer to and continue to refer to with stultifying unoriginality as Patient X. Some of you may discover his true identity during the course of his treatment, others will not, and that is the way it should stay. His identity must never reach the public domain. Absolute confidentiality is a must. Is that understood from the outset?'

Everyone nodded.

'While I am perfectly sure that all of you will be as good as your word, I am duty bound to point out that the confidentiality clause you signed when accepting your Hotspur Foundation grant made it clear that any breach would result in your being made to refund the entire sum, and would also render you liable to a breach-of-contract action which, I assure you, would be pursued . . . with vigour.'

Motram, who hadn't read the small print in the grant papers, noticed that the looks passing between a few of the others suggested he wasn't alone in this oversight.

'Patient X has a severe form of leukaemia. He also has un-limited financial resources, which may provide some of you with a clue to which part of the world he comes from . . .'

Polite laughter.

'He wants the best and he can afford it. But, as we all know, disease is not impressed by money. After trying everything else for Patient X, we have now arrived at the last chance saloon, a bone marrow transplant. This hospital has all the facilities neces-sary and we think we have identified a suitable donor. Without stepping on anyone's toes, we would like you to oversee every aspect of the procedure. According to your individual expertise, some of you will only be required for a short time, others for longer. Those who will be here for longer will be accommodated in the excellent patients' relatives' quarters they have here in the hospital until their job is done. Rather like members of a jury, you will be required not to discuss Patient X or any aspect of his treatment "out of hours", so to speak. As the physician in ultimate charge of Patient X, I'd now like to discuss with each of you in turn what will be required of you on an individual basis, starting with . . .' Samson referred to his notes, finding the right page at the third attempt, 'Dr John Motram.' He looked up and Motram responded with a half-hearted raise of the hand. It had been a long time since he'd held up his hand in class and he felt slightly silly.

'Kate will show the rest of you to one of the private rooms, where you'll find tea and coffee and some excellent chocolate biscuits.'

Samson seemed more relaxed when the others had left. He smiled at Motram and said, 'I think you'll be the chap getting off most lightly from all of this. The donor will be here shortly.' He glanced at his watch. 'We need you to set up the comprehensive range of tests we have detailed for you on this sheet.' He handed the A4 paper to Motram. 'In short, we would like you to confirm that our putative donor is indeed a perfect match for Patient X . . . compatible in every way.' He saw a questioning look appear on Motram's face and added, 'We are not looking for a donor who ticks some of the boxes and might be all right with high immuno-suppression for the rest of the patient's life. We need a perfect match – blood type, tissue type, sub-markers, the lot. We think we've identified such a donor: we need you to confirm this. We will supply you with the lab report we already have on Patient X; you can collect your own samples from the donor in order to make the comparison.' He handed Motram his card. 'Let us know your findings as soon as you're sure.'

After a tour of the hospital and its facilities, during which Motram decided that this was what all hospitals would be like if the world were perfect, he met the donor in a consulting room where, instead of a desk between them, there was a coffee table with a cafetiere containing the best coffee he'd tasted in ages sitting on it.

The young man facing him, dressed in jeans and a denim jacket, appeared fit and healthy. He was clean-shaven and had fair, close-cropped hair which was fashionably slightly longer on the top than at the sides. He smiled but appeared slightly nervous when he got up to shake hands. After some small talk about traffic and the weather, Motram told him what samples he would like to take and why. 'Nothing to it really. Anything you'd like to ask?'

'Sir Laurence told me this would be an absolutely straightforward procedure. Is that right?'

'Absolutely right,' said Motram. 'Walk in the park.'

The young man smiled at the expression but didn't seem entirely convinced. 'I had an older cousin, see, who donated a kidney to his brother . . .'

'It's nothing like that,' Motram interrupted. 'Organ transplant is a major undertaking, a completely different kettle of fish. You'll just be donating some of your bone marrow. It'll be replaced in no time at all. No scars, no after-effects, no nothing: it's very like donating blood really.'

'Thanks, doc,' said the young man, visible relaxing. 'That's more or less what Sir Laurence said, but it sounded better coming from you.'

'Good. Let's go through to the lab and I'll see about getting these samples from you.'

Cassie Motram handed her husband a large malt whisky when he came in and watched the look of appreciation appear on his face as he settled down in a chair and kicked off his shoes. 'How did it go?' she asked.

'I could tell you but I'd have to kill you.' Motram took another sip.

'Do you want any dinner or not?'

'Ah, my Achilles heel.' Motram grinned. 'They've got a leukaemia patient who needs a bone marrow transplant, a Saudi billionaire by the sound of it. They've found a donor for him and want me to check out his suitability.'

'Is that all?' Cassie sounded disappointed. 'Do we know anything about this Saudi billionaire?'

Motram shook his head. 'Nothing at all apart from the fact that he's to be referred to as Patient X, although I suspect Prince X might be a better bet judging by the money the foundation have been throwing around. Probably goes to sleep to the sound of oil slurping into barrels.'

'Will you have to go back to London?'

'I don't think so. I set up some basic tests in the hospital lab – their technicians can send the data to me when they have the results – and the more complicated things I'll do in the lab up here on the samples I brought back with me. When I've collated everything, I'll phone in all the results along with my conclusions and that'll be an end to it. Money for old rope.'

'So, it'll be back to Black Death now?'

'You bet,' said Motram with a grin.

EIGHT

The sun shone brightly as John Motram drove north into the Scottish Borders: it matched his sunny mood. He liked the rolling hills and valleys of the border country, which always seemed so calm and peaceful despite their bloody history of almost continual conflict between England and Scotland down through the centuries. He slowed as he crossed the River Tweed, perhaps one of the most famous salmon rivers in the world, and enjoyed the sight of the sun playing on its rippled surface for a few moments before driving on.

The first thing he saw in the abbey car park was a commercial vehicle with Maxton Geo-Survey written in red along its white side. A cartoon of a drilling rig at one end emphasised the point. Two men in company overalls were standing beside the vehicle; they were talking to a man in a suit who was carrying a clipboard.

'Alan Blackstone, Historic Scotland,' said Clipboard Man as Motram parked his car beside them and got out.

'You chaps are on the ball,' said Motram, stretching his limbs after the long drive and then looking at his watch. It was five to nine.

'It's never a problem to get up and out on a day like this,' said Blackstone, glancing up at the sky. This brought smiles of agreement from the two Maxton men, who introduced themselves as Les Smith and Tony Fielding.

'Tell you what,' said Motram, looking over his shoulder at the Dryburgh Abbey Hotel, which stood adjacent to the abbey, 'why don't we get ourselves some coffee and have a talk about what we're going to do?'

When the coffee arrived, Motram spread a modern-day plan of the abbey ruins out on the table and told the others about his findings. 'I think the chamber lies under the ground approximately here,' he said, tracing a rectangle with the end of his pen out from the east wall of the abbey, using the three windows of the chapter house as a starting point. 'I don't know just how far out it stretches, but hopefully that's something you chaps can determine?'

'We certainly can,' Fielding assured him.

'Depending on what you guys come up with, we can perhaps discuss with Alan here whether or not an excavation might be in order and whether we approach from the east end or try to come in from the side if the end should prove too near the trees.' Motram looked to the man from Historic Scotland.

'Sounds good,' said Blackstone. 'It's a big plus having the chamber outside the perimeter of the abbey. That being the case, there shouldn't be any objection from us, providing, of course, it doesn't turn out to be a very short chamber, very close to the back wall of the chapter house; we couldn't risk having the foundations undermined.'

'I hadn't even considered that,' Motram confessed. 'It shouldn't be that short if it's holding sixteen bodies, but I suppose there's only one way to find out . . .'

Fielding and Smith unloaded their equipment and Motram and Blackstone followed along behind as the electric-powered transporter vehicle – a sort of motorised trolley – moved everything along parallel to the north wall of the abbey before turning south and parking outside the windows of the chapter house. 'About here?' Fielding asked.

Motram nodded, emphasising with his right hand where he thought the hidden chamber might be. 'Assuming the entry to it was from here,' he indicated a point on the abbey wall directly below the chapter house windows, 'and there were, say, ten steps down to it to give some ceiling height, I reckon about ten to fifteen feet below where we're standing now.'

Smith and Fielding started up their machine and began a slow sweep of the ground. Motram watched their every move with bated breath while Blackstone turned away to examine the condition of the stone along the base of the chapter house wall.

Fielding removed his earphones and pointed to something on a graphic readout to his colleague before turning to Motram and saying. 'You're right. There's no doubt about it . . . there's a hollow space down there.'

'Brilliant! Can you tell how far out it stretches?' Motram asked, knowing that a great deal was riding on the answer to his question.

The machine resumed its sweep, stopping when Fielding and Smith were about ten metres east of the abbey wall. 'This seems to be the end of it here,' said Fielding.

'Great,' said Motram, relieved that the possibility of the chamber's turning out to be a sort of cupboard in the wall that went down rather than out had been removed. He walked over to join the two men and noted that the nearest tree was only about two metres away. He turned to Blackstone. 'Too close for an end approach, do you think?'

'I think so,' said Blackstone. 'Apart from anything else, the roots of these trees must be quite extensive. In fact I'd be surprised if they hadn't invaded your chamber over the years – maybe taken it over completely.'

'Not a happy thought,' murmured Motram, inwardly agreeing that Blackstone had a point. 'What do you think about a side approach?'

Blackstone nodded thoughtfully before saying, 'Let's not rush things. Let's wait until the chaps have finished mapping the whole thing out.' He led the way to a bench on the grassy area beside the abbey cloisters where they sat in the sun and exchanged bits and pieces of information about their respective careers until the survey was finished and Fielding came to join them with a printout in his hand.

'Here we are,' he said with a smile. 'More or less what you thought, an underground chamber about ten metres long by three metres wide and about four metres down. There's a blip on the north side – some kind of alcove cut in the wall – but the south wall is smooth all the way along.'

'Then we should approach from the south side, if you're agreeable?' said Motram, turning to Blackstone. 'About halfway along, do you think?'

Blackstone nodded, but added, 'Maybe an extra metre out from the wall, if you don't mind. If it's a choice between damaging tree roots and undermining the chapter house wall . . . let's err on the side of keeping me in a job.'

'Point taken,' smiled Motram. 'Wonderful. Look, I have to go to London early next week but I'll make arrangements before I go for all the gear we'll need. We can start work as soon as I get back if that's okay with you?'

With everyone in agreement Motram said, 'I can't tell you how much this means to me.'

'I think we sort of guessed,' said Fielding to the amusement of the others.

'Lunch is on me!' said Motram.

*   *   *

Smith and Fielding who, as it turned out, had worked all over the world, held the interest of the other two with tales of their past employment on archeological digs and, in Smith's case, oil exploration.

'You know, we could all be on the verge of making history here,' said Motram over coffee. 'We could be about to solve a seven-hundred-year-old mystery. There's something really exciting about uncovering the secrets of the past, don't you think?'

The others smiled indulgently at Motram's enthusiasm but Fielding said, 'I'm not so sure about what you'll be uncovering. The idea of anything to do with the Black Death ...' He shivered at the thought. 'Are you sure you know what you're doing? I mean, are you absolutely certain you won't be resurrecting some nightmare from the past?'

'You have my word for it. It's seven hundred years since anything down there has seen the light of day. Apart from that, no one is going to ask you guys to go inside the chamber. That's my job.'

'Actually, I'd quite like to see inside,' said Smith. 'The thought of being the first human beings in there in all these years is absolutely mind-blowing ... I mean, like wow.'

'I think I'll just be happy if the abbey walls don't fall down,' said Blackstone, getting sympathetic laughter.

The sight of some visitors arriving at the abbey made Motram ask about the policy on restricting public access while they were working.

'There aren't that many visitors at this time of year,' replied Blackstone. 'I thought we'd leave it officially open while the preliminary groundwork's going on but close before the chamber walls are breached.'

'Makes sense,' Motram agreed.

'We'll ribbon the site off when we start work,' said Fielding.

'People will probably think we're working on the drains.'

'You know,' said Smith thoughtfully, 'I'm surprised the press haven't caught on to this. You'd think it would be a natural for them. *Black Death tomb to be reopened* and all that . . . They usually don't miss the chance to hit the panic button.'

A sudden damper fell over the proceedings and there was a long silence before Motram said, 'You know, you're quite right. I didn't think of that.'

'Me neither,' said Blackstone. 'I guess it can only be because they don't know anything about it.'

'Please God we can keep it that way,' said Motram. 'I suggest we all be very guarded about what we say from now on.'

NINE

'Who can that be at this time of night?' exclaimed May Kelly as the doorbell rang in the council flat she shared with her husband, Brian, in the east end of Glasgow. It was nine o'clock.

'Only one way to find out,' replied her husband, not bothering to take his eyes from his newspaper.

May gave him a dark look but he didn't lift his eyes, even as he reached out for the can of lager that sat beside him. 'I take it it'll not be you doing the finding,' she murmured, putting down her knitting and getting up from her chair. She returned a few moments later but not alone. 'It's an officer from Michael's unit,' she announced.

This time the comment did get a reaction from her husband. 'Jesus Christ,' he exclaimed, getting to his feet, dropping the newspaper and peering at the newcomer over his glasses. 'What's happened?'

'I am very sorry, Mr and Mrs Kelly, but I have to tell you your son Michael, Royal Marine Michael Kelly, has been killed in action in Afghanistan.'

'Oh, Jesus Christ, no . . . no, no, no.' May threw herself at her husband, who stood there as if turned to stone, seemingly unaware of the presence of the woman seeking comfort from him.

'What happened?' he said numbly.

'I'm afraid he died of a wound infection in the treatment facility at Camp Bastion in Helmand Province. The medical staff did their best but the infection didn't respond to treatment. I'm so sorry. By all accounts, he was a fine marine.'

'Wound infection?' exclaimed Brian. 'No one even told us he'd been wounded. when did it happen?'

'I'm afraid I don't have the actual details of the action that led to his being injured. I believe he suffered slight shrapnel wounds which were not thought to be severe at the time. I understand your son dismissed them as being of no consequence. It was when infection set in that the problem arose and he had to be transferred to hospital.'

'Bastards,' murmured Brian. 'Bloody bastards.'

May, finding no comfort in her husband's anger, detached herself and took a handful of tissues from the box sitting on the sideboard. She held them to her face as the three of them stood there in an uncomfortable tableau. Seconds ticked by before Brian asked, 'What happens now?'

'Michael's body will be flown home to the UK for burial with full military honours. You will, of course, be consulted about specifics in due course, when you've had time to come to terms with your great loss.'

'Come to terms? And just how long's that going to take?' muttered Brian, bristling with indignation. 'He's our only son . . . sent to some godforsaken hellhole . . . and for what? Tell me that.'

'I'm so sorry,' said the officer.

May finally removed the tissues from her face and thought the time right to intervene. She gave a final sniff and asked, 'Would you like a cup of tea?'

'That's very kind, Mrs Kelly, but I think it best if I just leave you two alone right now. Someone from family liaison will be contacting you over the next few days about the arrangements and perhaps I should warn you that there's a possibility that the press might want to have a word. I'll leave you this number to ring if you find you need any help with this. I'm so sorry to have to bring you this sad news.'

Brian seemed lost in a world of inner conflict. Grief, anger and frustration were demanding an emotional response from a man not used to giving them. He stood, staring into space, apparently oblivious of what was going on around him. May asked the officer, 'Was Michael alone when he died?'

'I would think not, Mrs Kelly. The field hospital is very well equipped and staffed.'

'I was just wondering if he said anything before . . .'

'I'm afraid I don't know,' replied the officer, sorry for not being able to offer the woman in front of him any crumb of comfort when she looked so vulnerable.

'I just wondered . . .'

'Of course, Mrs Kelly. I'll make enquiries.'

'Thanks, son.'

The officer left and May made tea. She put a cup down beside Brian, who didn't acknowledge it. He simply said, 'You'd better start phoning around. People will have to be told.'

'Maybe you could get off your arse and give me a hand,' snapped May in an uncharacteristic outburst as her grief spilled over into anger.

Brian looked at her in amazement, suddenly unsure of his ground. 'Right, well, maybe I'll go round and tell Maureen . . .' he said, getting to his feet.

'You do that,' said May. 'Tell her her wee brother's . . . been killed . . . Oh, Christ! Sweet Jesus Christ, what am I going to do?' She dissolved into floods of tears, her shoulders shaking silently as Brian tried awkwardly to put an arm round her.

'Easy, hen,' he murmured. 'I'm hurtin' too.'

'Maureen'll want to come round,' said May, as she fought to

compose herself. 'Tell her no. I need some time to myself. I'll talk to her in the morning. Give my love to the bairns.'

'Right you are,' said Brian, putting on his jacket. 'Will you be all right? Is there anything . . .?'

'I'll be fine,' said May, giving a final blow of her nose and throwing the tissues in the bin. 'I'll drink my tea, then I'll start phoning folk.'

'Good girl . . . I'll see you later.'

Brian returned two hours later, after telling his daughter Maureen and her husband what had happened and watching Keith trying to explain to their two young children, who'd been woken by the noise, why Granddad was there and their mummy was crying. 'I'm back,' he announced.

There was no response. The living room was empty; it seemed cold and alien with the television off. Thinking that May might have gone to bed, he had started in the direction of the bedroom when he glanced along the hall and saw a light under the door of Michael's room. He went along and opened it slowly to find May sitting on Michael's bed with photographs in her hands and spread all over the bedspread. She didn't look up when Brian came in but knew he was there. 'Do you remember the holiday in Kinghorn?' she said, holding up a print. 'That awful, bloody caravan and the sound of the rain on the roof . . .'

'Aye,' said Brian. 'Rained every bloody day.'

'But Michael loved it . . . happy as Larry in his wellies, he was.' She finally looked up, pain etched all over her face. 'What am I going to do?'

Brian sat down beside her, hands clenched between his knees. 'We'll get through it, hen. You and me, eh? We always do.'

May had a faraway look in her eyes.

TEN

'Did you get your report off to St Raphael's?' Cassie Motram asked her husband when she arrived home from evening surgery to find him preparing what he'd need for the excavation at the end of the week.

'I did.'

Thinking that she detected some unspoken qualification in the reply, Cassie asked, 'A problem?'

'Far from it. The donor seemed a perfect match for his highness in every way . . .'

'But?'

'What I really can't get my head round is why they asked for my opinion in the first place. Many of the tests they asked for seemed utterly pointless in the circumstances.'

'As you said, they wanted the best and they could afford it,' said Cassie. 'You're the top man in your field.'

'All they needed to do was make sure that blood group and tissue type were compatible for the transplant. All the other stuff they asked for was quite superfluous, an attempt to inflate the bill, if you ask me.'

'Always better to have too much information than too little,' said Cassie. 'And it's their money.'

'I suppose.'

'Why look a gift horse in the mouth? If they want you to dot all the i's and cross all the t's, it's their business, and if it helps to pay for your excavation at Dryburgh, who are you to complain?'

'You're right.' Motram smiled. 'I should just take the money and run.'

'At last, some sense. Expecting wet weather?' Cassie was looking at her husband's Wellington boots, standing beside the rest of the gear he was getting together.

'The weather forecast from Thursday onward isn't good,' said Motram. 'Heavy rain across the north of England and the Scottish Borders.'

'In which case you should pack sunscreen,' said Cassie. 'You know what long-range forecasts are like.'

In the event, the forecast proved accurate. Motram had to drive up to Dryburgh on Friday through torrential rain propelled along by a gusting westerly wind. His hope that the latter might help the rain clouds pass over quickly was not encouraged by a persistently dark sky to his left. There was no sign of Blackstone or the two Maxton Geo-Survey men when he arrived although their vehicles were in the car park, as was a surprising sign saying that the abbey was closed to visitors for remedial work. Motram guessed rightly that the others had sought shelter in the hotel. He joined them for coffee and asked about the sign.

'Change of plan,' said Blackstone. 'After what Les said about the press last time, I thought it would be wise to keep the place completely closed off during the dig. We can do without that kind of attention.'

Motram looked out of the window at the rain. 'Doesn't look as if we'll be inconveniencing too many people on a day like this anyway.'

'Mmm,' agreed Blackstone. 'We've just been discussing whether or not to call the dig off until the weather improves.'

Motram felt a wave of disappointment wash over him but managed to hide it. 'I suppose it's up to you guys,' he said, looking at Smith and Fielding. 'I don't want anyone putting themselves in danger because of unstable ground or mud slides.'

'It's not so much the instability I'm worried about as the possibility of flooding,' said Fielding. 'We plan to create a forty-degree slope down to the wall of the chamber. If it's still raining when we reach the stonework, the water's just going to run down the slope and start accumulating.'

'Couldn't you use a pump?'

'We could, but it's a question of where would we pump the water to. There's a fair stretch of ground to cover before you reach the ditch to the south of the abbey; that's about fifty metres away and we don't want excess water seeping down into the abbey foundations.'

'We certainly don't,' Blackstone put in.

'Well,' Motram sighed philosophically, 'I suppose our hosts have been waiting seven hundred years; another day or two isn't going to make that much difference.'

It rained all day Saturday and Motram paced indoors at home like a caged animal, bemoaning his luck and insisting to Cassie that God had it in for him personally. Always had done, he insisted.

'It's just Britain,' countered Cassie. 'When have you ever known it not to rain when you've planned something outdoors? When I was a girl I used to think all invitations had to have "If wet, in church hall" on them.'

John asked if Cassie would like to go out somewhere. 'We could go into town. Dinner? A film?'

'Let's just stay in,' said Cassie, joining him at the window and giving his arm an encouraging rub. 'We can open a bottle of Côtes du Rhône and watch some telly?'

'Celebrity paint drying?' said John.

'As a prospective celebrity nail technician, you should be taking notes about how to behave on these programmes. You could be on next week . . . toenail cutting . . . on ice.'

John watched some rugby on the television in the sitting room, then went through to the kitchen to get some coffee when the final whistle blew. A news bulletin was showing on the small TV set that Cassie kept in a corner next to the coffee machine. The sound level was low – background noise as Cassie, who was sitting at the table reading a cookery book, called it – but Motram's arm shot out to turn the sound up as a photograph of a young man appeared on the screen.

'What on earth . . .?' exclaimed Cassie as the sudden increase in volume startled her. Her annoyance faded when she saw the look on her husband's face. 'What's the matter?' she asked. 'Are you all right? You look as if you've seen a ghost.'

'I have.' Motram had gone pale. He sat down beside Cassie at the table, eyes still glued to the screen until the report concerning the death of a young Royal Marine in Afghanistan had ended. 'I knew him.'

Cassie's eyes opened wide. 'How?' she asked.

'He was the donor I was asked to screen in London.'

'Did you know he was a soldier?'

'No. He wasn't in uniform when I met him and the subject of what he did for a living didn't come up. We were under instructions to keep everything on a professional level. No idle chit-chat.'

'His poor family,' said Cassie; then, as doubts entered her mind, 'Mind you, I wouldn't have thought there had been time to get back to Afghanistan . . . Are you absolutely sure it's him? Did you get his name?'

Motram shook his head. 'He wasn't introduced to me at the hospital. It was part of the secrecy thing: the patient was Patient X and the donor was, well, the donor. But I'm sure it's him. I liked him; he was a nice chap, a bit nervous about the procedure, ironic really when you consider what he was engaged in abroad.'

'How bizarre,' said Cassie. 'How on earth did a Royal Marine serving in Afghanistan come to be donating bone marrow to a Saudi prince in South Kensington?'

'It is bizarre,' agreed Motram. 'He must have gone back to Afghanistan almost immediately after donating his marrow . . . and been in action immediately after that. How unlucky was that?'

'You know what I think?' asked Cassie, leaning across the table conspiratorially and patting John's arm.

'What?'

'Mistaken identity. You're getting to an age when all young men start to look the same to you.'

Motram smiled but still seemed preoccupied. 'You know, I think I'm going to give Laurence Samson a ring . . . *Sir* Laurence Samson of Harley Street, by the way.'

Cassie made a face to feign how impressed she was, and returned to reading her cookery book. 'Give him my best . . .' she murmured.

Motram retuned a few minutes later looking crestfallen. 'Well?'

'You were right. Mistaken identity.'

'There you are then. Still, it obviously gave you quite a shock.'

Motram seemed deep in thought.

'John, are you all right?'

'I just can't believe it wasn't him,' said Motram. 'That marine was the absolute spitting image . . . I need to see his photo again, get some more details. Maybe the BBC News website will have something.' He went off to turn on the computer he shared with Cassie while she, with a slight shake of her head, returned to her reading. She had made her decision about dinner and was in the early stages of making a risotto when Motram returned and said, 'The report says he was wounded by shrapnel on the 8th: the wounds became infected and he died some days later in a field hospital . . . I saw the donor at St Raphael's on the 8th.'

'So it couldn't have been him.'

'I suppose not.'

After a long silence during which John fidgeted a lot, to Cassie's annoyance, he suddenly said, 'They said the dead marine came from Glasgow.'

Cassie looked at her husband, wondering why that should be significant.

'The man I saw had a Scottish accent.'

ELEVEN

Drier weather moved in late on Sunday and there was even a glimpse of sun on Monday morning when Motram set off for Dryburgh in much better spirits. It was agreed upon his arrival that work should begin right away. Fielding and Smith checked their data from their ground-radar survey and placed stakes in the ground at appropriate intervals before firing up a miniature JCB and beginning the excavation. Motram and Blackstone exchanged smiles as its shovel scooped out the first bucket of earth. Motram was as filled with excitement as Blackstone was with apprehension: the Historic Scotland man kept eyeing the distance between the work and the abbey walls.

After thirty minutes, Fielding signalled to Smith, who was operating the digger, that he should cut the engine. The noise died, leaving only contracting metal noises and the sound of birdsong in the air. Fielding negotiated his way down the sloping trench carrying a number of long steel rods in his hand, and started inserting them horizontally into the wall of earth at its face. He turned with a smile on his face as the rods met resistance. 'Stone,' he announced. 'We're right on the money.'

Taking great care, Smith removed another half-metre of soil with the digger before he and Fielding changed to manual clearing of the final section with their hands and small trowels to leave an area of stone wall of about two square metres exposed.

They climbed up out of the trench to allow Motram to descend and take a look for himself. He did so and ran his hand over the stone with barely suppressed pleasure. 'Well done,' he said, with a broad smile on his face. 'We're almost there.'

The smile faded when he emerged from the trench to see a man with a briefcase walking towards them. The others followed his gaze.

'Please God, it's not the press,' murmured Blackstone.

The four men stood in silence, awaiting the arrival of the newcomer, who did not smile when he reached them. 'Dr Motram?' he enquired, looking from one to the other.

'That's me,' said Motram.

The man removed a card from his pocket. 'Norman Bunce, Health and Safety. I understand you are about to open a tomb containing victims of the Black Death . . .'

Motram closed his eyes, hoping that divine inspiration might provide him with a better opening line than *What the fuck do you want?* He opted instead for, 'Seven-hundred-year-old victims of Black Death, Mr Bunce.'

'Be that as it may, doctor . . .' said Bunce, starting out on a soliloquy that ended with the edict Motram had been fearing throughout. Nothing more was to happen on site until Health and Safety had sanctioned it.

Details of contact numbers were exchanged as the four men accepted the inevitable. 'I must say I'm surprised at you, Mr Blackstone,' said Bunce. 'Historic Scotland are usually very much on the ball when it comes to safety.'

'We still are,' said Blackstone sourly.

'No need for that attitude,' said Bunce.

'There's no danger to anyone. The corpses, if they're there, will be seven hundred years old,' said Blackstone flatly.

'Let's leave that to the professionals to decide, shall we?'

'What professionals are we talking about here, Mr Bunce?' asked Motram.

'I'll make my report and my superiors will take the necessary decisions about whom to seek advice from,' Bunce announced, aware of the growing aggression in the air.

'They can't be too few on the ground,' murmured Fielding.

'Good day, gentlemen.'

'Oh, I don't believe it,' Cassie exclaimed sympathetically when she heard what had happened. 'What will you do now?'

'We just have to wait for a decision.'

'But surely they couldn't stop it altogether?'

Motram shrugged. 'Who knows?'

'At least you won't have this sort of thing to deal with when you become a celebrity nail technician.'

'Absolutely not,' said Motram. 'Mind you, nail scissors can be extremely dangerous in the wrong hands . . .'

Two days later Motram got the call he had been waiting for. The excavation and opening of the burial chamber could go ahead subject to the meeting of certain conditions. Health and Safety wanted to inspect the equipment and protective clothing the men would be using when recovering samples from the chamber. They also wanted a Public Health doctor to interview the four of them on site before the chamber was opened and administer any protective injections he thought necessary.

'Probably anti-tetanus,' said Cassie when she heard. 'I could give you that.'

'You'd probably also have to give me a certificate signed by two independent witnesses and a justice of the peace,' growled Motram. 'Best let them do it.'

'They're only doing their job,' Cassie said soothingly. The

look she got in return suggested she might be on her own in holding that view. 'Be positive. You are going to get in to your chamber.' She hugged Motram and persisted in looking at him until he gave in and smiled.

'You're right.'

With all the formalities finally out of the way, health checks over and injections administered, Motram and the others were left on their own to open up the chamber. Motram watched the official vehicles depart and then joined the others in a slow walk over to the site. 'Quite a day,' said Blackstone.

Motram nodded. 'Days like these don't come along too often in science,' he said. 'Research can be a bit of a plod when things aren't going well but when a moment like this pops up . . . by God, it's worth waiting for.'

'I only hope it lives up to expectations,' said Blackstone.

Motram paused to look at the abbey in its beautiful setting, parts of its ruined walls as old as the secret he was about to unlock, and felt the excitement of anticipation rise inside him. He put on his white cover-all suit while Smith and Fielding prepared their tools for the breach of the chamber wall. They had already erected a sealable plastic entrance 'vestibule' over the area they would open up. They would chisel out the mortar and make sure the stones were loose enough to be moved easily before retreating to allow Motram to enter on his own.

Blackstone chose to pace slowly up and down, leaving Motram alone with his thoughts. John sat on the grass, listening to the sound of chisels on stone and watching the crouched shapes of Smith and Fielding through the plastic screen. The noise stopped and the world seemed deathly quiet for a moment before the pair emerged. Fielding lowered his mask and said simply, 'All yours, doc.'

'Good luck,' said Blackstone.

Motram accepted the stone chisel handed to him by Smith as he passed by – just in case he needed it – and entered the plastic 'vestibule', closing the entrance flap behind him. He knelt down and tested the stones by rocking a couple before pulling out the first without any trouble. The gap grew as the stones piled up in neat rows on either side of him, but he resisted the temptation to stop and shine his torch in through the hole until the gap was big enough for him to enter. He took a slight pause to get his breath back, reminding himself in the process that he needed to take more exercise, then crawled head first into the chamber and got slowly to his feet.

TWELVE

In what little light was coming through the breach in the wall behind him, Motram could see that there were stone benches lined up along both sides of the tomb. It had been sheer good fortune that Smith and Fielding had picked a spot between two of these benches. He clicked on his torch but, strangely, the world remained black. The walls of the chamber were black, the benches were black and the bodies lying on them appeared to be black – or at least what they were wrapped in was black.

It was impossible not to draw parallels with the mummified occupants of the Egyptian pyramids, but in this case nothing had been left to accompany the departed on their journey to the afterlife, no colourful ceramics, no gold, no wine jars, just the blackened shapes of corpses that had lain undisturbed for seven centuries.

The first hurdle had been cleared. The bodies had been found, but the big question remained to be answered. The sixteen occupants of the benches looked like human bodies but until he had penetrated the outer wrapping he wouldn't know for sure how successful the Le Clerks had been with their preservation methods and how well the bodies had survived their long wait. Everything now depended on that. He shone the torch beam down into the bag he had brought with him and took out a bubble-wrap roll containing a number of surgical instruments.

Spreading it on the ground, he selected a scalpel and a pair of latex gloves. The big moment had arrived.

Motram knew immediately that something was wrong when he gently placed a hand on the torso of his chosen body. He could tell at once that it lacked substance. He had only sought to steady himself with his left hand while he inserted the tip of the scalpel into the wrapping material in the neck area, but now he felt forced to investigate and apply more pressure with the flat of that hand. It didn't take much before what little resistance there was gave way and his hand went clean through the corpse-shaped wrapping, leaving only a gaping hole and a cloud of dust which swirled mockingly across the beam of the torch he'd temporarily propped up on a neighbouring bench. Dust and dry, brittle bones was all that was left of the bodies after seven hundred years in their underground lair. Nothing of substance had survived.

Motram pulled the mask from his face and felt a wave of disappointment sweep over him. He supposed that this had always been the most probable outcome after such a long time, but he had failed to take the likelihood on board to any significant degree. Foolishly, he had allowed himself to believe that the preservation of the bodies was a realistic possibility and he had been seduced by the idea of going down in history as the man who solved the riddle of Black Death. He was now paying the price in crushing disappointment.

His spirits were so low that he actually felt physically weak and had to support himself on one of the stone benches while he tried to summon up the energy to leave and face the others outside with the news of failure. But, as the minutes passed, he didn't recover: instead, he started to feel worse. Disappointment was becoming anger and anger was threatening to become rage. The lines between one emotion and another were becoming blurred. Sweat broke out on his brow and he started to feel very ill indeed . . .

Blackstone looked at his watch and asked, 'Do you think he's all right?'

'Let's not grudge him his moment of glory,' said Fielding with a smile. 'This is probably the pinnacle of his whole career.'

'I'm still looking forward to seeing what's in there myself if he'll let me,' said Smith. 'It's dead exciting.'

'Here he comes,' said Fielding as he caught sight of movement behind the plastic. The three men moved towards the sloping trench, anxious to hear what Motram had to say. When he saw that the scientist seemed to be having difficulty, Fielding moved in to help him with the plastic door flap.

'Well?' asked Blackstone.

Motram, still carrying the torch in one hand, started to move slowly up the steep slope without answering. Blackstone exchanged a puzzled glance with the others and leaned forward to ask, 'Everything okay, John?'

Motram looked up at him, eyes burning like coals. Without warning, he swung the heavy torch into his face.

Blackstone's left cheekbone shattered and he screamed out in pain as he fell over, grabbing at Fielding in an attempt to stop himself slipping into the trench. Smith tried to help Fielding who was in danger of being pulled in too but unwittingly came within reach of Motram, who swung the torch again, this time connecting with the back of Smith's head. All three men tumbled into the trench behind Motram, Blackstone desperately trying to shield his shattered face and Fielding half somersaulting over him before the deadweight of Smith landed on top of him.

Motram continued his slow, ponderous journey up the slope

and started out across the grass towards the digger. He climbed on board and punched the start button, mumbling to himself as he struggled with the unfamiliar gears.

Smith was unconscious and Blackstone barely knew what was going on around him because of the excruciating pain in his face, but Fielding was all too aware of the little yellow digger beginning to trundle towards them and the pair of murderous eyes looking directly at him. 'What the fuck are you doing, man?' he cried out in panic. He knew he had to get out of the trench but it was taking him an eternity to free himself from the weight of Smith on top of him. He felt as if he were caught in a living nightmare.

The digger had almost reached him by the time he had managed to free his legs and swing one up over the lip of the trench. Motram saw his intention and responded by steering the digger to that side and lowering the bucket sharply.

Fielding fell back into the trench, crying out in pain and clutching his injured knee. He could only watch as Motram managed to reverse after several abortive tussles with the digger's control levers. It was clear that he intended to drive the digger down the slope and over the bodies of the three men lying there, perhaps to continue straight on through the wall of the burial chamber.

To Fielding's relief, Motram misjudged the alignment of the digger's tracks as it lurched forward after an uncertain change of gear. He missed the narrow entrance to the trench so that the left track stayed above ground while the other started down the slope. The angle of tilt was too great for the digger and it toppled over to the night, coming to rest against the lip of the trench and throwing Motram out onto the grass, where he lay holding his throat and seemingly fighting for breath before rolling over and lying still.

The digger's engine died, restoring peace to the abbey and its surroundings, making everything that had gone before seem quite surreal to Fielding, who stared at Motram's motionless body, willing it not to recover, before looking briefly up at the sky. 'Mad bastard,' he mumbled, searching through his pockets for his mobile phone.

'He did what?' exclaimed Cassie Motram when the police told her what had happened.

'He appeared to take leave of his senses, doctor. Ran amok, according to the others; almost killed one of them and severely injured the other two.'

'But this is my husband you're talking about,' protested Cassie. 'He's an academic, for God's sake. He's the kindest, most gentle man on earth. He goes to enormous lengths to avoid killing spiders. There just has to be some awful mistake.'

The senior of the two policemen sent to break the news gave an apologetic shrug. 'I'm afraid the medics have had to restrain him and place him in an isolation facility at the hospital,' he said. 'They say they haven't ruled out some kind of . . . reaction to what was in the tomb.'

'Reaction? What d'you mean? What kind of reaction?'

The policeman looked helpless. 'The doctors say they can't rule out some kind of poisoning or infection . . .'

Cassie sank into a chair, holding her head in her hands, unwilling at first to even consider what she was being told. 'Let me get this straight,' she said slowly, trying to adopt a rational approach when she really just wanted to scream. 'You are telling me that John entered the chamber sane but came out mad?'

'That's pretty much what we've been told, doctor.'

Cassie shook her head as if trying to clear it. 'I have to go to him,' she said, getting to her feet. 'Borders General Hospital, you say?'

'Yes, doctor. Sorry to be the bearer of such bad news.'

Bad news became tabloid news the following morning. The redtops had a field day. The Black Death, the opening up of a centuries-old tomb and the resulting insanity of the principal investigator was the stuff of editors' dreams. It didn't take them long to invent an accompanying curse that had come down through the years, which enabled them to draw parallels with the families of those who'd incurred the supposed wrath of the pharaohs when the pyramids were opened up in Egypt.

THIRTEEN

'Girls,' complained Peter. 'Why do they always have to take so long?'

Dr Steven Dunbar smiled at his young nephew's impatience. They were standing outside the changing rooms at Dumfries swimming pool waiting for Steven's daughter Jenny and his niece Mary to emerge. 'It's just the way things are, Peter. One of the things in life we blokes have to accept.' Seeing that Peter remained unconvinced, he added, 'The pizza will taste all the better when we finally get there.'

Steven, a medical investigator with the Sci-Med Inspectorate, based at the Home Office in London, had been on leave for the past month. He had escaped to Scotland for some respite after a particularly tough assignment, which had threatened his life and exhausted him both physically and mentally. He lived in London but his daughter Jenny stayed up here in the village of Glenvane with Steven's sister-in-law Sue and her solicitor husband, Peter, along with their own two children, Peter and Mary – an arrangement that had been in place since the death of Steven's wife Lisa from a brain tumour. Jenny had been a baby at the time so she had never known anything else.

In the normal course of events, Steven would spend every second weekend in Scotland, but the hell of his last assignment had meant not seeing Jenny for over six weeks so he was trying to make amends. A favourite outing for the children was always to the swimming pool in Dumfries, followed by pizza and as much ice cream as they could eat. Tradition had it that he would receive a mock telling-off from Sue when they got home but, for the children, this was part of the enjoyment.

'At last,' exclaimed Peter as the girls emerged. 'What do you do in there?'

'We have lots of hair to dry,' said Mary. 'You don't.'

'Talking to do, more like,' grumbled Peter.

'Are we going for pizza and ice cream, Daddy?' asked Jenny.
'You bet.'

'Even if it makes Aunty Sue angry?' she asked, suppressing a shared giggle with Mary.

'I'll fix things with Aunty Sue,' Steven assured her.

They emerged into the sunshine and took hands as they crossed the main road at the traffic lights to walk on the broad pavement by the River Nith.

'Can we go out on the bridge for a moment, Daddy?' asked Jenny as they were about to pass an old stone bridge crossing the river.

'Oh, yeah, let's,' said Peter, starting to look around for pebbles.

'Me too,' said Mary.

Jenny was content to hold her father's hand as they stepped out onto the bridge. 'I like this bridge. It's very old, isn't it?' she said, running the flat of her hand along the stones.

'Hundreds of years,' replied Steven.

Jenny paused to read a signboard. 'Dev ... Devor ... Devorgilla.'

'Devorgilla's Bridge, nutkin.'

'Funny name. Why is it called that?'

'It's named after a very grand lady named Devorgilla. She

lived a very long time ago with her husband, John, here in Galloway. The history books say they loved each other very much. They even had a son who became king of Scotland.'

Jenny seemed thoughtful for a few moments before asking, 'Do you love Tally very much, Daddy?'

Steven swallowed. He hadn't seen the question coming. During the course of his last assignment, he had met a woman – Natalie Simmons, a doctor at a hospital in Leicester – whom he'd come to care for and knew could be special in his life. He had brought her up to meet Jenny the week before and thought it had gone well.

'Would it bother you an awful lot if I did, nutkin?' he asked, looking for clues in Jenny's eyes, but she looked down at the ground.

'Do you love her more than me?'

Steven knelt beside Jenny and cuddled her tightly. 'I could never love anyone more than you, Jenny.'

Jenny smiled contentedly but then pressed on with her interrogation. 'If you and Tally get a house together . . . will I come? Will I have to leave Aunty Sue and Uncle Peter?'

'What would you like to do?'

'I think we should all live together. There's plenty of room.'

Steven smiled at Jenny's perfect solution. 'That might not be possible, sweetheart. Tally is a doctor in a big hospital in England and she has lots of children to look after. They would miss her terribly if she had to leave.'

'Mmm,' said Jenny, deciding the conversation was over. 'Can we go for pizza now?'

The children were in bed when Steven told Sue and Peter about Jenny bringing up the subject of his relationship with Tally.

'It's only natural that she should,' said Sue. 'Poor sausage.

It's not easy being nine years old when you think your very foundations might be under threat from an outsider.'

'I don't want them to be under threat,' said Steven. 'You know how much Jenny means to me, but . . . I do have feelings for Tally. God, I feel like I'm walking on broken glass at the moment.'

'Poor Steven. But be assured, whatever you decide, we regard Jenny as one of our own and always will. She's welcome to stay here with us as long as she wants to.'

'Absolutely,' said Peter. 'In fact – and I know this isn't going to help your decision making – we'd hate to see her go.'

'Thanks, you two. You know how I feel about you guys and what you've done over the years.'

'We do,' said Sue, who was always uncomfortable with high praise. 'Just keep us informed.'

Steven phoned Tally from the privacy of his own room and exchanged details of the day with her.

'Lucky you,' said Tally. 'I've been run off my feet; didn't even have time for a sandwich at lunchtime.'

'But the NHS is the envy of the world, Tally.'

'Just as well you're at a distance, Dunbar,' Tally growled. 'Talking about you being at a distance, what are our chances of meeting up soon? Or don't you have time for the number two lady in your life any more?' Before he could respond, she said, 'Sorry. That was unfair. I know this must be difficult for Jenny as well as you.'

'You two seemed to get on well together, I thought.'

'I thought she was a super kid.'

'But?'

'No buts. I just don't think we should rush things, that's all. I don't think I should suddenly be there every time she turns round. She needs time alone with her dad and I need time alone with my man. Let's not push the happy families button too soon.'

'Okay.'

Steven was thinking about the conversation and feeling less than happy about it when his phone, which he'd put down on the bedside table, came to life with a text message. He hoped it was Tally wishing him sweet dreams but it wasn't. It was the duty officer at Sci-Med, telling him his leave was over and he should return to London on the first available flight.

FOURTEEN

Brian Kelly was getting ready to go out. He stood in front of the hall mirror, examining his image, turning this way and that and appearing well satisfied with what he saw. The reality was a sixteen-stone man with a pot belly, wearing a Glasgow Celtic football shirt and scruffy jeans. Round his neck he wore a club scarf as a further mark of allegiance. A woollen hat in the colours added the final touch to the ensemble.

'Is that you off, then?' asked May, passing him in the hall. 'Who's it today?'

'Aberdeen. We'll stuff them and go six points clear at the top.'

'I hope so,' said May, who didn't care either way but felt that Brian in a good mood was a better prospect than Brian in a bad one.

'See you whenever.'

Brian had just reached for the door handle when the bell rang. The immediate opening of the door took the young Royal Marine standing there by surprise. 'God, that was quick,' he said.

'I was just going out,' explained Brian, fighting back conflicting emotions as he took in the uniform and saw that the caller was around the same age as Michael.

'I'm Jim Leslie. I was a friend of Mick's.'

'Oh . . . right . . . right,' said Brian as thoughts of the game evaporated. 'C'mon in, son.' He turned his head and called out, 'May, it's a pal of Michael's.'

May's face lit up with pleasure as she fussed over their caller. 'It's so nice of you to come and see us, Jim. Have you come far? Are you hungry? Can I get you anything?' She turned to Brian. 'Brian, maybe Jim would like a beer.'

'I'm fine, Mrs Kelly, really I am. I'm home on leave. I left the base in Arbroath this morning: I'm on my way to my girlfriend's place in Salford so I thought I would stop off in Glasgow and say hello to you folks.'

'I'm so glad you did, son,' said May.

'Aye,' echoed Brian. 'That was real nice of you. Are you sure you won't have a beer?'

Leslie declined again with a smile.

'Did you know Michael well?' asked May.

'Mick and I didn't train together but we got to know each other in Afghanistan – you get to know people pretty quickly when you're out on patrol with them: you've got to trust the guy who's covering your back, if you know what I mean. We got on well. He often spoke of you folks . . . and his sister, Maureen and her kids. He was really proud of being an uncle.'

'Tess and Calum adored him,' said May, her eyes beginning to fill.

'It must have been a hell of a shock,' said Leslie.

'You can say that again,' said Brian.

'How much d'you know about Mick's death?'

The sudden question seemed out of context in the otherwise comfortable and comforting exchange and took Brian and May by surprise. 'How do you mean, son?'

'How much do you know about the circumstances of Mick's death?

Brian shrugged, feeling uncomfortable and somehow filled with foreboding. 'Just what they told us, I suppose; he died in a field hospital of a wound infection that didn't respond to treatment.'

'That officer never got back to me,' interrupted May, her eyes filling with sadness. 'He said he'd find out if Michael had said anything before he died but he never did . . .'

'Did the rupert say anything about how Mick got wounded?'

Brian shook his head. 'We did ask him but he said he wasn't sure, said something about the wound being . . . well, nothing much: it was really the infection that killed Mick.'

'He'd been back in the UK.'

Brian and May looked at each other in surprise which quickly changed to confusion. 'We didn't know that. He never told us he was coming home. He never came to see us.'

'I don't think he could,' said Leslie. 'It was all very hush-hush. He said he couldn't tell me either when I kidded him about having friends in high places and getting special treatment.'

'How long was he back for?' asked Brian.

'Between two and three weeks, I reckon. He must have been on his way back to join the unit when the *incident* happened.'

The inflection Leslie put on the words caused an electric pause in the room. Brian looked for clues in the young marine's face. 'What are you trying to tell us, son?' he asked suspiciously.

Leslie drew up his shoulders and spread his hands. 'I wish I could be more specific, Mr Kelly, but it's just that no one seems to know what really happened to Mick. Like I say, he'd been home in the UK and was on his way back to the unit when next thing I knew was that he had been wounded and was lying in a field hospital. I tried to get down to see him but when I got there he'd been transferred to the bigger medical unit at Camp Bastion. A few days after that we were told he'd . . . died.'

'Are you saying there might have been something funny about how he got wounded?' asked Brian, beginning to sound angry. 'Like it was his own side who shot him, for instance? Friendly fire? Is that what you're saying?' He managed to inject such distaste and loathing into the phrase that Leslie recoiled a little. 'Tell me, son, were those American fuckers involved . . . shooting' at people from miles up in the sky to keep their own arses away from trouble?'

'I really don't think it was anything like that, Mr Kelly, Mrs Kelly. But whatever it was, it happened before he re-joined the unit because he never made it back. I would have known if he had. That means that something must have happened between the airport and the camp – and the airport road's pretty busy and well defended. If anything had happened – an ambush or an IED going off or any kind of air incident – we would have heard about it. But there was no word of anything happening, then or afterwards, when you'd expect the guys to be talking about it . . . absolutely nothing. That sort of suggests that Mick was alone at the time . . . so where were the others who came in on his flight? There's something not right and no one's talking.'

'We've obviously not been told the whole story, son,' said Brian. 'But by Christ . . . I'm going to get to the bottom of this.'

May looked as if she'd just become involved in something she'd rather not pursue.

FIFTEEN

Steven caught the nine o'clock British Airways shuttle from Glasgow to London in the morning and found himself circling over West Drayton an hour later while the aircraft queued for a landing slot. For once, he didn't mind the delay. He had mixed feelings about returning to work – perhaps as an aftermath of his last assignment. It wasn't just the danger he'd found himself in – danger had been part of his life for a very long time – but more a case of hoping that nothing like it would happen again, particularly not on his next investigation.

He'd done his best to assure Tally that last time had been a one-off and that his job was usually much more routine, involving paperwork rather than guns and car chases. Tally, who'd been caught up in the nightmare, clearly needed the assurance and he feared that the long-term relationship he hoped to have with her might well founder if he found himself in trouble again.

He'd fallen in love with Tally and she with him, but she was an intelligent woman who knew that love needed firm foundations. The big question was whether or not his job with Sci-Med could ever be compatible with that requirement. Steven reflected on this as he watched the shadows on the cabin wall change as the aircraft continued to circle. He considered how different life might have been had he marched to the drum of convention and followed a career in medicine.

Steven had been born and brought up in the village of Glenridding in the Lake District where he'd enjoyed an idyllic childhood, playing and climbing in the Cumbrian mountains. He'd done well at school and, like so many bright children, been pushed towards a medical career. He'd complied with this pressure – mainly to please parents and teachers – but, after graduating and doing his registration year, he had admitted to himself and everyone else concerned that he had little heart for a future in medicine.

Instead of drifting along as many did, he took the major decision of resigning from the hospital where he was working as a junior houseman and joined the army. His strong build and natural athletic ability ensured that at last he now felt like a fish very much *in* water. His career had progressed through service with the Parachute Regiment to membership of the Special Forces, with whom he'd served in trouble spots all over the world. The army, always keen to maximise resources, never lost sight of his medical degree and he had become an expert in field medicine – the medicine of the battlefield, where deserts and jungles had been his emergency rooms.

With his middle thirties approaching and Special Forces being the young men's game it was, he had been faced with an uncertain future as a civilian. The medical profession had little need of the skills he'd acquired in the military and he felt it was too late to retrain. This left some kind of peripheral job – perhaps with a pharmaceutical company or as an in-house physician with some large commercial concern. In the end, however, he had been saved from the humdrum by John Macmillan – now Sir John Macmillan – who ran a small investigatory unit, the Sci-Med Inspectorate, inside the Home Office. The unit looked into possible crime or wrong-doing in the high-tech areas of science and medicine where the police had little or no expertise.

Macmillan recruited science and medical graduates but never the newly qualified: he insisted that all Sci-Med investigators must have held demanding jobs in the real world before joining the unit and proved themselves in high stress situations. Weekend paintball fights and white-water rafting with the chaps in the office didn't count; coming under fire in Kosovo did. Above all else in his people, he valued common sense.

Over the years, Steven had quickly become Sci-Med's top investigator, but at some expense to his personal life. It was a very long way from being a nine to five job and, although he persisted in downplaying the risks – even to himself – it could be dangerous and had proved to be so in the past. His denial had its roots in guilt, the guilt he felt in acknowledging that he had wilfully continued in a hazardous job when he was the father of a little girl who had already lost her mother. However happy and settled she was with Sue and Peter in Scotland, his responsibility remained.

Steven's belief when Lisa died that he would never find another woman he would want to spend his life with had been challenged on several occasions over the years, as time proved to be the great healer it was always mooted to be. Such incidents had always caused him to re-examine the situation with regard to Jenny and family life, but circumstances had always changed before the Rubicon had required to be crossed. Looking back, he had been profoundly unlucky in love for a whole variety of reasons, ranging from tragedy to simple, practical incompatibility. But now Tally had come into his life and all the old questions were lining up again.

Tally had had a first meeting with Jenny and the early signs were good, but Tally had a successful career of her own to consider. She was currently a senior registrar at the hospital in Leicester but would soon be thinking about applying for a consultancy, and that could be anywhere in the country. She couldn't be expected to throw all that up in order to come and play *Little House on the Prairie*.

'Sorry for the delay, ladies and gentlemen, We've now been given permission to land,' said the captain's voice, bringing Steven's train of thought to an abrupt end.

As Steven opened the door to his apartment in Marlborough Court, he reflected on the fact that this was something he hated doing if he had been away for a while. There was something about coming home to a cold, empty apartment that he found depressing and invariably reminded him of the great loss in his life. As usual, he compensated by switching on everything from the central heating to the TV and the kettle; this time there was no call for lighting as it was mid-morning and it was sunny outside.

The directive to return to London had not said anything about urgency so he made himself coffee and took it to his favourite seat by the window where, through a gap in the buildings opposite, he could see the river traffic pass by. He started preparing a mental list of the things he should do. He'd been away for two weeks so he should check to see if his car in the basement garage was okay and whether it would start after its battery had been maintaining the Porsche security system without charge for that length of time. He would also have to replenish the fridge and larder, which he'd run down before going up to Scotland. A trip to the supermarket was on the cards, but he'd do that late at night to avoid crowds.

He finished his coffee and showered before changing out of his comfortable travel clothes of jeans and polo shirt. John Macmillan was very much old-school when it came to dress codes. The 'herd', as Macmillan called them, might have stopped wearing ties and started wearing trainers to work but his people hadn't. Steven's dark blue suit, Parachute Regiment tie and polished black Oxfords would pass muster.

He decided to let the lunch hour pass before going into the Home Office just in case Macmillan was having one of his working lunches. It was usual for him to have sandwiches at his desk, but at least once a week he would invite someone in the corridors of power to have lunch with him at his club. It was his way of keeping in touch with what was really going on in Westminster. He might – and did – look the very essence of the Whitehall mandarin, tall, elegant and patrician, with silver hair and charming manners, but Macmillan was in many ways a maverick, a man who jealously guarded Sci-Med's independence from all attempts to have it put on a 'more structured basis' as the parliamentary jargon went.

Steven settled for a sandwich and a Czech beer at a riverside pub before completing his walk to the Home Office. Showing his ID, he shared a joke with the man on the door who noted that it had 'been a while'. Jean Roberts, Macmillan's secretary, said much the same thing when he put his head round the door of her office. 'Hello, stranger.'

As always, Jean enquired about Jenny and how she was getting on at school and, as always, Steven asked about the Bach Choir – Jean's main interest outside work – and what they were doing at the moment. There was a slight pause before Jean asked, 'And you . . . what about you?'

'I'm fine.' Jean looked over her glasses at him, the gesture prompting further comment. 'Really I am . . . but thanks for asking.'

'Good,' said Jean, deciding to accept his assertion this time. 'It's good to have you back.' She pressed a button on her desk and announced his arrival.

SIXTEEN

'He's currently in isolation at Borders General Hospital near Melrose,' said John Macmillan in reply to Steven's question when he'd finished. 'He's being kept under heavy sedation for the safety of nursing and medical staff, and he'll stay there until lab tests are complete.'

'Quite a story,' said Steven. 'What made them excavate at Dryburgh Abbey in the first place?'

'According to his wife, the Master of Balliol College approached him. The college had come into possession of some old letters which suggested that the bodies of a number of Black Death victims – members of the Scottish army, which had been camped in the Selkirk Forest in the mid thirteen hundreds waiting for their chance to invade – had been recovered at the request of their kinfolk, preserved by some Borders family who specialised in that sort of thing and hidden away in a secret tomb. Apparently this family had been responsible for preserving the heart of the Lord of Galloway, John Balliol . . . so that his wife could keep it with her in a little box.' Macmillan made a face. 'Not exactly your usual sort of *memento mori*.'

'Devorgilla,' said Steven.

'You know about this?' exclaimed Macmillan in surprise.

'You forget, my daughter lives up in that area of the country. The lady is well known in Dumfries and Galloway. Jenny and

I were standing on Devorgilla's Bridge in Dumfries the other day. Why did Balliol College approach Motram?'

'Motram has an interest in old plagues and their causes – he's actually a specialist in cell biology and an expert on the mechanics of viral infection. His personal hobbyhorse is a belief that Black Death was caused by a virus and not by bubonic plague as the rest of us were taught. This was his chance to get some proof, if the bodies in the tomb had been preserved well enough.'

'But they weren't.'

'A case of dust to dust, I understand.'

'What's our interest?'

Macmillan placed his elbows on his desk and rested his chin on his folded hands. 'It might well be that this chap Motram suffered some sort of breakdown – maybe in response to the disappointment he felt when he found the bodies inside the tomb were just dust and bone – but on the other hand it just might . . .'

'Have had something to do with the dust,' said Steven, filling in the blank.

'Exactly. The tabloids have been doing their best to whip up fear and alarm with tales of curses coming down through the centuries; it would be nice to have a more objective view of what happened.'

Steven nodded. 'I take it the site is sealed off?'

'And the abbey closed to all visitors. The last thing the UK needs right now is any kind of epidemic coming on top of everything else.'

Steven smiled. 'No doubt the tabloids would construe that as the wrath of God coming to bear on the lot of us . . . What about the others on site at the time? I take it Motram wasn't alone?'

'There were three others, a couple of chaps from a company

called Maxton Geo-Survey who had located the burial chamber and did the actual excavation of the site, and an inspector from Historic Scotland who was overseeing things . . .' Macmillan flicked through his notes. 'Alan Blackstone. No one actually entered the chamber apart from Motram, but the others sustained a variety of injuries when Motram ran amok. The worst affected was Blackstone: Motram smashed the side of his face in with a heavy torch. He's awaiting maxillo-facial surgery in hospital in Edinburgh. The other two are on the mend. One was knocked unconscious with a blow to the back of the head and other suffered leg injuries when a mechanical shovel was dropped on his knee, but all three seem perfectly sane and free from infection, you'll be pleased to hear.'

'Maybe I should talk to them first.'

'Jean has prepared a file for you with relevant names and addresses.'

'Who else is involved in the investigation?'

Macmillan smiled. 'The usual suspects, although the police have backed off with Motram being held in hospital and possibly in line for sectioning under the Mental Health Act and the others being unwilling to press charges in the circumstances.

'But Public Health, Health and Safety, and major incident groups in the area will all have some input. Porton Down have also expressed an interest and will be having their say.'

It was Steven's turn to smile at the mention of the UK's chemical and biological defence establishment. 'There's a surprise,' he murmured.

'I think we can assume that they'll want to examine the chamber, swab it down and take samples of the dust. They'll probably put a mobile lab on site, like some of the others, but you have as much right as they have to be there and to ask questions. Don't let them push you around.'

'As if,' said Steven. He'd come into conflict with Porton Down on a number of occasions in the past. 'Anyone else I have to worry about?'

Macmillan adopted a pained expression. 'There's a degree of religious interest,' he said. 'There's some sort of inter-faith discussion going on over what should happen to the inmates of the chamber and how their remains – the dust – should be disposed of, but that won't affect you. There's nothing anyone can do until the closure notice on the site is lifted and that won't be until Public Health is satisfied that there isn't a problem. I've informed the relevant authorities in the area that Sci-Med is taking an interest.'

'Best get started then.'

Steven took the file back to his flat and read it through. There was very little to assimilate. John Motram was a 52-year-old lecturer at Newcastle University, and an acknowledged expert on how viruses infected people. He lived with his wife Cassandra in the village of Longthorn, a little north of Newcastle, where she was a partner in the group medical practice that served the surrounding area. He had no known history of mental illness or any other medical problems. In all respects, he seemed a perfectly normal, well-respected man who had, for no apparent reason, flipped his lid after entering a seven-hundred-year-old tomb harbouring victims of Black Death.

Steven appreciated that it was the Black Death connection that had attracted Macmillan's attention, and reflected on the fact that the mere mention of a disease that had inspired such fear and dread down through the years, having wiped out a third of Europe's population in the fourteenth century, was enough to precipitate a Sci-Med investigation in the twenty-first.

His first impulse was to dismiss any possible connection between Black Death and Motram's illness, but he had to acknowledge that in doing so he was assuming the very thing that Motram was arguing against, that Black Death had been caused by bubonic plague. It was certainly true that bubonic plague could not have survived in the dust of decayed bodies for such a long time and had no history of including madness among its extensive and horrifying repertoire of symptoms, but none of that would be relevant if Black Death had been caused by something else entirely. This was not a comforting thought.

Knowing that Porton Down was involved did little to lift his spirits either, especially when he started to wonder how likely it was be that their scientists would share their findings with the wider scientific community if evidence of a previously unknown microbial agent should come to light. He concluded that it wasn't very likely at all. It would be par for the course if they and the Ministry of Defence were to classify the whole affair under the Official Secrets Act. The sooner he got up there the better.

Steven held a particular loathing for the very notion of biological warfare. The idea of intelligent people teaming up with the microbial world – so long the sworn enemy of mankind – to design ever more dangerous bacteria and viruses seemed to embody the very essence of evil. He knew that the UK's Porton Down facility would insist that their interest was solely concerned with defence of the realm, but that would be the claim of every military microbial research lab on earth. It made him think of the labs full of smallpox virus that had been discovered all over the old Soviet bloc after the Berlin Wall came down – at a time when the World Health Organisation had been debating whether or not to destroy what they had believed to be the last remaining lab stocks of the virus on earth to create a smallpox-free planet.

Steven turned his attention to transport. He would need a car once he was up in Scotland, so should he fly up to Edinburgh or Glasgow and hire one for the duration of his stay or should he use his own car to drive north? He decided a phone call would help him with the decision and looked through the file Jean Roberts had given him for the number of the relevant Public Health authority in the area.

He spoke to Dr Kenneth Glass, the Public Health director, who told him the good news that his people had been first on site after the incident: they had already been inside the chamber under strict bio-safety conditions and had taken a large number of samples for analysis. The fear that Porton Down and the MOD might get there first and stop anyone else collecting samples was no longer an issue. Steven decided to drive up to Scotland.

SEVENTEEN

Steven left early next morning. He was looking forward to his first long-distance try-out of the new Porsche Boxter he'd bought to replace the one destroyed during the course of his last assignment. Luckily, Sci-Med took care of insurance matters for their people and it hadn't been necessary for him to explain the reasons behind his somersaulting from the M1 into a field and the resulting fireball.

Steven was up in Scotland by early afternoon but it wasn't until he'd left the motorway to follow the winding border country roads that he really started to enjoy the car. The exhilaration of good acceleration and limpet-like road holding ensured that he was in a good mood when he drew into the car park at Borders General Hospital and cut the engine. Not only was Dr John Motram being held here in isolation but the man he'd injured by dropping a mechanical shovel on his leg, Tony Fielding, was a patient in the orthopaedics department.

Unlike those of inner-city hospitals, where parking was always difficult and a constant bone of contention, the car parks here were extensive. He had found a space without any difficulty, enabling him to maintain his good mood as he left the car and walked over to Reception, where he asked for Dr Toby Miles, the man the file informed him was responsible for Motram's care.

Miles turned out to be a short, tubby man with wiry, dry-looking hair and a florid face. He was dressed in a grey pin-striped suit, a pink shirt and a purple tie which didn't help with the complexion problem. He examined Steven's ID at some length before returning it and asking, 'What can I do for you, Dr Dunbar?'

'I understand you are the psychiatrist in charge of John Motram's case, doctor. I'd like to know your thoughts on what you think might have happened to him.'

Miles appeared thoughtful for what seemed an age, and Steven was beginning to wonder whether the man had an interest in amateur dramatics when he finally said, 'I'm sorry, Dr Dunbar, but the truth is I simply don't know. John Motram is out of his tree.'

'Too technical for me, doctor,' said Steven with a smile and the ice was broken between them.

'I've never seen anything like it before,' said Miles. 'I was told that he'd had a mental breakdown but I'm now inclined to think that it's not a psychiatric problem at all. It's more like some form of delirium, and the fact that he has breathing difficulties tends to support this. I'm told that tests are also showing signs of liver damage, so the ball is moving rapidly out of my court and into the realm of the physician. I suppose it was natural to assume at the time that he'd had some sort of breakdown associated with stress or disappointment, but he hasn't. It's really beginning to look much more like a case of poisoning or even an infection of some sort.'

This was not what Steven wanted to hear. The spectre of something reaching out from a centuries-old tomb to cause modern-day havoc refused to be banished. 'Let's hope it's a curable sort,' he said without any trace of humour.

Miles shrugged. 'Maybe things will look brighter when the lab finishes its tests.'

'Is he conscious?'

'He drifts in and out. We have to keep him under a certain level of sedation for the safety of the nursing staff. He gets violent if we don't.'

'Has he said anything at all about what happened?'

'Words, but not sentences. Nothing that ever gives a clue to what's going on inside his head.'

'Are the words in English?'

'Oh, yes. He's not speaking in tongues if that's what you mean. They're English words, but apparently generated randomly so no train of thought is ever revealed.'

'Poor man.'

'Would you like to see him?'

Steven nodded. 'May as well put a face to the name,' he said, and got up to follow Miles.

John Motram was in a locked room under constant camera observation. He would remain there until the possibility of his suffering from an infectious condition had been ruled out. He was awake but obviously having difficulty breathing: an oxygen mask obscured half his face. Steven's immediate thought was that he just looked like the 52-year-old academic he was, but on closer inspection the look in his eyes suggested a failure to recognise anything around him. He was awake but he wasn't seeing. Steven pointed this out to Miles.

'He's not blind,' said Miles. 'His eyes follow the nurse when she goes in to see to his needs. He doesn't seem to acknowledge her as a person but he can see her, we're sure of that.'

He turned up the sound on the monitor. Motram was saying something but, as Steven had been forewarned, it sounded like random words. 'Red, seventeen, blue, twist, curl, burst, diamonds, diamonds, grass, yellow, sky.'

Steven nodded his thanks to Miles and got up to leave.

* * *

In the orthopaedic unit, he found Tony Fielding doing the *Times* crossword. He was alone in a room that was designed for two patients and had a pleasant view out to the hills. His left leg was in plaster and several visitors had added their signature. Steven smiled when he inclined his head to read the message in red crayon and found that it said *Love you Dad, Lewis.*

'He's seven,' said Fielding.

Steven smiled. He told Fielding who he was and about Sci-Med's interest.

'Good luck,' said Fielding. 'No one else can work out what came over him. He came out of that chamber like a man possessed by the devil. God, I'm even starting to sound like the tabloids.'

Steven smiled again, taking a liking to the man. 'It's an easy habit to develop,' he sympathised. 'Makes life so simple.'

'I promise not to use that particular expression if the press come back again,' said Fielding.

'I take it you've no idea what happened to Dr Motram?' asked Steven.

'Haven't a clue. Before he went into that chamber he was the nicest sort of bloke you'd ever want to meet, but when he came out ...' Fielding made a face. 'He'd only one thing on his mind and that was murder. God, I'm doing it again! I wonder if the *Sun* does a decent crossword ... I might think of changing. Anyway, I consider myself lucky to have got away with only this,' he said, tapping his plastered leg. 'If he'd actually managed to get that digger down the ramp, well, none of us would be here to tell the tale.'

'It sounds horrendous,' said Steven. 'I take it you personally didn't go in the chamber?'

'None of us did apart from John,' said Fielding. 'Do you really think it was something in there? Something from the past?'

'Common sense says not,' said Steven. 'On the other hand I haven't the slightest idea why John Motram is the way he is right now. But, just for the record,' he added, bringing out a small notebook, 'do you think you can talk me through everything that happened that day up until the time Dr Motram entered the tomb?'

Fielding puffed his cheeks and exhaled slowly. 'Not much to say really. The four of us – John, Alan Blackstone, Les and myself – met in the car park at the abbey and allowed the Health and Safety people to inspect the equipment we'd be using on site. When they'd finished ticking their clipboards and giving us the OK, we crossed over to the hotel to meet the doctor from Public Health, who interviewed each of us briefly about the state of our health, gave us a tetanus shot and basically said everything was fine by him. Then the four of us walked round to the site and Les and I set about loosening the stones in the wall of the tomb. When we'd finished we let John take over and watched him remove enough of them to gain an entrance. He disappeared inside and we waited – he was actually in there for more than twenty minutes, but we supposed that was because it was his big moment, if you like, and he was sort of savouring the experience.'

'What happened when he did come out?'

'I have to say he seemed a bit odd . . . he was having trouble with the plastic sheeting across the entrance so I gave him a hand, then Alan tried to talk to him, then . . . well, all hell broke lose. John really lost the plot. He smashed Alan in the face with the torch he was carrying, and then hit Les when he tried to help Alan. The three of us ended up in a ball in the trench with John doing his best to murder us with the digger. Luckily, he wasn't too familiar with the controls and that's really what saved us in the end. He ended up tipping it over on to its side and being thrown out.'

'Was he knocked unconscious?'

'No,' said Fielding thoughtfully. 'I mean he didn't hit his head on anything. He seemed to be having difficulty breathing.

He lay on the grass for a while, gulping for air, and then seemed to pass out, thank God.'

Steven thanked Fielding for his help and made his way to the exit. He checked his watch and saw that there would still be time to talk to Kenneth Glass at Public Health if he got a move on. He decided to do this rather than visit the site at Dryburgh because, at four o'clock on an early March day in Scotland, the light was already failing. He would visit the abbey first thing in the morning.

Glass turned out to be a pleasant, helpful man in his late thirties with his feet firmly planted on the ground, who seemed keen to put any notion of curses or plagues from the past to rest. 'It's early days for some of the tests,' he said, 'but I think I can tell you what happened to John Motram.'

'You can?' exclaimed Steven. 'That's wonderful . . . or maybe not if we're on the brink of an epidemic.'

'Nothing like that,' said Glass. 'We've been working closely with the hospital lab and we've discovered that Motram was poisoned with a mycotoxin from the genus *Amanita* – a large dose.'

'I'm all ears,' said Steven.

'Although we don't think there were any living organisms inside the tomb we think that there was a large accumulation of fungal spores present in the dust that Motram stirred up when he went inside. We think that inhaling them when he took off his mask was the cause of the problem. It would also account for his apparent breathing difficulties and the liver failure that's beginning to show up.'

'And the mental derangement?'

'There's no telling what a massive dose of this toxin can do. It's a very powerful poison.'

'Well, I think we're all in your debt, doctor. John Motram did not have any kind of mental breakdown and he wasn't infected by some super-bug from the past. He was poisoned.'

'That's certainly the way it looks,' agreed Glass. 'There is one embarrassing thing, though . . .'

'What?'

'We haven't been able to find any more of the spores in the air samples we took from the chamber. Everything so far seems to suggest there's nothing but harmless dust in that tomb.'

'I take it you and your people were wearing full bio-hazard gear when you went in?'

'Absolutely. But we carried out extensive tests. The air inside the tomb is not the sort of stuff you'd want in your air freshener, but as far as we can see there's damn all wrong with it in a biological sense. John Motram must have been really unlucky: the spores must have been present in the residue of the one cadaver he chose to disturb.'

'Poor guy,' said Steven. 'But thank God you've found the answer. The sooner the tabloids return to exposing thieving bankers the happier I'll be.'

'Amen to that,' said Glass. 'Incidentally, our mobile lab is still on site up there. You're welcome to use it for anything you need. We're going to disinfect the site when everyone's finished taking samples.'

Steven got back in the car feeling very relieved. There was no danger of an epidemic arising from the opening of the tomb. Motram had been poisoned by inhaling fungal spores, something which had absolutely nothing to do with Black Death. The only problem Steven had now was that he didn't have anywhere to stay for the night if he still intended taking a look at the excavation site in the morning. Then he remembered reading in the file that Jean Roberts had given him that the Dryburgh Abbey Hotel was situated right next to the ruins. He called and booked himself in.

EIGHTEEN

It was dark when Steven drew up at the Dryburgh Abbey Hotel. He was glad his working day had come to an end, pleased at his progress but tired after the long drive up from London and the interview of two key players in the drama – although interview was probably the wrong word to use in John Motram's case. All he was looking forward to now was a long, hot shower, a couple of gin and tonics and a decent meal.

It was dark, but he could see how close the hotel was to the ruins of the abbey, and the fact that he could hear running water when he paused to look up at the night sky told him how close he was to the River Tweed. An idyllic setting, he thought.

In the exchange of small talk at the desk, Steven asked if the hotel was full.

'It was last week, after what happened to Dr Motram, but now it's back to normal – about a third full,' came the reply. 'It'll start to pick up again around Easter.'

'You knew Dr Motram?' Steven asked, surprised at hearing the name mentioned.

'He and his colleagues used to come in for coffee and some-times lunch when they were on site. As you can see, we're right next door. A nice man, much nicer than the press who turned up in their droves afterwards.'

Steven smiled.

'Oh, God. You're not a journalist are you?'

He laughed. 'No. I'm sort of looking into what happened.'

'Whew.'

'Any chance of a room overlooking the abbey?'

'No problem. I'll give you the one all the journalists were after last week. It was like having a plague of locusts on the premises,' said the girl. 'But like all plagues, it moved on to pastures new.'

'How about scientists?' asked Steven, wondering about Porton Down's reported interest. 'Any of them around?'

'If they were, they didn't say.'

Steven took his time signing the register, running his eye down the list of names to see if any were familiar. None was. When he'd finished, the girl handed him his key. 'The abbey should look good tonight,' she said. 'The skies are clear and there's a full moon.'

Steven spent some time in the lounge after dinner, drinking coffee and brandy and reading tourist pamphlets about the abbey and the surrounding area. This, when allied with the fact that the moonlit abbey did indeed look wonderful from his window, decided him on going outside and taking a walk around for himself. He took a small plan of the ruins – courtesy of one of the pamphlets – with him.

He had discovered in his reading that the abbey was the resting place of both Sir Walter Scott and Field Marshal Douglas Haig, two very different characters. The famous novelist had romanticised the Scottish Highlands and its clan culture beyond all recognition, while the soldier had sent men to their death in their thousands in the hell that was the First World War – the war to end all wars that didn't. Steven reflected on the disparity as he stood before Scott's tomb, only a stone's throw from Haig's grave.

A frost was beginning to settle on the grass, accentuating the moonlight which was already wonderfully bright in an atmosphere free from air and light pollution. He moved on to the east end of the abbey, where he knew the chapter house to be, wanting to experience the atmosphere of a place which had seen so much history. Frost was sparkling on the east cloister stairs as he descended carefully and made his way round to the chapter house, where he stood at the head of a flight of stone steps leading down into darkness. There was a strong smell of wet plaster coming from below, and something else . . . Almost at the same time as he realised it was – after-shave lotion, he heard the metallic click of an automatic weapon being primed and flung himself backwards to roll over on the frosty grass and out of sight of whoever was down there.

He was scrambling to his feet, preparing to sprint to the cloister stairs but fearing he wouldn't make it, when he heard the sound of male laughter. A voice said, 'You're fast, Dunbar, I'll grant you that, and it's just as well for me you don't carry.'

Steven recognised the voice but couldn't put a name to it. Whoever it was knew his name and also knew he didn't carry a weapon – something he didn't do on principle unless he knew his life to be in danger. 'Who the hell are you?' he snapped.

A tall man climbed the stone steps and out into the moonlight. Steven took in the high forehead and slightly protruding chin. 'Ricksen, MI5,' he exclaimed, recognising an intelligence officer he'd come across before. 'What the hell d'you think you're playing at?'

'Couldn't resist, old boy. I've just arrived. When I saw your name in the register and the girl on the desk told me you'd just stepped out for some air . . . well, like I say, I couldn't resist putting you to the test.'

Steven felt angry but relieved at the same time. He occupied himself with brushing frost and grass from his clothes until he'd calmed down sufficiently to ask, 'What in God's name are you doing here?'

'Babysitting,' replied Ricksen. 'Porton Down have a couple of their boffins coming in the morning. I'm here to look after them, make sure they get their samples or whatever it is that they want from down there.' Ricksen inclined his head back towards the chapter house stairs. 'What's Sci-Med's interest?'

'We wanted to know what happened to John Motram.'

'Scientists have nervous breakdowns all the time,' said Ricksen. 'What makes this one different is the fact that he had his in a seven-hundred-year-old Black Death tomb and the papers heard about it.'

'I take it you haven't heard yet,' said Steven. 'It wasn't a breakdown. The lab boys have shown that Motram was poisoned with fungal spores.'

'Well, that saves us all a lot of trouble,' said Ricksen. 'Also buggers up a good tabloid story, I'm delighted to say. Buy you a drink?'

'After that performance, I think you owe me one.'

Steven took a last look out the window at the abbey ruins before drawing the curtains and getting into bed. He felt ill at ease about something but couldn't quite put his finger on what. Maybe it was just the stupid joke that Ricksen had played on him, but somehow he felt it was more than that. He'd always had a slightly uneasy relationship with MI5. Ostensibly he and they were on the same side but there was an important difference: Sci-Med operated independently of government while

MI5 were instructed by them. There had been occasions in the past where John Macmillan's people had ruthlessly exposed what government and MI5 would have preferred be covered up. That made them a bit of a loose cannon in the eyes of the establishment, although successive governments had been quick to realise that any attempt to neutralise Sci-Med would be seized upon by Her Majesty's opposition and used as a heaven-sent opportunity to make political capital.

As he lay in the darkness, Steven thought about the coming day. He would take a look at the burial chamber and then what? He'd originally planned to visit both Alan Blackstone and Les Smith but, in view of what the labs had found, there really didn't seem to be much point. They could only tell him what Tony Fielding already had, and Kenneth Glass had more or less assured him that, apart from the fungal spores, there was nothing sinister lurking down there in the tomb.

He thought a bit more about the mycotoxin that appeared to have been the cause of Motram's condition – a large dose, Glass had said, which made it all the more puzzling that the lab staff had failed to detect any more of the spores in the air samples they'd taken. Even if Glass had been right about Motram's being unlucky and the spores being confined to the dusty remains of the cadaver he'd examined, he would have expected there to have been some evidence of them inside the chamber.

NINETEEN

Steven was still thinking about Motram at the breakfast table when Ricksen appeared and sat down beside him. 'My guys should be here by ten o'clock,' he said. 'What are your plans?'

'I'm going to take a look at the burial chamber,' said Steven.

'Make sure they didn't overlook the angel of death sitting in the corner?' joked Ricksen.

'That sort of thing,' Steven agreed. 'Then I'll check with Public Health to make sure their microbiological tests haven't come up with anything else. After that, I think it'll be home sweet home. And you?'

'Should be out of here by lunchtime if the Porton guys get what they want. Shouldn't take too long to pack up a few samples of dust.'

Steven looked at his watch. 'If I get a move on I should be out of the way by the time they arrive.' He got to his feet.

'See you around,' said Ricksen.

Steven hadn't been quite honest with Ricksen; he hadn't mentioned that he intended to have a word with Motram's wife before returning to London. It was probably something to do with the little niggle at the back of his mind, but he felt he wanted to know a bit more about the man.

He walked over to where the Public Health mobile lab was parked and made himself known to the technician in charge.

'Dr Glass said you might turn up,' said a young red-haired woman who was setting up equipment for disinfecting the chamber later. 'You'll be wanting a grave-robber uniform then?'

Steven was suited up inside ten minutes, masked and ready to enter the burial chamber through the makeshift airlock. There was no need for him to use a torch; the Public Health people had already rigged up temporary lighting inside. He could see the entire contents of the vaulted stone chamber as soon as he entered, crouching, through the gap in its wall. His first thought was that it was a dormitory for the dead, sixteen black body shapes lying on stone benches, eight on either side.

On closer inspection, he could see that a circular area on the torso of each corpse had been opened up, presumably subjected to examination to make sure they had all decomposed like the one examined by Motram, he thought. Alternatively, Motram might have put his fist through each in turn after his disappointment with the first. Steven made sure his mask was fitting well before putting his gloved hand into one of the exposed areas. It went straight down to the stone bench without impediment; the shroud was an empty shell with nothing inside but dust and bones.

He tried to imagine the utter dejection Motram must have felt when he'd discovered it. Seeing the apparently preserved body shapes in the tomb would surely have been the cue for elation, but then to find that they had no substance and would crumble to nothing when touched, as Steven proved now with the tip of his finger on a thigh, must have been a crushing blow. He could understand Motram tearing off his mask and cursing his luck, inadvertently breathing in the dust and the poison spores.

There was no point in lingering any longer. Steven went

through the shower and decontamination procedure in the Public Health vehicle, suspecting it was more of a gesture than a necessity, and checked with the technician that no word of any new findings had come in from the lab.

'I spoke to Dr Glass first thing this morning,' said the technician. 'Harmless dust, he said. He thought that going to the local swimming pool was probably more dangerous.'

Steven set off for the village of Longthorn, noticing as he left the car park that an unmarked white van had just arrived. From the complex filtering vents on its roof, he deduced that this was the mobile lab facility from Porton that Ricksen was expecting. Seeing it brought the uneasy feeling back again. He was missing something here.

Dr Cassie Motram was on compassionate leave from the group practice where she worked, Steven had learned when he phoned earlier that morning. According to the senior partner he'd spoken to, she had tried carrying on working as normal – to take her mind off things as much as anything else – but when press interest entered the equation she had found dealing with patients well nigh impossible. A number of them believed she might give them Black Death. 'And it's going to take them a while to get their heads round *Amanita* mycotoxin,' he added.

The look of exasperation that appeared on Cassie Motram's face when she answered the door prompted Steven to assure her immediately that he had nothing to do with the press. Cassie looked at his ID but said, 'Never heard of you.'

'Not many people have,' said Steven with a smile. He explained briefly what Sci-Med did and Cassie shrugged and invited him inside the pleasant cottage where she and John lived.

'I'm busy in the kitchen,' she said. 'We'll talk in there if you don't mind.'

104

'Not at all.' Steven perched on one of stools at the breakfast bar and watched Cassie busy herself collecting ingredients, which he assumed had to do with the open recipe book lying on the bar. His immediate thought was that here was a woman who was keeping herself busy for therapeutic reasons. He could sympathise. 'How is he this morning?' he asked.

'Not good.'

'I'm sorry.'

'So what is it you are investigating exactly?' asked Cassie as she weighed flour out on a set of digital scales.

'I was sent to find out what happened to your husband in the tomb at Dryburgh Abbey,' said Steven.

'And whether it had anything to do with the Black Death corpses lying there,' added Cassie with a wry smile.

'That was our fear,' agreed Steven. 'The idea of Black Death making any kind of come-back certainly concentrated minds in Whitehall, but now we know what really happened – a combination of fungal spores and sheer bad luck.'

Cassie glanced at Steven sideways. 'I'll be frank with you, Dr Dunbar. When John told me he was planning to open up a seven-hundred-year-old Black Death tomb, I was far from delighted. I knew such fears were groundless – I'm a doctor; I can work out the odds – but even in the twenty-first century the thought of Black Death tends to grip the imagination.'

Steven nodded. 'I know what you mean. I went inside the tomb this morning. Whatever you tell yourself beforehand, your mind starts working overtime as soon as you're inside.'

'But your fears were groundless, doctor; mine weren't,' said Cassie, pausing in what she was doing. 'My husband didn't come back to me. They were considering putting him on life support this morning when I phoned.'

'I'm so sorry.' Steven saw the sadness in Cassie's eyes and felt a lump come to his throat.

Cassie quickly recovered her composure. 'Would you care for some coffee, Dr Dunbar?'

'Thank you,' said Steven, collaborating in the restoring of normality. 'Black, no sugar.'

As they grew comfortable in each other's company, Steven tried to inject some encouragement into his words. 'Now that the hospital know what the problem is with John, they'll be better placed to come up with treatment,' he said.

'There's really nothing they can do right now,' said Cassie. 'Dr Miles has withdrawn from the case and the toxicologist I spoke to admitted it's down to life support and good nursing at the moment. He thinks John must have inhaled a massive dose.'

Steven nodded. 'That's what I heard from the Public Health people too,' he said. 'But their lab failed to find any spores in the dust. They were quite embarrassed about it.'

Cassie shrugged but didn't respond. Steven continued: 'I was puzzled, so I asked the Sci-Med lab about it. The other possibility is that it wasn't a massive dose but that John was in some way hypersensitive to the *Amanita* toxin. Was he the type to suffer from allergies?'

Cassie moved her head one way and then the other, as if suspecting this line of inquiry was not going to go anywhere. 'Cats,' she said. 'He liked them but he started itching if he was in their company for any length of time. If he patted one, he had to wash his hands afterwards, but that was all.'

Steven continued undeterred. 'Another possibility would be stress. I'm told that that can render people more susceptible to the effects of toxins. Was John under any pressure? Had he had any problems in his life recently?'

Cassie shook her head slowly as she thought. 'I really don't think so. Opening up the chamber at Dryburgh has been the single thing uppermost in John's mind for weeks – ever since he got the letter from Oxford.'

Steven nodded to indicate he knew about the Balliol connection.

'I suppose you could say he was a bit stressed when Health and Safety got involved and delayed the start of the excavation, but that didn't last long. He was more pissed off than stressed.'

'They get up everyone's nose.'

'And had to make a trip to London. I suppose that was a bit out of the ordinary for him but hardly stressful. Everything seemed to go all right.' Steven's expression invited further elaboration so Cassie continued, 'He was called down to a hospital in London to screen a man who was due to donate his bone marrow to a patient with advanced leukaemia.'

'Why John if it was a London hospital?'

'It was a *quid pro quo* for the funding John got for the excavation at Dryburgh. Under the terms of the agreement, the funding body had the right to call him in as a consultant. He was just away the one day and then he had some work to do in his own lab on the samples he brought back with him. But it seemed quite straightforward, no stress or pressure involved.'

Steven nodded.

'Actually, it's probably nothing, but there was one odd thing that came out of that trip . . .'

'Yes?'

'Some time after John came back, there was a report on television about a young marine who'd died in Afghanistan. When he saw the picture on the screen, John was convinced he was the donor he'd seen in London.'

'And was he?'

'It turned out to be a case of mistaken identity. The marine had been wounded in Afghanistan on the very day John saw the young man in London.'

'Ah,' said Steven.

TWENTY

Steven called Tally in Leicester.

'Steven! Where are you?'

'I'm up in the north. I'm just about to start back to London. I thought I might stop off at your place tonight unless you have other plans?'

'No, that would be great. I've been wondering how you were getting on. I kept getting your answering service.'

'And I yours,' said Steven. 'Let's go out to dinner and catch up.'

'So, I'm a romantic at heart,' said Steven as he drew up outside the French restaurant where he and Tally had eaten together shortly after meeting for the first time. His investigation had led him to the children's hospital in Leicester where Tally worked.

'It's nice to be back,' said Tally, looking at the Provençal posters on the walls. 'I think I was a bit hard on you earlier in the week. I didn't really mean to suggest there was some kind of competition between Jenny and me for your affections.'

'I never imagined that having two women in my life would be easy,' said Steven with a grin that suggested he knew he was embarking on a dangerous course.

'As long as the other one's called Jenny and she's nine years old,' said Tally with an icy glance.

'You know how I feel about you.'

'Pretty much how you feel about your Porsche is probably the best I can hope for,' said Tally. 'How did you find the new one, by the way?'

'Not a patch on you,' said Steven.

'Is the right answer. But pretty pathetic, Dunbar. Still, I suppose I should be grateful it's not on fire in some field somewhere and bullets aren't coming in through the windows of the restaurant as we speak.'

'That was an exception,' Steven insisted. 'Sci-Med investigations are usually quite straightforward and often very dull.'

'So how's the current one going? Or can't you tell me?'

'Of course I can. I've been up to Dryburgh Abbey in the Scottish Borders where an academic went off his head and started attacking his colleagues after entering a seven-hundred-year-old tomb which was home to sixteen Black Death victims.'

'I read something about that in the papers,' said Tally.

'Sci-Med were worried in case the academic's condition had anything to do with the contents of the tomb.'

'And had it?'

'The tomb contained nothing but dust and bones, which was a big disappointment for everyone, but unfortunately for the chap in question the dust contained a large quantity of poisonous fungal spores. He breathed them in and ended up with severe mycotoxin poisoning: it's touch and go whether he'll recover. But now that the panic's over, Public Health will disinfect the chamber and that'll be an end to the investigation. See, I told you you were exaggerating the dangers of the job.'

'Mmm,' said Tally, not convinced. 'So, what's next?'

'Don't know yet. I'll make out my report on Dryburgh when I get back to London and see what John Macmillan has lined up for me.'

'Exciting.'

'Probably mundane and boring,' said Steven with a one-up smile.

'All right, Dunbar. Don't over-egg the pudding.'

'What have you been up to?'

'Working my socks off in an under-staffed, under-funded, over-administered excuse for a hospital where management – and I use the term humorously – are more concerned with ticking boxes than they are with treating sick children.'

'So no change there then.'

'NHS, the envy of the world? It's as fucked as the banking system. People just haven't realised it yet.'

'Obviously time for a change,' said Steven. 'How does the idea of being the full-time mother of a nine-year-old girl sound?'

Tally fixed him with a stare. 'Don't be flippant, Steven. We've been through all that. I have a career; it's important to me. I love medicine; I love the kids; it's the crummy system I hate.'

Steven nodded. 'Sorry,' he said. 'I know and, believe me, I do understand.'

'Do you?' asked Tally, searching his face for the truth.

'Yes,' Steven assured her. 'But it's also true that I love you . . . and it's unconditional.'

Tally was about to say something when Steven's phone went off. He apologised but said he had to take it. Switching off his Sci-Med mobile was never an option. He left the eating area to take the call in a small cocktail bar adjoining the restaurant which was currently empty, and perched on a bar stool with one foot on the ground.

'Dr Dunbar? It's Cassie Motram.'

Steven remembered giving Cassie his card and inviting her to call if she thought of anything relevant. 'Hello, Dr Motram. What can I do for you?'

'Have you seen the TV news this evening, doctor?'

'I've been on the road most of the day, Dr Motram. Why, was there something interesting?'

'I'll leave that for you to decide, doctor. I found it very strange. Do let me know what you think when you see it.' The line went dead, leaving Steven looking at his phone with a slight feeling of embarrassment.

'Problems?' asked Tally when he sat back down.

Steven shrugged. 'Don't know. That was Cassie Motram, the wife of the chap who was poisoned in the tomb. She's a GP. She wanted to know if I'd seen the TV news tonight.'

'What have we missed?'

'She didn't say.'

Tally looked surprised. 'How odd.'

Their starters arrived and they tried to get their evening back on track, but the phone call was ever present at the back of their minds. 'Would you like to go home?' Tally asked half way through the main course, when she saw Steven's attention wander yet again. He did his best to assure her that there was no need to rush off and the news item was probably something trivial anyway, but Tally said, 'On the other hand there just might have been an outbreak of Black Death in the Scottish Borders . . .'

'Oh my God,' said Steven. 'Would you mind?'

Tally smiled. 'I think this is the bit in those police programmes where I accuse you of being married to the job and storm out in high dudgeon . . . but as we're both staying at my place there's not much point really.'

'Good.'

'Mind you, if this should turn out to be an elaborate subterfuge to ensure an early night, Dunbar . . . you'll be spending it on the sofa.'

*   *   *

It was nine thirty when they got home: Steven turned on the TV and tuned to Sky News, waiting for a headline update while Tally made coffee. 'Anything?' she asked coming in with a tray and putting it down on the coffee table in front of the sofa.

'Nothing yet.'

Tally patted the sofa with the palm of her hand. 'Won't be too bad . . .'

Steven was about to respond when he froze and stared at the screen. A news item, *Dead Marine's Family Seek Answers*, had captured his undivided attention. It was reported that the family of a Scottish Royal Marine, Michael Kelly, who lost his life in Afghanistan, were claiming that they had not been told the whole truth about their son's death. They claimed to have information that he had been sent back to the UK on a secret mission and that the circumstances surrounding his death were clouded in mystery. They were demanding answers.

The report ended but Steven continued to sit staring at the screen unseeingly.

Tally seemed incredulous. 'Is that it?' she exclaimed. 'What on earth has that to do with Black Death and the excavation at Dryburgh?'

'What an awfully good question,' replied Steven distantly. He finally moved his attention away from the screen to face Tally. 'Cassie Motram told me that her husband saw the original report of that marine's death on TV and thought he recognised him as the donor in a bone marrow transplant he'd been asked to advise on. Then they heard he'd been wounded in Afghanistan on the same day that John Motram saw the donor in London, so they put it down to mistaken identity. But now this . . .'

'So, if what the marine's family is saying is true, he could have been the donor after all?'

'Apparently.'

Tally left Steven alone with his thoughts for a moment. She returned with two brandies and handed him one. 'Do you know what I think you need now?'

'What?'

'That early night.'

TWENTY-ONE

'You still seem troubled,' said Tally as they sat having breakfast together with the sun streaming in through the kitchen window, creating an oasis of light.

'I thought this investigation was over but it's not,' said Steven. 'Someone's been playing me for a fool.'

'In what way? I thought you said everything was straight-forward.'

'That's what I thought. But that's what I was meant to think. I've just realised what's been niggling away at me ever since I went up to the Scottish Borders. The timing was all wrong.'

Tally looked blank. 'Whose timing? What timing?'

'MI5.'

Tally's eyes opened wide. 'Am I missing something here?' she asked, a look of bewilderment on her face. 'What on earth have MI5 got to do with anything?'

'When Motram lost his mind and there was a possibility that his entering the tomb at Dryburgh might have had something to do with it, John Macmillan told me that Porton Down were interested.'

'The microbiological defence establishment?'

Steven nodded. 'And that made sense. You'd expect them to be, in the circumstances. In fact, I was worried about them getting there and stopping anyone else gaining access, but the Public Health people beat them to it: they had already been inside the tomb to take samples by the time I phoned. Porton still weren't on site when I arrived. An MI5 officer who'd been detailed to look after their interest did turn up but he arrived after me and told me he was expecting the Porton people the following morning. They were just pulling into the car park when I was leaving.'

'So?'

'They were going through the motions,' said Steven. 'They knew damn well that Motram's condition had nothing to do with any new virus inside that tomb. They turned up to collect samples for my benefit.'

'Oh, God,' said Tally. 'You're about to cross swords with MI5 again, aren't you?'

'Not deliberately,' said Steven. 'But I'm not going to end the investigation just yet.'

Tally suddenly realised she was going to be late if she didn't get a move on. She went into overdrive, muttering about what she had to do at the hospital, gathering her bits and pieces together, hopping on one foot while she pulled a shoe on to the other and finally kissing Steven on the cheek before rushing out the door. Steven smiled at the ghost of Tally past and cleared away the breakfast dishes, still wondering how best to approach what now seemed to be an entirely new investigation – one that he would have to seek John Macmillan's approval for before proceeding. But if MI5 and Porton Down had not been in any great hurry to investigate what had caused John Motram's condition . . . it suggested they already knew.

'Aren't you reading too much into this?' asked John Macmillan. 'I mean, it could be that Porton were just a bit slow in getting their act together.'

'Porton *and* MI5 slow off the mark when the possibility of

a new killer agent was in the offing?' exclaimed Steven. 'I don't think so. Public Health had had time to examine the chamber, take samples, confer with the hospital guys and actually work out what had caused Motram's illness before they arrived. If the security services had really believed there was a possibility of something new and nasty being down there . . .'

'Public Health would never have got near the place,' Macmillan conceded.

'They were putting on a show of turning up and taking samples for our benefit.'

'But why?'

Steven took a moment before saying slowly and deliberately, 'I thought about that all the way down. The only explanation I could come up with was that MI5 knew exactly what happened to John Motram: they might even have been the cause of it, with or without the collusion of Porton Down.'

Macmillan wore the expression of a man who had just been given some very bad news. 'And why would they do something like that?'

'I've no idea. I may be quite wrong, but I'm now pretty sure Motram's illness has more to do with a dead marine and a bone marrow transplant than it does with mouldering corpses in a medieval Scottish tomb.'

'What do we know about this dead marine you've suddenly become interested in?'

'Nothing as yet. I thought I'd talk to you first, see what you thought.'

'I take it that means you'd like to run with it?' asked Macmillan, without much enthusiasm.

'If only because someone at 5 or Porton thought they'd put one over on us.'

'Not a good reason,' said Macmillan flatly.

Steven tried again. 'Cassandra Motram is a very nice woman, a hard-working GP whose husband – also a decent person by all accounts and a brilliant academic in his field – is now close to death. I think MI5 had something to do with it, or know who did.'

'Better,' said Macmillan, 'much better. I'll have Jean come up with what she can on the dead marine. Meanwhile, perhaps you can find out something about the transplant Motram was involved in?'

'On my way.'

The sun was shining when Steven left the Home Office so he chose to walk back home along the Embankment, pausing to sit on a bench and watch the river traffic pass by. He planned to phone Cassie Motram later to ask for more details about her husband's dealings with the London hospital, but for the moment he concentrated on the toxic spores and how they came to poison Motram. If Steven was right about MI5's knowing more than they were letting on, it raised the possibility that Motram had been poisoned deliberately.

No one had been in the tomb before Motram so the spores couldn't have been planted there: the poisoning must have taken place *before* Motram went into the tomb. This would explain why Kenneth Glass and his people had failed to find the deadly spores in the air samples they'd taken from the chamber. There never had been any spores in the chamber.

But if this were so, Motram's attacker would have had to be in a position to administer the toxin at exactly the right time in order to create the red herring of his being affected by something in the tomb, something that the lab would uncover and blame on the dust. That surely narrowed the field down to Motram's three colleagues; the two men from the geo-survey firm, and the on-site observer from Historic Scotland, Alan Blackstone.

Not a promising cast of suspects, but then Steven remembered that others had been present on site that morning. Tony Fielding, lying in Borders General Hospital, had told him that people from Health and Safety and a doctor from Public Health had been present before work started, and what's more, the four involved in the opening of the tomb had been given injections just before they started work. Injections.

Steven called Kenneth Glass at Public Health.

'Hello, Steven,' said Glass, thinking he would be calling about the screening of the chamber. 'All samples from Dryburgh are still negative, you'll be relieved to hear.'

'Thanks, Kenneth, but it's actually something else I'm calling about. One of your medics was on site the morning the tomb at Dryburgh was opened. He took some health details from the guys involved and gave them anti-tetanus injections.'

'Really? That's news to me. Do you have a name?'

Steven felt his blood run cold at Glass's response. 'Afraid not. I'll try and get one if you like.'

'No, it's okay. I'll ask around and get back to you.'

Steven realised that he didn't have names for the Health and Safety representatives either but maybe Motram had mentioned them to his wife. He'd ask Cassie later when he called.

His phone rang and he just knew it was going to be bad news.

'Hi, Steven. I'm afraid no one here knows anything about giving anti-tetanus shots to the guys at Dryburgh. In fact, at that time, we didn't even know it was happening.'

'Thanks,' said Steven. 'I was afraid of that.'

He ended the call and shivered as he thought about his latest discovery. It now seemed likely – even probable – that someone had turned up at Dryburgh Abbey, purporting to be from Public Health, and injected John Motram with the mycotoxin that had scrambled his brain. That explained perfectly the absence of spores in the air samples and the 'large dose' hypothesis. But only John Motram had been targeted. Three others had received injections without any ill effects. It had been a specific attack on Motram . . . because . . . he knew something about a marine who had been killed in Afghanistan?

This changed everything. He decided that a phone call to Cassie Motram would not be good enough; he'd go back up north and talk to her personally. He also needed to see Tony Fielding again to find out what he could tell him about the people from Health and Safety and Public Health or, more correctly, the people who weren't from Health and Safety and Public Health. He'd phone Cassie to let her know he was coming and then drive on up to Borders General to talk to Fielding.

Steven was still thinking about it all when he got back to his flat. He didn't know much about mycotoxins but Porton Down certainly would. Someone somewhere had taken the decision not to kill Motram but to scramble his brain instead. 'All heart, you bastards,' he murmured as he filled the coffee holder and switched on the espresso machine.

TWENTY-TWO

Steven collected the file on the dead marine from the Home Office before setting out for the north. Jean Roberts apologised for the lack of detail but she had only had time to get her hands on the official press release from the MOD and add in what she could garner from the newspapers. John Macmillan wasn't in the office so Steven didn't get the chance to tell him about the bogus Public Health official and what he'd deduced. He told Jean he'd call him later.

After an uneventful drive with only one stop for coffee at a service station, which had given him the chance to read through the slim file on Michael Kelly, he drew up outside Cassie Motram's cottage: it was shortly after one o'clock. Cassie told him that she'd made sandwiches in case he hadn't stopped for lunch. Steven smiled, thinking that this was exactly the kind of thing Cassie Motram would do. He accepted gratefully.

He was invited to take a seat in the small conservatory stuck on the back of the house where he sat and looked out on a picture-book country garden while Cassie went to fetch them, calling through from the kitchen that she had hoped to have been able to talk outside in the garden.

'I thought when I saw the sunshine this morning . . .' she said as she put the heaped plate down. 'But it was false optimism; I'm wishing the winter away. I always do; but it's still far too early and far too cold. So, put me out of my misery, Dr Dunbar. What did you make of the TV news item?'

'That's really why I'm here,' Steven admitted. 'Seeing that report after what you'd told me about John thinking the donor and the dead marine were one and the same started alarm bells ringing. It's just too much of a coincidence. I need to know everything you can remember about John's London trip and the transplant operation he was involved in: how it came about, the names of those involved, absolutely everything, no detail too small.'

Cassie looked serious. 'Do you think this could have had something to do with what happened to John?' she asked.

'Yes. I do.'

'So it had nothing to do with the excavation at all?'

'I don't think so.'

'Then what?'

'That's what I'm determined to find out. Let's start from the beginning.'

Cassie took a sip of her tea. 'When Balliol College told John about the letters raising the possibility of preserved bodies of Black Death victims lying in a secret tomb at Dryburgh, John was over the moon. But he didn't have the funding to take on such a project: he'd more or less been told his grant for the historical work wasn't being renewed. However, the Master of Balliol said that funding might be available from a new source called the Hotspur Foundation. All John had to do was agree to act as a consultant in his specialty when called upon and without being given too much notice. Well, of course, John agreed, seeing it as a lifeline for his research and his chance to settle the argument over the cause of Black Death. He signed on the dotted line, as they say, and a few weeks later he was called to London, to a private hospital in South Kensington. It was called St Raphael's.'

Steven wrote the name down. 'Who called him?'

'A firm of London solicitors representing the Hotspur Foundation.'

'Do you still have the letter?'

Cassie left the room for a few moments and returned with it. 'Apparently the person or persons behind the Hotspur Foundation are very reclusive so they use the solicitors as a front to protect their privacy. The Master of Balliol College told John he thought it was probably a billionaire atoning for past sins.'

Steven smiled. 'Quite a few of those around,' he said. 'They usually pop up in the honours list.'

'When John turned up at the hospital there were some other people there, all specialists in their own fields . . . I think he said six but I'm not sure.'

'Names?'

'Sorry, John didn't mention any, but the man in charge of proceedings who told them why they were there was a Sir Laurence Samson. Of Harley Street, no less.'

'And they were there because they were to be involved in the treatment of a patient who was to have a bone marrow transplant?'

'Yes. The patient had advanced leukaemia. As a last resort they were going to try replacing his bone marrow. It was John's job to screen the donor for compatibility. He told me there was a tremendous air of secrecy surrounding everything. The patient was only ever referred to as Patient X, although there was a strong hint that he was fabulously wealthy. The donor was simply called the donor. The consultants weren't allowed to talk to each other about the case unless it was professionally necessary and no names were to be mentioned. There were to be severe financial implications for anyone stepping out of line, although I don't think John ever understood why such threats were necessary. He saw his role in screening the donor as being very simple and straightforward – any hospital lab could have done the essentials, according to him. He couldn't understand why he – or rather the university – was being paid all that money for a piece of routine work. I think we concluded that the patient was buying the best of everything simply because he could.'

'Am I right in thinking that John never saw the patient, only the donor?'

'That's right.'

'And he didn't know the donor's name?'

'No. He was a young man with a Scots accent. That's it.'

'Who looked a lot like the young marine on the television,' said Steven.

'John was sure he was the young man he'd seen in London, but Sir Laurence convinced him otherwise and the dates made it impossible. But then when I saw the story on the news last night . . .'

'So John actually voiced his suspicion to Laurence Samson?' asked Steven, seeing this as a crucial point.

Cassie nodded. 'He was so sure. He called him up almost immediately after seeing the report of the death on TV. Sir Laurence assured him he was mistaken.' She refilled Steven's cup. 'So who's lying?' she asked.

'And why?' Steven wondered.

Steven decided against telling Cassie anything yet about his suspicions surrounding the false Public Health doctor and the possibility that John had been deliberately poisoned, but he did tell her something about the dead marine. 'If the soldier really was the donor John saw in London, his name was Michael Kelly and he came from Glasgow. The official report says he was wounded by shrapnel in an incident in Helmand Province in southern Afghanistan. It wasn't thought to be a serious wound but it turned septic and didn't respond to treatment. He died from blood poisoning in a military hospital at Camp Bastion where he was taken after being transferred from a smaller field hospital. His body was returned to the UK for burial with full military honours.'

Cassie looked perplexed. 'So what exactly are his family going on about?' she asked.

'Michael Kelly's parents have complained to their local member of the Scottish parliament that they haven't been told the full story about their son's death. They claim he was flown home secretly to the UK shortly before his death but haven't been told why. They also complain of a lack of information about the incident he was supposedly wounded in. Their MSP has decided to run with it and has passed on their concerns to the Ministry of Defence – defence is not a devolved power in Scotland. He's also briefing the news media, by the look of it.'

Cassie shook her head in a gesture of hopelessness. 'So it *is* possible this young man was the donor. God, I wish I knew what the hell was going on.'

'Well, it's going to be my job to try and find out,' said Steven, getting up to go. 'If you remember anything else you think could be useful, let me know.'

As he headed north-west to Borders General Hospital, Steven reflected on what he'd learned from Cassie Motram and tried to match it to what he already knew or suspected. If John Motram really had been the subject of an attack, it was difficult to see the motive, particularly if MI5 were party to it. It was possible that Motram had been targeted to shut him up about something to do with the secret transplant, but what? He didn't know anything. He had said, however, that he thought the donor and a dead Royal Marine were one and the same. Had voicing that suspicion been enough to seal his fate?

TWENTY-THREE

'I didn't think I'd be seeing you again,' said Tony Fielding, when Steven put his head round the door of his room.

'I was back in the area; I thought I'd pop in and see how you were,' said Steven. 'How's the leg?'

'They say it's mending well; it's amazing what they can do with nuts and bolts these days. I'll be going home the day after tomorrow. And now tell me the real reason for your visit, doctor.'

Steven smiled. 'I need to ask you about the people from Health and Safety and Public Health who came to see you on site at Dryburgh.'

'What about them?'

'Names . . . descriptions.'

Fielding looked shocked. 'Are you saying those people weren't who they said they were?'

'Let's just say I'm having trouble tracing them,' said Steven.

'Jesus,' murmured Fielding, subconsciously rubbing his upper arm as he thought about the injection he'd been given. 'Why?'

'That's what I'm trying to establish.'

'Bunce,' said Fielding. 'Norman Bunce was the Health and Safety guy. White, five-seven, brown hair, balding, suit, brief-case, clipboard, had a permanent air of disapproval about him, mouth like a cat's arse, seemed pretty genuine to me.'

Steven wrote down the details. 'How often did you see this Bunce?'

'Twice, the first time on his own when he appeared on site and told us we'd need permission. The second time was on the morning of the excavation when he turned up with two of his mates to check over our equipment.'

'Descriptions?'

'Big guys. I remember thinking they looked more like bouncers than safety inspectors. White, six feet plus, didn't say a lot but had English accents like Bunce.'

'Anything else?'

Fielding shrugged. 'Not really, I didn't pay them too much attention.'

Steven nodded. 'How about the Public Health doctor?'

'Dr Morris,' said Fielding, 'Dr Simon Morris. White, well spoken, six-one or two, well built, short dark hair, balding at the front, wart on his . . . left cheek.'

Steven looked at him questioningly, finding this a surprising observation.

'I was wondering how he shaved round it while he was asking me questions about my health,' explained Fielding.

Steven smiled. 'What sort of questions?'

'Routine stuff: had I had any serious illnesses, did I have high blood pressure, did I smoke, did I drink . . . you know.'

Steven nodded. 'And then he gave you an injection . . .'

'Anti-tetanus.'

'Any after effects?'

'None . . . Good God, is that what happened to John? The injection?'

Steven held his hands up. 'It's too soon to say anything like that, but I'd be really obliged if you'd keep this to yourself for the time being.'

Fielding nodded and said wryly, 'No problem. Frankly I wish I could just blot out the whole bloody episode from my memory.'

Steven nodded his understanding. 'I hope you're up and about again soon.'

Steven had already decided to visit the family of the dead marine in Glasgow, but it was too late to go up there that day. His first thought was to stay overnight in nearby St Boswells or Melrose, but then he reminded himself it was only a short drive to Dryburgh. If he stayed at the Abbey Hotel again, he might be able to glean some more information about the fake Public Health official from the staff. His gamble on there being a vacancy at the hotel – it still was a couple of weeks shy of Easter – paid off and he was even given the room he'd had before. 'Nice to see you back, doctor,' said the receptionist. He recognised her from his last visit and asked her if she remembered anything about Simon Morris. The question brought about an uneasy pause before she said – as if reading from a cue card – 'I'm afraid I'm not at liberty to discuss other guests, doctor.'

Steven smiled and showed her his ID. 'It's OK,' he assured her. 'You won't be breaking any rules.'

The girl seemed relieved at being released from the obvious embarrassment she felt in toeing the company line. 'What about him?'

'You do remember him?'

'He was the doctor from Public Health. He was the only guest we've had this year who paid in cash. He'd lost his credit cards.'

'Bad luck,' said Steven, thinking, *Smart move. You can't trace cash.*

'He was here to examine the people working at the abbey. We gave him a little room on the ground floor.'

Steven nodded. 'Did he leave an address when he left?'

The girl shook her head. 'He just wrote Public Health Service in the book.'

'Don't suppose he left anything behind, did he?'

Another shake of the head.

'Do you think I could see the room he used to see his patients?'

The girl smiled as she came out from behind the desk. 'It's not exactly a consulting room,' she said. 'It's the ground floor linen store. We just made space for him on the day.'

Steven could see that the room had been restocked with linen. 'I hope he cleared up after him,' he said, 'and didn't leave any syringes and needles lying around . . .'

'He was very good,' said the girl. 'Cleaned up everything when he was finished. Just as well. I hate needles and all that stuff.'

'A true professional,' said Steven, although he was thinking about a different profession entirely. He went upstairs and called John Macmillan at his home number, beginning with the usual apology for doing so.

'Better that than silence,' said Macmillan. 'I hate being kept in the dark. Jean told me you'd uncovered something about the excavation at Dryburgh?'

Steven told him about the impostor who had given injections to the four men at the site.

'You're certain he was a phoney?'

'Absolutely. Public Health had never heard of him: I checked.' Steven told Macmillan that the man had paid in cash at the hotel.

'So you think *he* engineered what happened to John Motram,' said Macmillan slowly, as if he were thinking at the same time as speaking.

'I think so,' said Steven. 'The other three were unaffected by their injections, but I think Motram was given something different.'

'Which makes him a specific target.'

'I think they wanted to keep him quiet about something.'

'Odd way of going about it.'

'But clever,' said Steven. 'If it hadn't been for the lab not finding spores in the air . . .'

'You did well,' said Macmillan.

'The point is, it's not exactly something private enterprise would come up with. It's more an intelligence services sort of thing, wouldn't you say?'

He heard Macmillan let his breath out in a long sigh before muttering, 'Damnation. This we don't need.'

'Did you find out anything more about the dead marine?' Steven asked.

'The MOD are sticking to their official line: anything else is pure fantasy, according to them. They have every sympathy with the dead boy's parents but what they're suggesting is, in the MOD's view, stuff and nonsense. They're keen to let it be known that the Kellys' MSP belongs to the Scottish Nationalist Party: they maintain he's seizing the chance to make trouble for the Westminster Labour Party.'

'Mmm,' said Steven. 'But in all honesty, I can't see the Kellys making something like this up, can you? Do we know anything about their reasons for suggesting their son had been back in the UK?'

'No one I spoke to could say,' said Macmillan.

'I'm going to visit them tomorrow,' said Steven. 'I'll try to find out.'

'Did you learn anything new from John Motram's wife?'

'She couldn't add much to what we knew already,' said Steven. 'Motram's research was being funded by something called the Hotspur Foundation. In return, he had to screen the donor for an unnamed bone marrow patient who was suffering from advanced leukaemia. The man in charge of the transplant was a Sir Laurence Samson, a Harley Street physician, and it was being carried out at a private hospital called St Raphael's in South Kensington. At some point after the screening, Motram contacted Samson and told him he thought the donor was the dead marine. Samson told him he was mistaken.'

'Then someone destroyed the synapses of his brain . . .' murmured Macmillan. 'The smell of rat is overpowering.'

TWENTY-FOUR

The Barony flats in the east end of Glasgow were as bleak and depressing as the area they were situated in. Steven had suspected the worst when the taxi driver gave him a funny look and asked if he was sure when he gave him the address. 'Why do you ask?'

The taxi driver looked him up and down and said, 'Three hundred quid leather jacket, designer jeans, Rolex watch: you don't belong there, pal. They'll know that too ... When you step oot ma cab they're gonae see it as Santa's sleigh ...'

'Drop me at the edge of the estate,' said Steven. 'I'll use the quiet streets.' He was determined that his only compromise was going to be not taking the car. He liked it just the way it was ... with wheels.

'Good luck,' said the driver with a knowing smile when Steven paid and tipped him well.

There were places like this in every city in the UK, thought Steven as he skirted round a group of young children blocking the pavement, maybe in every city in the world. They were universally described as poor areas, but it wasn't just money missing from the equation, it was optimism, self-respect, enthusiasm, hope. There would be exceptions – there were always exceptions, people who tried hard against all the odds – but, in the end, the rubbish would win; the rubbish always won. The lazy, the feckless, the stupid, the criminal, the serially disaffected would smother and destroy the seeds of hope and make sure the wilderness remained in perpetuity.

It was no surprise to find that the lift going up to the Kellys' floor was broken. The smell of urine in the ground floor area suggested this was probably a blessing and Steven took the stairs, picking his way through the accumulated litter of fast-food wrappings and beer cans. He paused at the third landing to look out at the view and reflected that Michael Kelly's decision to join the military couldn't have been that difficult. He found the Kellys' door and rang the bell. The name tag above the button had 'Kelly' written on it in Biro: dampness had made the lettering run.

The door was opened by a woman who immediately changed her mind and said, 'We've nothing more to say to the papers. Please go away.' She made to close the door and Steven stopped her by putting his hand against it, moderating his action with what he hoped was a friendly smile. 'I'm not from the papers, Mrs Kelly. My name's Steven Dunbar. I'm trying to establish the truth about your son's death.'

May Kelly still seemed suspicious. 'How do I know you're not lying?' she asked.

Steven took out his ID with one hand and showed it to her.

'It says here you're a doctor.'

'Yes, but I work as an investigator. I really am trying to find out the truth about Michael's death.'

May Kelly relented. 'You'd better come in.' She showed him into a small sitting room and gestured to him to sit down.

'I take it Mr Kelly's at work?'

'Sleeping.'

'Sleeping?'

'Off sick.'

'Nothing serious, I hope?'

'A couple of Rangers guys gave him a doin'.'

Steven made a face. 'I take it he's a Celtic supporter?' He was well aware of the loathing between supporters of Glasgow's two biggest football clubs. His wife had been a Glasgow girl.

May nodded. 'Everyone is round here. He was wearing his Celtic top coming out of a pub and these guys jumped him, gave him a right goin' over.'

Steven shook his head. 'I'm sorry. I suppose you know what I'm going to ask you?'

'Same as the others. Where did we get our information about Michael's death not being as straightforward as they were making out.'

Steven nodded. 'More or less. In particular, what makes you think your son was back here in the UK on a "secret mission", as the papers called it?'

'I can't tell you that,' said May. 'The guy who told us would get into big trouble. But take it from me, he knew what he was talking about.'

Steven was about to say something when he was interrupted by the opening of the room door and the appearance of Brian Kelly in a Celtic top and his underpants: his bulk filled the doorway. 'What did I tell you about talking to these buggers?' he asked May.

'He's no' the papers,' said May. 'He's an investigator.'

'Investigator my arse,' stormed Brian, the heavy bruising to his face making his anger appear even more ferocious. He made a grab at Steven, who rose expertly from his seat, avoided Brian's grasp and put him in an arm-lock. Lowering him very slowly and gently into the chair he had been sitting on he said, 'I'm Steven Dunbar of the Sci-Med Inspectorate. I'd like to ask you a few questions, Mr Kelly.'

Kelly looked balefully at his wife and said with an air of resignation, 'Make us some tea, will you?'

May left the room and Steven sat down opposite Kelly, and took in the state of his face. 'God, you have been in the wars.'

'Rangers bastards,' said Kelly, touching his bruises. 'I take it you're here like the others tae find oot who blew the whistle on those lying bastards at the MOD? Well, we're no' talkin'.'

'It might help me find out a bit more about your son's death.'

'No it wouldnae,' said Kelly. 'We've told everyone all they need to know to get the answers we want but they're a' more interested in getting hold of the guy who told us.'

'Well, he's obviously the one who knows what really went on,' said Steven. 'You could have made the whole lot up.'

'Yer arse,' said Kelly angrily.

'No matter,' said Steven. 'Your wife's already told me that you folks aren't going to say anything about your source so I'll have to respect your decision.'

Kelly looked at Steven and Steven was surprised to see fear in his eyes. 'We promised,' he said. 'We promised the guy we wouldn't tell anyone . . .'

'Of course.' Steven sensed there was more going on inside Kelly's head. 'But?' he prompted.

'That's what those Rangers bastards wanted to know,' mumbled Kelly.

Steven felt stunned. 'What?' he exclaimed. 'The men who attacked you wanted to know who told you about Michael's death not being straightforward?'

Kelly remained silent and looked at the floor.

'I take it your silence means that you told them?'

'I had to; they were kicking eight kinds o' shit out of me.'

'So the cat's out of the bag anyway.'

Kelly appeared ashamed. 'It was Michael's pal,' he said. 'Jim Leslie.'

'He's a marine too?'

Kelly nodded. 'He asked us no' tae tell anyone it was him but he was well pissed off over what happened to Michael.'

'And what exactly did happen to Michael?' Steven probed gently.

'Jim said Mick was called back to the UK but he didn't know why; it was a secret. Michael said he couldn't tell him. The next thing Jim knew, Michael was back in Afghanistan, lying in a field hospital. They said he'd been injured by shrapnel and the wounds had turned septic but nobody knew anything about the incident and Jim didn't get to see Michael . . . until it was too late.'

'Too late?'

'They let him pay his last respects after he died.'

Steven had to make absolutely sure of his facts. 'So Jim Leslie saw your son's body in Afghanistan after he died?'

'That's what I just said,' said Kelly. 'And now he's goin' tae get in real trouble because I blabbed.'

'I don't think you had much choice in the circumstances, Mr Kelly,' said Steven, but he saw it was cold comfort.

May Kelly returned with three mugs of tea and three chocolate biscuits on a circular metal tray with a picture of the Grand Canal in Venice on it. She looked suspiciously at each of the two men in turn as if trying to work out what had been going on. They had their tea and biscuits in an uneasy silence before Steven said, 'Well, I'm sorry you can't help me with my investigation, Mr and Mrs Kelly, but of course I do understand.' The look he got from Kelly was thanks enough. 'And I'm very sorry for your loss.'

TWENTY-FIVE

Steven left the Barony flats. It was his intention to walk until he found a main road and catch either a bus or a taxi back to town, depending on which came along first. He felt like a deer in a concrete forest; the eyes of the hunters were on him, and he had to stay alert. A group of three youths standing in a doorway looked as if they might consider bidding to become the new owners of his wallet and mobile phone, but perhaps the fact that he was over six feet and in good physical condition caused them to reconsider. He kept up his quick pace, however, anticipating a possible call for reinforcements; he'd seen one of them talking into a phone inside his hood.

In the event, he made it to a main road without incident and got on the green and yellow bus that turned up shortly afterwards. Up on the top deck, he thought through what he'd learned from Brian Kelly on the fifteen-minute ride back into the city. The fact that Kelly had been beaten up for reasons other than football rivalry or sectarian bigotry was scary. The real motive had been to find out where he'd got the information about his son's death and that could mean that Marine James Leslie was in real danger. He'd alert Sci-Med as soon as he was somewhere less public. On a more positive note, he could now be sure that Michael Kelly had died in Afghanistan; Jim Leslie had seen his body there, which removed the lingering possibility that Kelly had met his death back in the UK. Even

if John Motram had been right about his being the donor –
and plenty was pointing to that – he must have returned to
Afghanistan immediately afterwards.

But then what? Sheer bad luck? Had he been killed as soon
as he'd stepped off the plane? He hadn't had time to return to
his unit. Apart from that, no one knew anything about the incident in which he'd supposedly been injured, according to Jim
Leslie . . . who'd seen Kelly's dead body lying in Camp Bastion
. . . Kelly's dead body . . . Kelly's dead body.

A cloud of doubt swirled back in. Maybe he couldn't elimi-
nate the possibility that Michael Kelly had died in the UK after
all. Maybe it was his dead body that had been returned to
Afghanistan.

More and more, his attention was being drawn towards the
London bone marrow transplant. How had a Royal Marine
serving in Afghanistan come to be selected as the donor? Who
was the patient? He must have had something more than money
going for him to merit this kind of hush-up. Unwittingly
echoing the Motrams' assessment of the patient's possible identity,
Steven supposed the ante could have been raised considerably
by his being a member of one of the ruling families in the Gulf
that the UK and US depended on for support; he could even
conceivably be a powerful figure in a not-so-friendly administra-
tion who had been forced to seek medical help in London
without the knowledge of the opposition in his own country
– a favour to be called in at a later date. But advanced leukaemia
at a stage that required a last-ditch bone marrow transplant
wasn't really something that could be hidden that well . . .

Steven got off the bus and found a quiet spot to call Sci-Med.
He asked that they make immediate enquiries at the Ministry
of Defence regarding the current location and welfare of Marine
James Leslie, serving with 45 Commando in the Northern

Battle Group in Helmand Province. He hoped that having Sci-Med express an interest might make others think twice about initiating any adverse action against him.

Steven had a beer and a sandwich in a city centre pub before calling Tally on his way back to the car park. He was redirected to her answer service. This was nothing new. Life as an NHS hospital doctor meant that she could rarely answer during the day. He left her a message, saying that he'd finished in Scotland and could stop off on the way back if that was all right with her. He asked that she leave him a message if it wasn't.

He stopped at a service station some three hours later to take on fuel and have a break. The sun had come out, so he took a stroll around the car park and found a spot where the boundary fence backed on to farmland to call John Macmillan. He told him about the attack on Brian Kelly.

'That explains your earlier call,' said Macmillan. 'The duty officer told me you'd requested information on Marine James Leslie from the MOD. Actually, it's just come in . . .'

'That was quick.' The slight pause that ensued made the hairs on the back of Steven's neck stand on end. 'And?'

'Marine Leslie died in a car accident yesterday. He'd been home in the UK on compassionate leave; his partner lost her baby recently. He was driving up to HMS *Condor* in Arbroath where 45 Commando are based.'

'But they're in Afghanistan just now,' interrupted Steven.

'They're due home in April,' said Macmillan. 'I suppose someone decided there was no point in sending him back out to Helmand if they were all coming home next month.'

'So they sent him up to Arbroath instead.'

'His car left the road between Dundee and Arbroath at around three p.m. yesterday. Police are appealing for witnesses.'

Steven let out a snort of anger. 'I think I want to call a Code Red on this.'

'Agreed,' said Macmillan without argument.

By agreeing to Code Red status, Macmillan was sanctioning the upgrading of Steven's preliminary investigation into a fully funded Sci-Med inquiry. Full Home Office backing would be accorded to him, including the right to demand police co-operation where necessary. He would also have access to a number of other facilities ranging from financial provisions to expert scientific analysis. A duty officer at Sci-Med would be assigned to him specifically – actually three, giving round-the-clock cover – and he would have the right to bear arms if he thought it necessary. Unlike chain-of-command organisations, Sci-Med investigators could conduct their inquiries exactly as they saw fit. Any repercussions would be left until after the inquiry was over.

'Any thoughts?' Macmillan asked.

'Route one.' I'm going to ask Sir Laurence Samson and St Raphael's Hospital what the hell's been going on.'

'And when you get nowhere?'

'I'm going out to Afghanistan. Michael Kelly's the key to this whole business. I need to know where and when he died.'

'And the why?'

'That'll come.'

'How was bonny Scotland?' asked Tally with a smile when Steven arrived at her flat just before eight o'clock.

'Less than bonny,' replied Steven. 'I've called a Code Red on the whole thing.'

Tally stopped pouring them a drink and turned to stare at Steven. 'What happened to dull, boring inquiries?' she asked.

'One academic with his brains scrambled and now two dead

marines,' said Steven, knowing that he was skating on thin ice with Tally.

'So what's in store for *you*, Steven? Brains scrambled or just plain dead?'

'Look, I know how you must feel after last time . . .'

'Do you, Steven? Do you really?'

'Look, Tally, I don't go looking for trouble . . . it just happens sometimes.'

'Maybe they'll say that at the service after your body is recovered from a burnt-out car or riddled with bullets. I'll stand there, dressed in black, being brave, hearing you being given the thanks of a grateful nation . . . Like fuck I will!'

There was an electrifying pause. Tally's temper was struggling with the tears running down her face. 'Why don't you just let the police investigate this?' she demanded.

'They wouldn't know where to start; the military are involved . . .' said Steven weakly.

'Well, the military police?'

'There are medical aspects to the case that . . .'

'Only Steven Dunbar understands,' interrupted Tally.

'If you like,' said Steven quietly.

Tally fixed Steven with a stare that seemed to go on for ever. 'I love you, Tally,' he began.

'And I love you too, Steven,' said Tally. 'But this kind of life is not for me. I'd like you to go now please.'

Steven drove back to London.

TWENTY-SIX

Steven sought comfort in the arms of gin and tonic when he got in. It was late; he was tired; he felt low and any argument from his conscience that he was just feeling sorry for himself was dismissed without further consideration as he refilled his glass and slumped back down in his chair by the window to gaze up at the stars in the cloudless sky – the ones he could see against the light pollution of the city. It was impossible not to think *here we are again* as yet another love affair looked set to founder on the rocks of his job.

Maybe Tally would come round or maybe she wouldn't and this really was the end. Maybe he should be soul-searching, analysing, considering his position as the doomed were always advised to do . . . No, gin was better. The pain was easing; the edges were already becoming blurred, so hazy even that a wry smile crossed his lips when he thought that at least he wouldn't have to tell Tally he was going to Afghanistan.

Next morning, Steven slept late before spending a long time in the shower and downing three cups of strong coffee before he even started to consider the day ahead. It eventually began with a call to Jean Roberts and a request that she make him appointments at St Raphael's and with Sir Laurence Samson.

'How insistent should I be?' asked Jean.

'Start nicely and move towards doing it at a police station if they'd prefer.'

'Remind me not to steal your toys,' said Jean.

'Sorry, Jean. Bad night.'

Steven had his appointment with the hospital secretary at St Raphael's at two p.m. He arrived a few minutes early and was invited to wait in a room with a view. There was no need to avail himself of one of the upmarket magazines – a wide choice and all current editions – while he could look out through a large picture window at the garden and enjoy the scent of the spring flowers that filled four vases in the room. Beethoven's 'Pastoral' Symphony was playing almost imperceptibly from a hidden speaker system in the room. The level was exactly right. He suspected that the level of everything in this hospital was exactly right.

'Mr Sneddon will see you now, doctor,' said a smiling girl in an immaculate white dress. She showed Steven to an office where a man in a Savile Row suit greeted him as if he'd been looking forward to his visit for weeks. He waved away Steven's ID card, saying, 'I'm sure you have every right to be here, doctor. How can we help?'

'I need information, Mr Sneddon. I need to know all about the operation that Dr John Motram acted as an adviser on some weeks ago.'

'Would you have a more exact date?' asked Sneddon, opening up a desk diary.

Not entirely convinced by Sneddon's apparent lack of recall, Steven said shortly, 'The eighth of March.'

'Ah, here we are,' said Sneddon, adjusting the frameless glasses on his nose. 'Oh, of course, I remember now. Dr Motram was here to screen a potential donor for a marrow transplant operation. The patient was suffering from advanced leukaemia . . .'

'Yes, I know that,' said Steven.

'Then what?' asked Sneddon, looking puzzled.

'I want to know who the donor was, who the patient was and the outcome of the operation.'

Sneddon did a good impression of a man shocked out of his skin. 'I'm sorry,' he began, with an excellent stutter. 'We can't possibly divulge such information. It's absolutely out of the question.'

Steven did a very good impression of a man who wasn't at all surprised. 'Mr Sneddon, I have the full backing of the Home Office in making my inquiries. I need that information.'

'Doctor, this hospital . . . this establishment . . . this business exists on an absolutely fundamental code of total confidentiality. That is more important than our consultants, our nurses, our operating theatres, our recovery rooms. Without it, we simply couldn't survive.'

'I have the right to demand answers to my questions,' said Steven.

The good nature in Sneddon's eyes was replaced by blue ice. 'I don't think you have,' he said. 'Unless you are pursuing a murder inquiry, I don't think I have to tell you anything.'

Steven silently acknowledged that he was right and took a moment to consider how he was going to proceed. He hadn't expected Sneddon to tell him anything: he was here on a cage-rattling exercise. 'Dr Motram is currently a very sick man,' he said.

'Yes, I heard,' said Sneddon, putting care and concern into his voice with consummate ease. 'Some kind of nervous break-down, I heard. Poor chap.'

'No, it wasn't a nervous breakdown,' said Steven. 'He was poisoned and his condition is in some way connected with his involvement in the operation he was advising on.'

Sneddon did 'taken aback' very well. 'You cannot be serious,' he said.

'I am,' said Steven flatly.

'But he was in the process of unearthing a centuries-old tomb,' protested Sneddon. 'There were suggestions of Black Death, I understand. How can there possibly be a connection between that and what he was doing here?'

Steven ignored the question. 'The donor Dr Motram saw here was a serving Royal Marine who has since died.'

'Oh, that was just a silly case of mistaken identity,' exclaimed Sneddon, as if relieved to be clearing up an old misunderstanding. 'Sir Laurence explained that to Dr Motram.'

'Dr Motram didn't believe him,' said Steven, getting to his feet. 'Neither do I.'

Sneddon lost his aplomb and seemed distinctly uncomfortable. 'Well, that's something you'll have to take up with Sir Laurence,' he said, starting to move some papers around on his desk like a TV newsreader at the end of a bulletin.

'On my way,' said Steven pleasantly. He left, feeling well satisfied with the cage-rattling he'd done. He would have bet his eye teeth that Sneddon was already on the phone to Samson.

His appointment with Sir Laurence wasn't until four p.m. so he picked up a sandwich and a soft drink and took a leisurely walk down to the park, where he shared his lunch with some ducks. It was therapeutic to interact with simple creatures who had no agenda but to survive. They had no convoluted notions of confidentiality and honour, didn't know what hypocrisy and lying were, or cheating and double-dealing. The irony that struck him was that despite the multiple layers present in human sociology, the underlying driving forces were really just as simple as those of the ducks. It might be important to remember that when you started rattling cages . . . If you get in my way, I'll push you out of the road . . .

It was impossible for Steven not to acknowledge that he was

in the very heart of the medical establishment as he sat waiting in Sir Laurence Samson's premises in Harley Street, but the rebel inside him couldn't help but reflect that there had been a time when the practitioners in this famous street really didn't know that much about medicine at all. But, as with witch doctors in darkest Africa, the mystique had survived.

'Dr Dunbar, I'm a few minutes late. I do apologise.'

Steven smiled at Samson. 'No need, Sir Laurence. Mr Sneddon has probably told you what it's all about.'

A look of irritation appeared in Samson's eyes, but only for a second. 'No, should he have done?'

Steven told him what he wanted to know and got the same response he'd got from Sneddon. He made his final gambit. 'Dr John Motram may die and a young marine has already met an untimely death – two young marines, in fact, although the second needn't concern you for the moment.' Steven looked for surprise in Samson's eyes and found it. He continued, 'There is a limit to how long you're going to get away with playing the confidentiality card before what you're doing simply becomes obstruction in a very serious criminal investigation.'

The look on Samson's face told Steven his cage had been well and truly rattled. 'Thank you for your time, Sir Laurence.'

TWENTY-SEVEN

'You've been busy,' said Macmillan when Steven called him.

'What makes you say that?'

'The phone's been red hot with calls from people who'd rather you stopped what you've been doing.'

'Anyone interesting?'

'People in high places. But . . .'

'But what?'

'I don't know – I should be used to this sort of thing by now, but there's something different about it this time: I can't quite put my finger on it. Usually I can work out the primary source of any flak that's flying, but not this time.'

'Maybe I've upset everyone equally,' suggested Steven, tongue in cheek.

Macmillan permitted himself a laugh before he said, 'Seriously, watch your back.'

'Will do.'

'How's Dr Simmons, by the way?'

'I'm sure she's fine.'

'Oh . . . I didn't realise.'

'Some other time, John.'

'Right . . . Are you still intent on heading off to sunny climes?'

'I've been in touch with my old pals in Hereford. They've been given a job to do in the Sangin Valley in the north of Helmand Province – that's where 45 Commando have been operating. I've arranged to fly out with them; they'll kit me out and provide me with a vehicle. After that, they'll go their way and I'll go mine. I plan to start at the field hospital where Michael Kelly was reportedly treated before he was transferred to Camp Bastion.'

'You do realise we could do all this through official channels,' suggested Macmillan.

'I prefer my way,' said Steven. 'Official channels can leak, and from what you've said about some folks in officialdom not being too happy, I'd rather not be a sitting target. The Regiment doesn't advertise its travel arrangements.

'And after you've checked out the field hospital?'

'I'll play it by ear. My Sci-Med ID should get me most of the answers I'm looking for unless there's some really big cover-up going on. If that should turn out to be the case, I'll let you know.'

'Don't forget your satellite phone.'

'Packed and ready.'

'Take care, Steven.'

Being back at the Hereford base of the SAS was like a trip down memory lane for Steven. It wasn't the first time he'd had to call on old friends since he'd joined Sci-Med, but the last time had been over three years ago. No longer being an active member of the Regiment meant, of course, that he was excluded from team briefings, and he knew better than to enquire about their mission. Likewise, he did not divulge the nature of his own assignment, but there was still a bond that members past and present shared and valued. As one ex-comrade had put it, you really don't know what being alive feels like until you're bloody nearly not. Sharing that experience was the basis of a special relationship. Steven took particular pleasure in learning from one young soldier, recruited from 2 Para – the same route that he himself had followed – that his reputation had preceded him and he was still well thought of in Hereford.

The flight out to Afghanistan followed a familiar pattern for Steven. For the first hour or so everyone on board was running on the adrenalin of anticipation, and good-humoured banter made sure there was lots of laughter around, but after that things started to quieten down, eventually to such an extent that John Donne's assertion was proved wrong – at least in the short term – and every man on board the aircraft became an island.

Steven was no exception: he became lost in his thoughts. He glanced at his watch and knew that Jenny would be at school, perhaps painting one of the animal pictures she liked to present him with when he went up to see her, possibly arguing with one of the other children over the colouring. Red elephants and green tigers were no strangers to Jenny's world. 'Just because you haven't seen them doesn't mean they're not there,' she would assert. Bossy little madam.

Tally would be on duty at the hospital, doing her best to restore sick children to good health, perhaps doing her morning ward rounds, reading charts, getting lab reports, discussing cases with colleagues and the nursing staff. He wondered if she was still angry with him or whether the passage of a few days had caused her to mellow and perhaps reconsider. Was there any way back for him? The idea of making up with Tally was, for him at that particular moment, a vision of paradise. Paradise lost? Please God, no.

When he closed his eyes, he could see them holidaying together in the Highlands of Scotland, in a cottage with no one else around, entirely lost in each other's company with no desire to be anywhere else on earth. Time would stand still and . . . Steven suddenly realised that Tally didn't know where he was right now. If she did . . . what was that word journalists used but no one else did? . . . incandescent, that was it. That's what she'd be. He closed his eyes again and tried to catch up on some sleep.

As he waved farewell to his travel companions and watched their Land Rovers move off into the desert, Steven felt a momentary pang of regret that he wasn't going with them. Not that he missed that awful feeling in the stomach when heading off into a dangerous unknown, but he did miss the camaraderie. They were off to take on the Taleban, and when their vehicles faded from sight he would be off to visit 179 Field Hospital where Michael Kelly had reportedly been taken after his wounds had become infected.

Steven checked the map and set a start point on his satnav. The hospital was only forty kilometres away but the ground was rough. He checked fuel and oil levels for a second time and took comfort from patting the plentiful supplies of drinking water he had with him in the Land Rover. He hoped he wouldn't need the automatic rifle and ammunition he'd also been given.

He paused for a final few moments to take in the scene around him before setting off. It wasn't the first time he'd been in Afghanistan: he'd been here with a Special Forces team on a 'fact-finding' mission a few years after the Russians had given up the struggle against the mujahideen and withdrawn from what would generally come to be thought of as their Vietnam. The talc-like sand and jagged-toothed mountains held memories, not all of them good.

Steven was a civilian now, but one well versed in the ways of the military. He had no trouble at all convincing the sentries at 179 Field Hospital that he had a right to be there. His request to be taken to see the commanding officer, Major Tom Lewis (TA), was acted upon without question.

*   *   *

Lewis, a stocky man in his mid-to-late forties with a complexion that was obviously ill at ease with the sun in his current surroundings, looked at Steven's ID at some length before confessing with a smile, 'Doesn't mean a lot, I'm afraid, doctor. Where's your base exactly?'

'The Home Office.'

'Bit out of your way, aren't you?' said Lewis, looking surprised.

'I could say the same about you,' said Steven.

'Fair point,' Lewis conceded with a smile. 'I'm an orthopaedic surgeon at Cardiff General in the real world.'

'Life's rich pattern.'

'What can I do for you?'

'Does the name Michael Kelly mean anything to you?'

'Certainly does. We all read the papers.'

'I understand he was brought here to your hospital?'

Lewis nodded. 'Marine Michael Kelly was brought here in a field ambulance. He was suffering from a wound infection. It was actually quite advanced by the time we saw him.'

'Advanced?' Steven repeated. 'Where had he been before?'

'That wasn't clear,' said Lewis. 'I was informed that Marine Kelly had been slightly wounded by shrapnel but had brushed off his injuries as being insignificant at the time. Unfortunately they turned septic and he was forced to stop ignoring the condition and seek medical help. That's when he was brought in here, but he must have been in considerable pain for some time before.'

'Didn't that strike you as odd?'

Lewis gave a slight shrug. 'I suppose I was more concerned with his condition at the time.'

'Didn't you ask him about it?'

'He was heavily sedated.'

'Then what happened?'

'After a brief examination, I decided that he needed a more

sophisticated medical environment than our tent village here if he was to have any chance of recovery, so I ordered him taken on to Camp Bastion.'

'I see,' said Steven thoughtfully. 'Did you examine Kelly personally?'

Lewis nodded. 'I did.'

'About these shrapnel wounds . . . where had he been hit?'

Lewis took a deep breath. 'Difficult to say really, the infection had made such a mess of his flesh, but it looked to me as if the epicentre was round about his mid region, upper thighs spreading across lower stomach.'

Steven thanked Lewis for his help and asked for an estimate of how long it would take him to drive to Camp Bastion.

'You'll be there before nightfall.'

Steven was awestruck by the sheer size of Camp Bastion. It seemed to stretch for miles, a huge artificial home for a very large military community, with proper buildings for a medical facility. He was given a tour of the hospital by its commanding officer, Lientement Colonel James McCready, a Scotsman who was obviously proud of what he and his colleagues had achieved in the desert. 'We can do most things here,' he said, 'outside plastic surgery. What's your specialty, doctor?'

'Field medicine,' replied Steven, something that caused McCready to raise his eyebrows.

'So you were military?' he said.

Steven nodded. 'For a good few years.'

'So this must all be familiar to you?'

'Not really,' said Steven, feeling slightly awkward. He was getting into a conversation he'd rather not have been in. 'I didn't actually serve with any medical unit . . .'

'Then what, might I ask?'

'2 Para and SAS.'

'Ah. Then you will have seen the odd cut thumb.' To Steven's relief, McCready seemed happy to leave things at that. 'What exactly about Marine Kelly did you want to know?'

'I understand he was admitted here?'

'He was,' said McCready. 'He was suffering from infected shrapnel wounds. 179 Field Hospital referred him to us. We admitted him and did our best to stabilise him. We put him on antibiotics but, despite our best efforts, he died two days later.'

'Why?'

The bluntness of the question caused McCready to exaggerate surprise. 'Because it happens, doctor. His infection didn't respond to treatment. It proved resistant to every antibiotic we tried.'

'Do you know what the infection was?'

'We have an excellent lab here,' replied McCready with some pride. 'It was a *Staphylococcus aureus* infection. Marine Kelly died from MRSA.'

'It may seem irrelevant, colonel, but can you tell me anything about the wounds that led to the infection?'

'Not really,' replied McCready. 'I was told they were very slight and he neglected – for whatever reason – to have them seen to right away. Unfortunately, he paid the price.'

Steven nodded. Outwardly, he remained calm and thoughtful but inside his head all hell had been let loose. Michael Kelly *had* died in Afghanistan, but not as the result of any shrapnel wounds. He'd died of an MRSA infection after being the donor in a bone marrow transplant in London. The bone marrow would have been extracted through wide-bore needles from his hip bones; the 'shrapnel wounds' were needle puncture marks which had turned septic. Instead of being treated in London, he had been flown all the way back to Afghanistan to die, complete with a phoney story about having been wounded in action.

TWENTY-EIGHT

'Are you all right, doctor?' asked McCready. Steven seemed to have been preoccupied for a long time.

He nodded and gave a resigned smile. 'What a tangled web we weave, colonel.'

McCready gave a slight, bemused smile. 'The ambulance crew that brought Marine Kelly in,' Steven went on. 'Can you tell me anything about them?'

McCready frowned and shook his head. 'We tend to be more concerned with the casualties than the soldiers bringing them in.'

'But they were soldiers?'

This time McCready appeared irritated. 'I didn't see them personally but I assume they were. If they'd been chartered accountants, I'm sure someone would have said.'

'Sorry,' said Steven. 'So no one did mention anything unusual about them?'

'No.'

'Do you have lab cultures of the organism that Marine Kelly died from?'

'Of course,' said McCready. 'As I said, we have excellent facilities here. Why d'you ask?'

'I'd like to take one back to the UK with me.'

McCready suddenly seemed suspicious. 'Is there some problem here?' he asked, all at once sounding more Scottish. 'Are we under some kind of scrutiny for our handling of Marine Kelly?'

'No, you're not. Is there some problem about giving me a culture of the organism that killed Michael Kelly?'

McCready shrugged. 'I suppose not. I'll have the lab grow one up for you: it'll be ready in the morning. Anything else?'

'Accommodation for the night would be good,' said Steven. 'I didn't have time to arrange anything.'

McCready looked appraisingly at Steven, as if he were seeing an enigma. 'No problem,' he said. 'Tell me . . . where exactly does the Sci-Med Inspectorate fit in with the military?'

'It doesn't,' Steven replied, matter-of-factly.

McCready remained impassive until a slight smile broke out on his lips and he said, 'Something tells me if I ask any more questions, I won't like the answers and this could all end up in a mass of paperwork.'

'Seems to me cold beer would be a better option,' Steven suggested.

A moment's hesitation, then a slight nod was the prelude to a very pleasant evening in the officers' mess, a good night's sleep and success the following morning in hitching a lift back to the UK on an RAF flight returning to Brize Norton. In Steven's pack, surrounded by absorbent packing material, was a small glass vial containing a culture of the micro-organism that had killed Michael Kelly.

'How was the graveyard of empires?' asked Sir John Macmillan when Steven turned up in his office.

'As inhospitable as ever,' Steven replied. 'But worth going: I made progress.'

Macmillan looked at the sun streaming in the window and

said, 'I think the least I can do is offer you lunch. Let's walk over to my club; we can go through the park.'

On the way, Steven told Macmillan what he'd discovered.

'So the military weren't involved in any shenanigans?'

'No,' said Steven. 'They all did what they could when Kelly turned up on their doorstep, but none of them thought to question how he'd come to be there.'

'But the military must have been involved in selecting Kelly as the donor for this damned transplant in the first place,' mused Macmillan.

'Or if not them officially . . . someone who had access to military medical records,' said Steven.

'What was wrong with civilian ones, I wonder?'

Steven mulled this over for a moment before suggesting, 'Maybe they weren't comprehensive enough . . . maybe the patient had a very rare blood or tissue type and Michael Kelly was the only one who fitted the bill?'

'Plausible. Did Motram's wife mention anything about that?'

'No, she didn't,' Steven conceded. 'In fact she mentioned at one point that her husband thought it was a really routine job – money for old rope, to use his expression. He didn't understand why they wanted such a comprehensive report.'

Macmillan nodded and said, 'You know what worries me most? This someone who had access to military medical records would also have needed the clout to put the knowledge to practical use. He or she wasn't some filing clerk.'

'Good point,' said Steven. 'And a worry. Maybe one of your people in high places who doesn't like me rooting around?'

'Well, like it or not, it's what we'll be continuing to do.'

Steven smiled at Macmillan's resolution. 'Have you had any more thoughts about who the opposition might be?' he asked.

'I still can't get a handle on it,' Macmillan replied. 'I'm

convinced it's not the usual suspects. It's not MOD despite the military factor we've just been talking about, and I'm sure I'd recognise the hand of our colleagues in the Home Office if it were them. The Department of Health I'm not so sure about, but that would still leave lots of things that didn't fit.'

'MI5?' suggested Steven, thinking of Ricksen's appearance on site at Dryburgh.

'All wrong for them,' said Macmillan. 'Doesn't have their mark on it at all, although I suspect they know more than they're letting on. Still, the more opposition we encounter, the more they'll give themselves away.'

'A comfort,' said Steven, tongue in cheek. Macmillan smiled his acknowledgement that it would be Steven who bore the brunt of any future 'opposition'.

They didn't discuss the investigation over lunch, preferring instead to talk about other things ranging from climate change to rumours of a scandal brewing over MPs' allowances, but when they got to the coffee and brandy stage it was time to get back to business.

'The way I see it,' said Steven, 'returning Michael Kelly to Afghanistan with a full-blown MRSA infection was tantamount to murder. He might well have survived had he been treated here.'

Macmillan nodded his agreement. 'It was a ridiculous thing to do.'

'But maybe he wasn't the only one to contract MRSA at St Raphael's,' said Steven, suddenly seeing a new line of inquiry opening up. 'If there were other cases, we could get the lab to do a comparison of the local MRSA and the strain I brought back from Afghanistan. If a DNA comparison showed them to be identical, it would prove Michael Kelly contracted the infection at St Raphael's and possibly turn his death into a murder inquiry. The hospital would then have to release details of the operation.'

'Brilliant,' said Macmillan. 'The only problem I can see on the horizon is that St Raphael's aren't going to admit to any MRSA problem.'

'Mmm.'

A club server appeared with a silver coffee pot and caused a hiatus while he refilled their cups.

When the man withdrew, Macmillan said thoughtfully but with a glint in his eye, 'Tell me, what d'you think a private hospital does when it encounters an MRSA problem in their patients?'

A smile broke out on Steven's lips. 'Transfer the patients,' he said. 'Transfer the patients to the nearest NHS hospital.'

'I'll put out discreet feelers to surrounding hospitals,' said Macmillan.

'I still think we need to find out what made Michael Kelly so special,' said Steven. 'But we're not going to get that from St Raphael's or Sir Laurence Samson.'

'We could request more details from the military,' suggested Macmillan. 'But if we do that . . .'

'We'd be alerting the opposition to what we're up to.'

'An alternative would be better.'

'John Motram's wife told me that her husband carried out some tests on the donor samples in his own lab up north . . . If we could get our hands on them, we could see what our labs could come up with.'

'Well worth a try.'

TWENTY-NINE

Steven returned to his flat and found an envelope lying behind the door. There was no stamp on it and his name had been written in violet ink in beautiful copperplate handwriting. It was from one of his neighbours, Cynthia Clements, a solicitor in a city law firm. She was informing fellow members that Ms Greenaway, the chair of the Marlborough Court Residents' Association, had been taken into hospital. She thought it would be a nice gesture if they clubbed together and sent her some flowers. Steven put ten pounds in an envelope and left it on the phone table to put through Miss Clements' letter box on his way out. He couldn't help but take on board the fact that there were no new messages on his answering machine. The green zero gave him a hollow feeling in his stomach. Each day that passed seemed to make it more unlikely he would hear from Tally again.

He called Cassie Motram. There was no reply from her home number so he tried the practice. He learned that she had in fact returned to work but was currently with a patient: the receptionist would pass on the message when she became free. Cassie called him back within ten minutes.

'You're back in harness,' said Steven.

'My patients have decided they're not going to get Black Death from me after all,' said Cassie. 'Their attention span has moved on to worries new – swine flu to be precise.'

'Good to hear,' said Steven. 'Can't have the public not panicking about something.' He asked about the donor samples her husband had analysed in his own lab at Newcastle University. 'D'you think there's a chance they might still be there?'

'Quite possibly. I can't think why anyone would throw them out unless John did when he was finished with them, but tidiness is not his strong point. They'll probably still be lying in some fridge in his lab.'

'Good,' said Steven. 'I was just checking it would be worth flying up there in the morning to take a look.'

'May I ask why?'

'I'm trying to find out what was special about the donor John saw at the London hospital. I think he's the key to everything. Mind you, samples from the patient himself would be just as good, but I don't suppose John had access to any samples from him?'

Cassie said not. 'He was supplied with a lab report listing details for him to compare.'

'Was it as comprehensive as the one he was asked to provide on the donor?' asked Steven, almost as an afterthought.

'Actually, no,' Cassie replied. 'I remember John remarking that it had the relevant details but nothing more, while he'd been asked to do all sorts of tests on the donor he couldn't see the point of.'

'Interesting,' said Steven. 'I don't suppose you have this report?'

'I haven't, but maybe it'll be in John's lab. Whoops, I can see old Mrs Jackson getting anxious in the waiting room,' said Cassie. 'She's started complaining to the reception staff about how long she's been kept waiting. I'd best get on.'

'Sorry to interrupt,' said Steven.

'Good luck tomorrow.'

* * *

Steven took a British Airways flight up to Newcastle in the morning and a taxi for the six-mile journey into the city itself. Jean Roberts had arranged a time for him to meet the head of the Department of Cell Science but the journey had gone so smoothly that he had an hour and a half to spare. He used the time to have a walk round on what was a fine morning, finishing up with a leisurely coffee in a café with a view of the Tyne Bridge.

Steven had always liked being near great iconic structures, be they buildings or bridges or natural features like mountains. There was something about proximity to them that promoted him from being a member of the 'audience' of life to having at least a walk-on part in the 'performance'. No fog on the Tyne this morning, he noted before leaving the river to head off for the university.

'Any word of Dr Motram coming back?' asked the smiling woman who shook hands with him and introduced herself as Professor Mary Lyons. She was a short woman in her late fifties with white hair that had once been blonde and wrinkles on her cheeks that suggested she smiled a lot. She wore a dark green two-piece suit over a silk blouse with a yellow floral motif on it.

'I'm afraid not.'

'What an absolute tragedy. Such a nice man, and one of our best researchers too. Everyone misses him – although some of us for more selfish reasons, it has to be said.'

Steven gave her a questioning look.

'John's work on viral cell receptors is one of the main reasons we have such a high research rating – we were rated 4 in the last Research Assessment Exercise,' explained Lyons. 'These things are important when it comes to attracting grants and students.'

161

'I see.'

'So, how can I help you, doctor?'

Steven explained about the samples he was trying to trace and Lyons nodded. 'I don't see a problem there. Perhaps Louise Avery can help. She's John's research assistant: she's been working with one of the other groups while John is ... indisposed.' Lyons picked up the phone and made a three-digit call.

A few minutes later, a tall, slim girl with brown hair tied back in a ponytail and wearing a white lab coat knocked and entered. Lyons explained what was required and she replied, 'No problem,' in a north-east accent. As they walked along the corridor, the girl asked the question Mary Lyons had and Steven had to disappoint her too.

'It's a right shame,' she said, unlocking a lab door. 'I miss him. John could be a right laugh.'

Steven had difficulty imagining the man he'd seen in the isolation unit at Borders General Hospital being 'a right laugh' but the girl persisted. 'He told me he was going to give up science and become a celebrity nail technician if his grant wasn't renewed.'

Steven grinned broadly – not least because 'celebrity nail technician' gained much from being said with a Geordie accent – and found himself warming to the man who'd said it. Some scientists took themselves awfully seriously. Motram clearly wasn't in that school. 'Was the grant renewed?' he asked.

'No, not for the historical stuff – John's passion – but he managed to get some money from something called the Hotspur Foundation. As one door closes another one opens, you might say.'

Steven nodded his agreement with Geordie-tinged philosophy.

'If John didn't chuck out the samples, they'll be in here,' said Louise, opening the top half of a large fridge freezer.

'Did you work on them at all?' asked Steven, suddenly realising that the girl might have the very information he was seeking, but the hope was short-lived.

'No. John said it was something he had to do himself. Delegation wasn't permitted.'

'I don't suppose you saw his results?'

Another shake of the head. 'I had no reason to. It was nothing to do with our work here. He was checking out a potential bone marrow donor . . . but I suppose you know that.'

Steven nodded.

'You're in luck,' announced Louise, removing a wire rack from the fridge. It contained a number of plastic tubes of various shapes and sizes. She gave a little laugh. 'Can't get much clearer than that,' she said, holding up the rack.

Steven read the label. *Bone Marrow Donor.*

Louise produced a small polystyrene box and some dry ice. Steven watched as she packed the samples. 'Have you been with John long?' he asked.

'Ever since I graduated,' she replied. 'About eight years now.'

'Quite a while. Any plans for the future?'

'I'm thinking of registering for a master's degree if John agrees. I could do it part time and still continue working here. After that, who knows?'

'PhD?'

'Maybe.'

What had started as small talk had given birth to a plan in Steven's head. 'You must know almost as much as John about research in receptor biology,' he said.

Louise smiled. 'It's one thing learning what's there, quite another coming up with what's not there.'

'What does that mean?' asked Steven, intrigued by her response.

'People think research is all about getting answers. It's not; it's more about asking questions, the right questions. Out of the hundreds of questions you can ask, only one or two will be the right ones. The others . . . well, they just keep researchers in employment.'

Steven was impressed. 'Hang on a moment,' he said as he saw she was about to seal the box. It had been his intention to take the samples back to London and hand them over to the contract labs Sci-Med used for analytical work. There had never been any trouble with this arrangement in the past and there was no reason to think there would be this time, but the paranoia that came with knowing there was some kind of establishment opposition to the current investigation was making Steven ultra-cautious. 'What would you say to the idea of Sci-Med commissioning you to carry out an analysis on these samples?'

'I don't know what Professor Lyons would say about that.'

'Assuming she was agreeable?'

'Then sure, no problem. What is it you'd want me to do exactly?'

'I need to know everything you can possibly tell me about the donor from the samples in these tubes.'

'Look, John actually mentioned in passing he was a perfect match for the patient,' said Louise, 'if that's what you're worried about. In fact . . .' She opened a drawer under the lab bench and rummaged around for a few seconds before coming up with a sheet of paper which she handed to Steven. 'These are the patient's details. I remember John saying they were too ordinary to be secret.'

'Thank you,' said Steven. 'May I keep this?' When she nodded, he went on, 'Look, this is going to be a belt and braces exercise. I want you to divide the samples in two: I'm going to get the

164

lab we use in London to do a second analysis. How do you feel about that?'

Louise smiled. 'It'll take more than a bunch of soft southerners to scare me,' she said.

THIRTY

Steven flew back to London with the small package of samples in his briefcase. Barring unforeseen circumstances, he planned to have them in the lab before the end of the working day. The flight landed on time at Heathrow – his least favourite airport – and he was about to start making his way through the anticipated throngs of people to catch the Heathrow Express into the city when he was stopped by two men who showed him Special Branch ID. They were accompanied by two armed airport police. Steven showed them his ID but to little effect.

'We know who and what you are, doctor, but we have our orders. Would you please come with us?'

Steven was led away to an interview room where one of the Special Branch officers took his briefcase from him and opened it. He removed the package containing the samples.

'What the hell do you think you're doing?' exclaimed Steven. 'I'm a Sci-Med investigator, on operational duty with the full backing of the Home Office. Take your hands off that.'

'I'm sorry, sir, but our information is such that we'll have to hold on to this and detain you for the time being.'

'What information?'

The officer held up the package. 'Regarding the contents of this, sir.'

'That package contains biological samples,' said Steven as calmly as he could in the circumstances. 'They are vital to my current investigation and they must be delivered to the lab before it closes or they'll deteriorate.' This was not strictly true: the dry ice packing would preserve the samples for a day or two, but Steven was in no mood to be reasonable. 'Give it here: I'll show you what's in it.'

The officer withdrew the package beyond his reach.

'I'm afraid that won't be possible, sir. Special Branch will be carrying out its own examination of the contents.'

'In which case there's every chance they'll fuck up an official Sci-Med investigation big time,' said Steven, losing all patience. 'And if that happens. I'll make a point of making sure you two spend the rest of your careers giving road safety talks to children in the Outer Hebrides.'

'We have our orders, sir.'

One of the officers left the room with the package; the other remained.

'What now?' asked Steven through gritted teeth.

'I'm afraid you'll have to remain here in the airport holding facility for the time being.'

'Great,' snorted Steven. 'Am I permitted to make a phone call?'

The officer nodded and Steven called John Macmillan. 'I'm being held at Heathrow Airport. Special Branch have confiscated the samples I brought back from the north.'

'What?' exclaimed Macmillan. 'Didn't you tell them who you were?'

Steven edited out *Of course I bloody did*. 'It made no difference.'

'We'll see about that,' stormed Macmillan. 'I'll be in touch.'

Steven spent ninety minutes in a holding cell at Heathrow before sounds of activity outside the door told him his detainment was coming to an end. Sir John Macmillan had arrived in person to oversee his release.

'A bit like having my dad bail me out,' said Steven.

Both men got into the back of the black, chauffeur-driven car waiting on the double yellows outside the terminal building.

'So what's going on?' asked Steven.

'I wish I knew,' said Macmillan. 'Special Branch have offered their apologies for what they say was a "regrettable mistake" but there's more to it than that; I know there is.' He seemed deeply troubled. 'There was no mistake. There's something going on. It's part of a pattern that's been emerging. People with power and influence are making things happen.'

Steven resisted the urge to say, *What's new?*

'But not in the usual way,' continued Macmillan. 'They're calling in favours, using the old school tie, invoking the old pals act. That's why I've been unable to get a handle on the people behind the opposition to your investigation. It's not a specific department or arm of government that's the prime mover, it's people in very high places asking favours of each other across a whole range of departments.'

'From the military to Special Branch,' said Steven. 'Did the apology include the return of our samples?'

'They should be on their way back by now,' said Macmillan. 'I asked them to return them directly to the Home Office.'

'So what was it all about?' mused Steven as they slowed yet again in heavy traffic. 'They stop me at the airport, take away the samples and now they say it was all a mistake. What kind of mistake are we expected to believe it was? Mistaken identity? They knew exactly who I was . . . A random search? They knew exactly what they were looking for.'

Macmillan nodded. 'It's quite clear they knew where you'd been, what you'd been doing and that you'd be flying into Heathrow. Someone could have a tap on your phone.'

'Or Cassie Motram's,' said Steven. 'She was the only one I

spoke to about flying up to Newcastle for the donor samples.'

'I'll get some IT technicians to check out both as soon as we get back,' said Macmillan.

'So, if they wanted the samples so badly . . . why are they now saying it was all a big mistake and giving them back?'

'I'd like to think it was because I created such a fuss,' said Macmillan. 'I told them the fallout from interfering with one of my investigators acting with the full authority of the Home Secretary would end in P45s fluttering down on Special Branch like leaves on a windy day in autumn.'

'Then maybe that was the reason,' said Steven. 'I don't suppose you found out where they were taking the samples?'

'I got the distinct impression that Special Branch didn't actually know anything about what the package contained,' said Macmillan. 'It's my guess that someone suggested to someone that they stop you, take the package from you and deliver it somewhere else . . .'

'A high-level favour,' said Steven.

'Exactly, but it didn't work out for them. We're getting our samples back and, with any luck,' said Macmillan as he stepped out of the car at the Home Office, 'they'll be waiting for us inside.'

The samples had been delivered some fifteen minutes earlier, according to the man on the desk. Macmillan asked Steven to check if the package had been interfered with in any way.

'I don't think so,' replied Steven, examining it briefly on all sides but acknowledging that, if it had been opened, it would have been easy enough to reseal it again. It was a simple white polystyrene box sealed with brown adhesive tape. 'But I can't be sure.'

'Maybe you should check the contents before I ask Jean to call a dispatch rider,' suggested Macmillan.

Steven opened the box in Jean Roberts' office and took a look inside. Everything seemed to be in order – there was still blood in the one tube he lifted out.

A motorcycle dispatch rider arrived within ten minutes and was briefed to deliver the box to the contract lab as quickly as possible, together with the patient's details Steven had obtained from Louise Avery. Jean had warned the lab to expect their arrival, and requested a fully comprehensive analysis of the donor samples.

'Another day of work and play,' sighed Macmillan as he sank into his office chair and sipped the sherry he'd poured for himself after handing a glass to Steven. 'Well, what's the lab going to come up with, d'you think?'

'I simply can't imagine,' Steven confessed. 'The whole thing just seems so bizarre. But there has to be something they don't want us to know about the donor. What are they trying to hide?'

'The identity of the patient?' suggested Macmillan half-heartedly.

'Surely it can't all be about that,' exclaimed Steven.

'Amateurish,' said Macmillan, causing Steven to raise his eyebrows at the choice of word. 'That's what it is, amateurish. Powerful people who don't have a proper understanding of what they're doing are pulling the strings of people who do but aren't being told why because it's a *secret*.' Macmillan managed to put a great deal of distaste into the word and Steven had to smile.

'Of course it could be we're just missing something,' he said. 'Something we haven't even thought of.'

'Yet,' said Macmillan.

'Did you have any luck asking round the hospitals about MRSA patients from St Raphael's?'

Macmillan gave a rueful laugh. 'I overlooked one factor,' he said. 'I should have realised that hospital secretaries would be very circumspect when it came to admitting they'd imported MRSA into their hospitals. I drew a complete blank. Mind you, I could see their point. Imagine what the papers would do with that kind of information.'

'*Filthy rich send their bugs to the NHS,*' Steven intoned.

'I think we can forget about official channels on that one,' said Macmillan. 'Any progress will have to be made at grass roots level.'

'Chatty nurses and disaffected cleaners,' said Steven.

Macmillan nodded. His phone rang and he answered. It was confirmation from the lab that they'd received the samples. They would be giving them top priority as requested.

'Maybe we need a Plan B,' said Steven. He responded to Macmillan's raised eybrows by adding, 'What are we going to do when the lab tells us that the donor was blood group A2, rhesus positive and an excellent tissue match for the patient, end of story?'

'We look at the small print – all the extra tests Motram was asked to perform. There has to be something.'

THIRTY-ONE

Steven spent a few minutes sitting by the river before going back to his flat. He was conscious of the fact that he hadn't said anything to John Macmillan about the duplicate analysis of the samples he'd requested and was feeling slightly guilty about it. He owed a great deal to Macmillan and would trust him with his life, but there was some kind of problem in the corridors of power at the moment and he didn't know how close to home it was going to come. It was like a cancer: people were seeing signs of metastasis but no one knew where the original tumour was lurking.

There had already been one attempt to prevent Sci-Med from examining the donor samples: he didn't want any more interference. His action in requesting Louise Avery to examine the samples had been unplanned and spontaneous, so it had not been mentioned in any discussion or phone call. This was a good way to leave matters. He resurrected a favourite old adage: two can keep a secret if one of them is dead.

He was still thinking about this when his phone rang. It was Macmillan, which made him feel guilty all over again. 'Jean tells me the technicians have finished checking out the phone lines I asked them to look at. Your line has not been interfered with but Mrs Motram's has. Quite a professional job, they said.'

'Might be useful to leave it that way,' suggested Steven. 'In case we need to feed guano to the opposition.'

'My thoughts too,' said Macmillan. 'I've asked them to take no action for the time being.'

Perhaps it was the unease he felt at learning of the phone tap on Cassie Motram's line, but Steven's senses seemed heightened as he resumed his walk home. He tried telling himself it was imagination when he started to think he was being followed. When he'd last crossed the road, he'd spotted a man in a dark suit about a hundred metres back and it immediately registered that he'd seen him a few minutes before when he'd got up from his seat by the river.

After another hundred metres Steven stopped, half turned and pretended he was looking for something in his briefcase while really glancing back out of the corner of his eye to see what the man was doing. He was still there but, as Steven prolonged his 'search', he turned off up a side street and disappeared from sight. Steven relaxed, feeling slightly embarrassed at having let his imagination run away with him. He was starting to wonder about his stress levels when he came to his own turn-off and started up the lane leading to the street where his apartment block was located. A faint smile at his own gullibility crossed his lips but disappeared in a trice when he caught the scent of aftershave on the breeze – it was a scent he recognised. He continued walking but, as soon as he had turned off to the right, he slipped into a doorway and waited.

The dark figure of a man passed the doorway and Steven had his arm up his back and his cheek pressed to the wall before his victim realised what was happening. 'This had better be good, Ricksen,' he hissed. 'Very good.'

'For Christ's sake, Dunbar,' stammered the MI5 man. 'I'm here for your benefit. I just wanted to talk to you.'

'You've been following me since I left the Home Office. You had every opportunity to talk to me but instead you've been tailing me for the past ten minutes. Then you circle round ahead of me and wait in a quiet lane . . .'

'That's because I didn't want anyone to see me talking to you,' groaned Ricksen.

Steven released him slowly, still unsure of the situation and remaining very alert as he watched as the MI5 man dust himself down. 'Go on,' he said.

'There's something going on and I don't like it,' said Ricksen. 'In fact, a number of us don't like it, including my boss, but for reasons I don't fully understand there's nothing he can do about it.'

'I'm listening.'

'An ex-MI5 man has reappeared on the scene: he's behaving as if he's back in the fold although I'm assured he isn't. The fact remains, however, that certain people are dancing to his tune whether we like it or not. Rumour has it he's been detailed to keep tabs on you . . . maybe more than keep tabs . . .'

'Why?'

Ricksen shrugged. 'I don't know. Nobody seems to. But you and I, we've always got on. I thought I'd warn you. I swear it's nothing to do with 5 officially, even though it might look like it.'

'Who is this guy?'

'Monk. James Monk,' replied Ricksen. 'He was with us for three years before being dismissed the service for being – as the euphemism goes – too enthusiastic in the execution of his work. Too many "accidental" deaths. People he was assigned to monitor as possible hostiles kept ending up "taking their own lives in the woods", if you get my drift.'

'If you can't solve a problem, remove it.'

'Exactly.'

'Psycho?'

'Borderline if not official, but comes from a "good" family. Daddy owns a chunk of Berkshire. Rumour has it, it wasn't Daddy's foxhounds that were tearing the foxes limb from limb . . . Any other background and Monk would be in a cage, but, with Daddy smoothing the way through public school and Oxford, Her Majesty's Secret Service ended up with the pleasure . . . until we got shot of him like a bad smell.'

'And now he's back.'

'Like I say, it's not official.'

Steven nodded. 'Thanks,' he said. 'I owe you one. This guy Monk: six-two, well built, wart on the left cheek?'

'That's our man. You've come across him?'

'Not personally, not yet.'

'Take care,' said Ricksen.

'You too,' said Steven. 'And if you'll take some advice? Change your aftershave.'

'What?' exclaimed Ricksen. 'My lady loves it: she bought it for me.'

'Then she's probably KGB. You'd be as well painting a bullseye on your arse.'

'She's the mother of my children,' protested Ricksen.

'Could be a quantitative thing,' said Steven, enjoying teasing the MI5 man. 'Maybe half a litre's too much.'

'I'm beginning to wish I hadn't bothered.'

'Seriously, I'm glad you did,' said Steven. 'Thanks.' He started to walk away.

'Aren't you even going to tell me what it's all about?'

'I don't know either,' said Steven. 'It's a secret.'

Steven showered and changed into jeans and trainers. There was a chill in the air so he pulled on a sweater before putting on his denim jacket and heading for the lift down to the garage.

His first port of call was going to be the Jade Garden restaurant, where he was a once-a-month customer. There were a number of restaurants he visited on a fairly regular basis, chosen first because they were good and second to interrupt the more usual packet-meals-from-a-supermarket foundation of his diet. He'd never learned to cook and had no plans to alter the status quo.

Chen Feng, the owner of the Jade Garden, who'd spotted he was a doctor from the first time he'd used his credit card, never failed to keep him apprised of her state of health and that of her family. Because he liked her, Steven tended to offer very general medical advice which often translated into extra dishes on the table but not the bill. It was a nice, simple arrangement between two people who were less than friends but more than strangers. More importantly, they liked each other.

As he walked back to the car after eating, Steven wondered how he should spend the rest of the evening. He could return to the flat and have an early night but he doubted if he would sleep: he was too uptight, particularly after what Ricksen had told him. It was unsettling to know that he was being targeted without knowing why. The investigation was on hold until the analysis of the donor samples was complete, but rather than just kick his heels he thought he might have a sniff round the hospitals that might have admitted MRSA patients from St Raphael's.

After a moment's thought, he changed his mind. If it was his intention to glean what he could from gossipy sources rather than the official ones Macmillan had already failed with, he would be as well trying to make contact with staff from St Raphael's itself.

He drove over to St Raphael's and started touring the surrounding area, looking for likely watering holes that the hospital staff might use. A wine bar called the Pink Puffin was nearest but Steven had reservations about the name. Thinking it might be a gay haunt, he decided to leave it for the moment and look for somewhere more inclusive.

Rene's looked as if it might be a possible. He found a parking place a couple of streets away and walked back, went in and ordered a bottle of Czech beer at the bar. The place was small and about half full of mainly couples although there was a group of four businessmen at a table with their briefcases tucked underneath at their feet, exuding the confidence of the mob-handed as they exchanged stories of their prowess in the commercial jungle. A couple of loners were at the bar, one reading an evening newspaper opened at the accommodation-to-let section and the other, a young woman, concentrating on the screen of her mobile phone.

Steven looked for a clue to suggest she might be a nurse on her way home – sensible flat shoes, black stockings, a glimpse of white uniform dress beneath her coat – but didn't find any. He lingered over his beer for twenty minutes or so before giving up and leaving. He thought about driving round the area some more but no longer felt confident that this approach was going to work. Most hospitals had a choice of pubs within easy reach where many of the staff would be regulars but St Raphael's was different. It was located in an upmarket, exclusive area: there weren't any pubs round here. On the way back, however, he decided he might as well give the Pink Puffin a try.

The name had indeed been a clue, Steven concluded when the barman looked him up and down and said, 'You're new.'

Steven smiled. 'Just arrived today.'

'And what brings you to the Puffin?' the barman asked, the smile in his eyes suggesting he knew the answer.

'St Raphael's,' said Steven. 'I'm starting work there.'

'A nurse?'

Steven nodded.

'So you won't know anyone round here if you've just arrived?'

'That's right, all alone in the big city.'

'Robbie works at St Raphael's,' announced the barman as if he'd just remembered. He turned away from Steven to scan the clientele. They were exclusively male and mainly in pairs, although there did seem to be a birthday gathering with six at one table wearing party hats. 'Robbie! Robbie!' he called out. 'Come over here and say hello to . . .' He turned questioningly to Steven.

'Steve.'

'Come and say hello to Steve.'

Steven watched as a short, tubby man broke up one of the pairs to come over to the bar. The barman introduced them and related Steven's story.

'Come and join us,' said Robbie. 'The smoke can be a lonely place if you don't know anyone.'

Steven followed Robbie back to his table, where he was introduced to Clive, who Robbie made a point of adding was his partner. 'So, hands off.' He made a slight smacking gesture with his hand.

Steven shook hands with a tall, handsome man.

'So you're a nurse,' said Robbie as they all sat down. 'Clive was a nurse too until he took to the skies and became a trolley dolly.'

'BA cabin crew,' explained Clive.

'I didn't know we were getting anyone new at Raffa's,' said Robbie. 'You must be Iwona's replacement, poor love.'

'Iwona?' asked Steven.

'Polish nurse,' said Robbie. He touched the side of his nose and said conspiratorially, 'Sent home in disgrace, you might say.'

'How so?' asked Steven, anxious to keep the conversation flowing and trying to appear as keen to garner scandal as Robbie clearly was to impart it. He imagined he was about to hear a tale of illicit sex in a linen cupboard.

'I shouldn't really,' whispered Robbie, leaning forward, 'but as you're staff anyway . . .'

Steven leaned forward to meet him halfway.

'MRSA,' announced Robbie, lingering over each letter.

Steven couldn't believe his luck. He wanted to hug Robbie – and it wouldn't have seemed out of place in his current surroundings – but instead he said in a low growl, 'No, you're kidding.'

Robbie shook his head, obviously pleased at Steven's reaction. 'A carrier,' he said. 'Infected three people before it was discovered that she was the cause of the problem.'

'Poor love,' said Steven, hoping he wasn't camping it up too much, 'that's going to be an absolute nightmare to live with. I just don't think I could do that. She wasn't an illegal, was she?'

'No,' exclaimed Robbie, exchanging shocked glances with Clive. 'Raffa's is the best, my man: the staff are the best, the pay is the best. Absolutely everything is pukka and above board at Raffa's. Iwona was fully qualified and a damn good nurse, it has to be said. The MRSA carrier thing was just . . . well, just one of those things. There but for the grace of and all that.'

'So the problem's been cleared up?' asked Steven.

'And without a breath of scandal,' whispered Robbie. 'We were lucky. The papers would have had us on toast if they'd found out.'

'Being the hypocrites they are,' added Steven.

'So where was your last job, Steve?' asked Clive, who had been quietly appraising Steven throughout with eyes that gave away nothing.

'Glasgow,' replied Steven after a momentary hesitation, suddenly aware that he didn't have a cover story. 'Western Infirmary.'

'Tough city,' said Clive.

'Reason I'm here,' replied Steven, once again hoping he wasn't pushing the pink button too hard. He had started to suspect that Clive was having his doubts about him.

'You'll love Raffa's, Steve,' said Robbie.

'What does MRSA stand for, Steve?' Clive asked suddenly, to the amazement of Robbie, who seemed embarrassed at his partner's behaviour.

'What's this, pub quiz night?' he exclaimed.

'Methicillin-resistant *Staphylococcus aureus*,' said Steven calmly, 'although people outside the profession often think it's "multiply-resistant".'

Clive smiled. 'Is the right answer,' he said. 'Sorry about that, Steve.' He turned to Robbie and added, 'I thought he might be press.'

Robbie's eyes opened like saucers. 'You're not, are you, Steve?' he asked like a child seeking reassurance.

'No,' said Steven, 'I'm not.'

He bought a round of drinks and left soon afterwards, citing tiredness after the long journey down from Scotland.

'See you at Raffa's then,' said Robbie.

'Thanks for being so welcoming,' said Steven, nodding to both as he got up and waving to the barman as he headed for the door.

'See you soon,' said the barman, using his eyes to impart more into the phrase as he polished a glass.

THIRTY-TWO

Steven returned to his flat and called the duty officer at Sci-Med. 'I need this information ASAP. St Raphael's Hospital employed a Polish nurse until recently; her first name was Iwona. Everything was above board so there should be no difficulty getting the information – but don't approach St Raphael's directly. I need to know her full name, how long she was at St Raphael's, the official reason given for her leaving and which Public Health lab might have been involved in her demise if any. Get people out their beds if you have to.'

'Will do.'

Steven was woken just after four a.m. by the duty man, who made a joke about including him in his 'get people out their beds' instruction.

'Very funny,' said Steven. 'What'd you get?'

'Iwona Tloczynska was employed at the hospital for four and a half months between December last year and the start of April. She came with excellent references and was working as a theatre nurse. She was highly thought of until a problem arose and the staff were screened as part of an investigation into post-operative infection. Iwona was found to be unsuitable for continued theatre work and subsequently decided to return home to Gdansk with what was described as generous severance pay.'

'Excellent,' said Steven. 'Did you find out who did the screening?'

'In the first instance it was the small hospital lab, but then it was referred to the private lab that does the microbiological work for St Raphael's. When they confirmed it was MRSA, sub-cultures of the organism were passed on to the Public Health authorities and the reference lab at Colindale in north London in compliance with the rules about these things.'

'Brilliant,' exclaimed Steven.

'Just what my mother always said,' replied the duty man.

Knowing that the people the duty man had disturbed during the night might well be complaining to colleagues about their rude awakening and, in doing so, alerting the opposition, Steven was at the Colindale lab before nine a.m., waiting for the staff to arrive. Once he'd established his credentials, it took less than fifteen minutes for the technicians to provide him with a glass vial containing the MRSA isolated from Nurse Iwona Tloczynska. Another twenty minutes and the culture was in the hands of the labs used by Sci-Med for scientific analysis and a comparison with the strain of MRSA he'd brought back from Afghanistan was under way.

Steven was at the Home Office before John Macmillan arrived. When he did, he took one look at Steven and said, 'You're looking smug, Dunbar. It doesn't become you.' He swept past into his office, leaving Steven swapping amused glances with Jean Roberts.

'Send him in,' said the small loudspeaker on Jean's desk.

Steven related the events of the previous evening to Macmillan and told him of the successful detective work of the duty officer through the night.

'The Pink Puffin, you say,' said Macmillan, foraging around in the papers on his desk. 'Wasn't it a blessing you spend your evenings there . . .'

'I don't spend my . . .' Steven had began before he saw the smile on Macmillan's face. 'I was following up an idea.'

'And a bloody good one as it turned out. Well done. Mind you, I'm not sure the lab will agree. They spent all last night analysing donor samples from the north and now they've got even more work to do. I understand we should be getting the donor results around noon today.'

Steven glanced at his watch. 'I'll go get some coffee, stretch my legs. See you at noon.'

He took a favourite stroll through St James' Park, enjoying the signs of spring and wondering idly what the year might bring. Spring had always been his favourite season, bringing with it signs of new growth and new hope. He found autumn heart-achingly sad and winter too icily sterile to engage with. Summer was more often than not disappointing but spring was full of optimism, the overture to the year.

He started to think again about the identity of Patient X and how the human cost of so much secrecy could ever be justified. Who in this world could be considered so important that keeping leukaemia a secret was worth the lives it had now either cost or ruined?

No one, he concluded, but there were clearly people out there who disagreed: powerful people, people with influence, the sort who got away with things. He knew they existed because he'd seen them do it often enough in the past. He'd felt the anger and frustration of watching the guilty walk free because it was 'not in the public interest' to pursue the matter further or 'not in the interest of the state to prosecute'. It would be nice if, just this once, they – whoever they were – were held to account for what they'd done. Perhaps a first step towards that goal was to be found in the lab report on Michael Kelly.

Macmillan already had the report open on his desk when Steven got back to the Home Office. He took off his glasses and leaned back in his chair. 'It's pretty much what we feared,' he said. 'Michael Kelly was blood group A, rhesus positive and a near perfect tissue match for Patient X.'

'Shit,' said Steven.

'Well,' sighed Macmillan. 'I think we're at throw-a-six-to-restart time, eh?'

'I just don't get it. There has to be something special about Kelly. Group A, rhesus positive blood is the second most common group in the country. Just about every second human being in the street has it.'

'There's the tissue match too,' Macmillan reminded him.

'True,' said Steven, 'but you still wouldn't need to scour the civilian and military medical records of an entire nation to come up with the match they've got here.' He held up the lab report. 'Bone marrow donors are much more plentiful than organ donors. It would be different if they were looking for a heart or a liver or any vital organ for Patient X but they weren't . . . they were attempting to save someone with terminal leukaemia . . . someone whose identity had to be kept secret at all costs. Why? We're still missing something . . .'

'The discovering of what I'll leave in your capable hands,' said Macmillan, getting up from his chair. 'I've got a meeting.'

'Can I hold on to the report?'

'Please do.'

Steven returned to his flat and spent a frustrating afternoon trying to see what was special about Michael Kelly. Reading and rereading the lab report didn't help: there was nothing unique about Kelly. The bottom line was that he was an ordinary squaddie with a common enough blood and tissue type who'd contracted an MRSA infection after donating his bone marrow. The attempted cover-up of what had happened and why he'd actually died was, to use Macmillan's word, amateurish, but the serious fact remained that anyone expressing the faintest interest in Kelly or the circumstances of his death was in danger of losing their life . . .

To break up a train of thought that was going nowhere, Steven phoned Louise at the University of Newcastle to ask how she was getting on with her analysis.

'It should be complete the day after tomorrow,' she said. 'Do you want me to email the report to you?'

Steven stalled for a moment. The day after tomorrow was Friday. On impulse, he decided he would go up to Scotland and spend the weekend with Jenny. 'No,' he replied. 'If it's okay with you I'll drop by the lab on Friday.'

'A long way to come,' said Louise.

Steven told her of his weekend plans and they spoke for a bit about Jenny, her circumstances and where she lived.

'That's a lovely part of the country,' said Louise. 'A perfect place to grow up. My parents have a holiday cottage there . . . near Southerness?'

'Know it well. Beaches that go on for ever.'

'Aren't they wonderful?' said Louise, sounding pleased to be speaking to someone who shared her affection for a part of Scotland so often neglected by the tourist guides. 'My brother and I adored our holidays there. In fact, now that you've mentioned it, I may go there myself this weekend. It'll be the first time this year. I always like opening the cottage up after the winter: it's like lifting the lid of a chest full of childhood memories. It's a bit early for my folks; they'll probably wait till it warms up a bit. They're not as young as they were.'

'Well, I'm glad I've sorted your weekend as well as my own,' Steven joked. 'See you Friday.'

THIRTY-THREE

As he gunned the Porsche up the M1 on Friday morning, Steven knew that it was not going to be the pleasant and relaxing weekend he might have hoped for. He was, to some extent, running away from an investigation that was coming close to grinding to a halt because he couldn't see the way forward. It was odds-on that Louise's analysis would be a formality and in agreement with the contract lab, so picking up the report was just a case of going through the motions. He would end up being no further forward in determining what was so special about Michael Kelly.

The only progress to be made after that would be through the lab analysis of the strain of MRSA that the Polish nurse was carrying. If that should provide proof positive that Michael Kelly had indeed been infected at St Raphael's, it should be possible to force the hospital to reveal the identity of Patient X.

Steven found that he couldn't work up much enthusiasm about that. It really wasn't what he wanted to know. Bringing the identity of Patient X into the public domain would only annoy those who'd been determined to keep it secret. There had to be more to the deaths of Michael Kelly and his friend Jim Leslie than met the eye, and under those circumstances there was a real risk that the reasons behind their deaths would remain a mystery, as would the motive behind the horrendous toxin attack on John Motram.

Steven had tried to manage things so that he would arrive in time to be able to take Louise Avery to lunch as a thank you for her help in analysing the samples. She would, of course, be paid officially by Sci-Med, but, as with most payments to academic staff, money had a habit of being siphoned off by the university, a bit like tips for the waiting staff at a bad restaurant. As Louise was expecting him, Steven didn't bother to announce himself at the front desk but went straight to the Motram lab and knocked on the glass door. There was no reply.

He checked his watch, fearing that she might already have gone to lunch, but it had only just gone twelve. Then he remembered Mary Lyons telling him that Louise was working with another research group in John Motram's absence and concluded that that might be the reason for her absence. He went back to the front desk to seek information.

'She's not here today,' replied the military-looking man sorting mail into pigeon holes behind the desk. 'Long weekend.'

'Are you sure? She was expecting me.'

'Must have forgot.'

'Is Professor Lyons here today? And before you ask, no, I don't have an appointment.'

The man gave Steven a sour look and picked up a telephone. 'Name?'

'Dr Dunbar, Sci-Med Inspectorate.'

Steven saw the puzzled look on Mary Lyons's face as soon as he entered the room and knew immediately that something was wrong.

'Dr Dunbar, this is a surprise.'

'I arranged to see Louise today,' said Steven. 'I'm here to pick up her report.'

'Yes, but your colleague came to see her yesterday . . . She gave him the report.' Puzzlement became confusion and then changed to alarm when she noted Steven's reaction. 'He wasn't your colleague, was he?' she asked slowly, visibly paling.

Steven shook his head as the pit fell out of his stomach. 'I work alone.'

'Oh, dear God.' Mary Lyons put both her hands to her head and massaged her temples. 'A man telephoned me yesterday morning, saying he was from Sci-Med. He wanted to check that all the samples Dr Motram had in his possession had been returned to London. I said yes, apart of course from the ones that Louise was currently analysing. I pointed out that you were due here this morning to pick up her report.'

Steven felt strangely helpless. 'What did he say to that?'

'He said there had been a development in the case and wondered if it might be possible for him to come a day early for the results. I asked Louise and she told me she could be finished by late afternoon: he could come any time after four thirty. He came around ten to five and Louise handed over her report and what was left of the samples. We thought that that was the end of it . . . but apparently not. I'm so sorry.'

'Is Louise here today?' asked Steven. His initial alarm at what had happened was being diluted by his failure to see what the opposition had to gain from making such a move. They'd got their hands on the samples, but Sci-Med had the other half and they knew that. And the Sci-Med lab had already come up with a report.

'No,' said Mary Lyons. 'She had to work so hard yesterday to get the report ready I told her to take the day off. I knew she was planning to go up to her parents' holiday cottage in Dumfries and Galloway this weekend so I told her to make it a long one . . .' Her voice trailed off. 'I've done something awful, haven't I? I didn't even think to ask the man for his ID after the telephone call. It all seemed so . . . plausible.'

'Don't blame yourself,' said Steven. 'You couldn't have fore-seen this happening.' The anger he felt was at himself for not having foreseen it either. The opposition knew about the exist-ence of the samples at Newcastle University from the bug on Cassie Motram's phone line when he and Cassie had discussed it. They were just being thorough and checking that there were no more lying around and they had come up trumps. 'Did you see this man?' he asked.

'Oh, yes. I thought it was only right that I be there. I waited with Louise until he arrived and then sat in on the discussion. Morris, he said his name was, Dr Simon Morris, a tall, well-built man . . .'

'With a wart on his left cheek,' said Steven. It came out as more of a statement than a question.

'Then you do know him? He is connected with your organ-isation?'

Steven shook his head. 'No, it's a long story,' he said. 'What did he and Louise have to say about the report?'

Mary Lyons shrugged. 'I think the general conclusion was that the donor was a near perfect match for the patient in question.'

The expected reply left Steven wondering again why on earth Monk had rushed up here to recover samples ahead of him or see a report Sci-Med already had – *particularly as there was damn all interesting in it*, was the frustrated rider he added to his own question.

'Actually, there was one thing Louise remarked on.'

'Really, what?' asked Steven, ready to clutch at any kind of straw.

Mary Lyons looked apologetic. 'I'm afraid I don't know,' she confessed. 'Louise pointed out something in her report to Morris that she thought was rather unusual: she did it with the end of her pen so I couldn't see what it was from where I was sitting.

Dr Morris dismissed it as having no relevance at all to the transplant and Louise seemed to agree, so I didn't ask.'

Steven nodded, feeling that the world was against him but finding consolation in the thought that Louise could tell him personally what she thought was 'unusual' when she got back from her weekend. He was on the point of getting up to go when he suddenly realised with a hollow feeling in his stomach that, if the unusual thing Louise had spotted in the report *did* have a significance, James Monk knew that she'd noticed it. That kind of knowledge could be fatal: Louise could be in great danger. 'Did Louise's weekend plans come up in the conversation at all?' he asked, trying to sound casual.

'You know, I believe they did,' said Mary Lyons. 'Yes, I'm sure they did. I remember Louise saying that she hoped the weather would be good enough to let her walk by the sea and maybe even have a paddle . . . A bit early for that, I thought.'

Steven felt things go from bad to worse. Only the close proximity of a distinguished female academic stopped him letting go a foul-mouthed tirade against the malevolence of fate. 'Can you tell me *exactly* where Louise was going this weekend?' he asked. 'I remember her saying it was somewhere near Southerness.' His tone betrayed the urgency he felt.

'Not the precise address . . . I've never needed that . . . but I do seem to remember the cottage is in a village called . . . let me think . . .' Steven reined in his impatience as the seconds ticked by. 'Leeford. Yes, that's it, Leeford, and you're right, it is near Southerness. We talked about the lighthouse there.'

Steven keyed the village into the satnav in the Porsche and roared off, heading west across the country to Dumfries and Galloway. He was stopped by traffic police when doing in excess of eighty-five mph on a straight stretch of road between

Annan and Dumfries after being held up for some minutes by a JCB bumping along at twenty. One officer walked round the Porsche while the other asked the usual question. Steven assured the officer that he knew perfectly well what speed he was doing and, as he was a Sci-Med investigator, fully operational and with Home Office authority, he would like to continue doing it at their earliest convenience. He showed his ID and pointed out the number to call for verification.

The reply brought about a sudden change in the officer's attitude and that of his colleague after a warning glance. Both men now seemed anxious to help in any way they could, and asked if Steven would like an escort to his destination. Steven looked at his Porsche and then at the police Volvo. 'Maybe not,' he replied. 'Just let your colleagues know I'll be on your territory for the next day or so.'

The road leading from the city of Dumfries to the Solway coast imposed further restrictions on Steven's progress. Apart from its twists and turns, it was busy with the Friday rush hour: Dumfries' commuters were heading home.

The traffic thinned as he neared the Solway and he was able to pick up speed on the switchback road that skirted the coast. Now that he was by the sea, he found himself wishing he had more time to enjoy his surroundings. The early clouds had cleared away and the evening sun was shining on the Solway Firth, reminding him of the happy times he and Lisa had spent on weekends in the area, exploring the sites or just enjoying each other's company on wild and lonely beaches. Steven had always loved the beaches here. The tide seemed to go out for miles, leaving huge expanses of flat sand that ran out to meet the sky, encouraging a sense of proportion when contemplating the problems of life. It was always good to be reminded how small one was in the great scheme of things.

Ten minutes later Steven turned off the main road and onto a single-lane loop on the coast side to enter the village of Leeford. The Porsche's engine settled down to an irregular and unhappy burble as it was reined in to almost walking pace to allow Steven to look for somewhere he could enquire about the location of the Averys' cottage.

For this purpose, Leeford proved to be inconveniently small: it comprised, as far as he could see, little more than a few cottages huddling together on a cliff top. It boasted no pub or garage, no shops and very few houses with lights on. A number had wooden shutters on the windows. Holiday homes, thought Steven: it was still very early in the season. Like many such places, Leeford would remain a ghost village until summer sun beckoned its absent owners from the cities. He recalled Louise saying that this would be her first visit of the year.

He passed a sign pointing to a cliff-top path leading to *The Harbour* and saw there was a light on in the second cottage down from the road. He stopped the car and walked back. He could smell the sea far below on the evening breeze and noted that the cottage he was approaching had seashells rendered into its front wall. A small tricycle lay on its side in the front garden beneath a swing with frayed ropes. Steven knocked on the door and apologised to the woman in her early thirties who answered.

'Gosh, you're the second person to ask about the Averys' cottage today,' she said with a smile and an accent that suggested she was not from around these parts. 'Is Louise having a party or something? I thought we were going to be the first of the outsiders to open up this year. Apparently not.'

The news stunned Steven into silence: it seemed that his fears had been proved horribly right. If the earlier enquiry had come from Monk, he *had* seen Louise as a potential threat and had come to . . . deal with the problem. Hoping against hope all the way here had come to nothing. He should have known better. Monk's background and reputation said he wasn't the sort to leave loose ends lying around.

'Are you all right?' asked the woman, obviously feeling slightly uneasy in a situation she was finding difficult to read. Her young daughter had joined her at the door and was clinging to her leg. 'Go back inside, please, Zoe,' she said.

'Yes, sorry,' said Steven, snapping out of his preoccupation. 'If you could just tell me where the Averys' cottage is?'

'Three doors along on the main street on the same side as us,' said the woman. She pointed briefly with one hand while closing the door with the other. 'The one with blue shutters.'

THIRTY-FOUR

The door closed and snuffed out the pool of yellow light, making Steven realise that daylight was rapidly becoming a reddish memory in the western sky. He walked back to the main street. The small size of the village meant that it didn't merit street lighting, something that made it difficult to tell if the east-facing cottage he picked out as Louise's had blue shutters or not, especially as there were no lights on in the windows. There was no space for a car; three were parked on waste ground on the other side of the road but he didn't know what Louise drove. He walked up the gravel path and knocked loudly on the front door.

The lack of lights predicted no response and that was what he got. He didn't bother with a second attempt but walked round to the back where there was more light. The rear of the cottage was high above the beach and faced west so that the red glow in the sky bathed the building in what Steven thought resembled the safe-light of a photographic darkroom.

He rapped on the stable-style split back door and called out Louise's name but again without response. His mind insisted he start imagining scenes of what might be lying inside but he tried to counter it by hoping that Louise might have changed her mind about coming here this weekend. An open window to the left of the back door, however, caught his attention and the hope died.

After a moment's hesitation, he tried the latch on the door and found it unlocked. He stepped inside onto the cracked linoleum floor of a small, whitewashed utility room containing a fridge and a washing machine. The washing machine was old, its front showing signs of rust where the enamel had been chipped. He called out Louise's name again but knew he was using it as a mantra to inject normality into a situation that was threatening to unfold into a nightmare. He ran the flat of his hand up the wall as he moved into the house proper and clicked on the light to reveal that everything seemed to be in order in the sitting room. There were no signs of a struggle, and a cardboard box full of groceries which presumably Louise had brought in from the car was lying in the middle of the floor, waiting to be taken through to the kitchen and unpacked. He moved on through the house but every door he opened was preceded by a vision of what he might find inside.

After drawing three blanks, he came to the last room, the bathroom, where he paused, preparing to find a corpse staring up at him through a tub full of water. The fear disappeared instantly when he found the room empty and smelling pleasantly of bathroom cleaner. Louise was not at home . . . but she had been.

He stepped out into the back garden and looked out over the Solway, trying to put himself inside Monk's head. He didn't like what he came up with. Monk was a professional; he wouldn't have murdered the girl and left her body lying on the floor or in the bath at the cottage where it would precipitate an immediate police murder hunt and press outrage. He would have faked her death, made it look like an accident, just as he'd disguised the attack on John Motram and probably engineered Jim Leslie's road traffic accident. Steven felt the chances were awfully high that Louise had had an 'accident' too and, standing in the back garden of a cliff-top cottage, he didn't have to be a member of MENSA to figure out what the likely kind would be.

He walked down the sloping garden to the picket fence which marked the boundary between the Averys' garden and a steep slope of rough grass leading down to the cliff-top path which zigzagged below. His heart sank when he noticed that a swathe of the grass had recently been flattened: something heavy had been dragged across it.

Taking care in the dying light, he scissored his legs over the fence and slid on all fours down the flattened grass trail to where it met the cinder path. Less than five metres to his right, where the path changed the course of its zigzag, he could see that the wooden guard rail between the path and a one-hundred-foot drop had been broken. It had given way . . . or someone had made it look that way. He felt sure he was looking at the site of Louise's 'accident'.

With a heavy heart, he made his way down the winding path and out on to the beach to discover the inevitable: Louise Avery, her neck broken and lower limbs at an impossible angle, lay spread-eagled on the sand, her eyes open but her life very definitely over. 'I'm so sorry,' he murmured, feeling almost overwhelmed by guilt. If only he hadn't asked her to analyse those damned samples. 'You bastard, Monk,' he raged, slamming his fist into the sand once, twice, three times. When his breathing finally subsided, he brought out his mobile phone and called the police.

An hour later, when Steven had finished with the police, he called John Macmillan and told him what had happened, starting with his request to Louise Avery that she carry out a duplicate analysis on the Michael Kelly samples and ending with the circumstances of her death.

'Ye gods, this is getting out of hand,' said Macmillan, quickly assimilating all the facts and asking the right questions. 'How much do the local police know?'

'I only gave them the bare facts when they turned up,' said Steven. 'With nothing else to go on, I think they might see it as a tragic accident – a fall from a cliff-top path after the guard rail gave way . . .'

'Whereas we know it was anything but,' said Macmillan.

Steven grunted, his anger still smouldering inside.

'So why did he kill her?'

'According to Louise's boss who was present when Monk came to pick up the report, Louise saw something unusual in her analysis and pointed it out to Monk. I think that may have been her undoing.'

'But we've seen a report on the samples,' protested Macmillan. 'There was nothing unusual about them at all.'

'I know,' sighed Steven. 'I don't understand it either.'

'I'm assuming Miss Avery's findings were the same as our lab's?'

Steven screwed up his face at the question. 'I didn't see Louise's report,' he said. 'She gave it to Monk.'

'And there's no other copy?' asked Macmillan, sounding astonished.

'I doubt it – most universities' policy on contract work is to hand over everything to the client when the job's finished. Contract work is always regarded as confidential so they don't keep copies – that's normal practice. Christ, I should have realised Monk would check there were no more samples lying around at the university. What a fool . . .'

'Don't blame yourself,' said Macmillan. 'None of us can think of absolutely everything. Apart from that, they were quick enough to give us our samples back after their "mistake" at the airport, so why should it matter if there were still some up north?'

'Another question I can't answer.'

'Are you still intending to stay over with your daughter this weekend?'

Steven sighed. 'No, I think I'm going to have to call off. I'll come back to London as soon as I've told Louise Avery's head of department what's happened. I don't want her finding out from the papers. The police will be telling Louise's parents.'

'Let me know when you get back. There's something else we need to discuss: the lab report on the MRSA cultures has come in. It's the same strain.'

Steven let out his breath in another long, slow sigh. There were times when he could turn off the day job and switch into family mode to spend time with Jenny but this definitely wasn't one of them. The cocktail of anger, frustration and guilt that simmered inside him was best not shared with anyone. He didn't want the dark world of his job to come anywhere near Glenvane. He called Sue and apologised for crying off.

As always, she was understanding. 'Don't beat yourself up over it, Steven,' she said. 'If you can't come, you can't; we all know there must be a good reason – probably one it's best we don't know anything about,' she added.

'Thanks, Sue. I'll call Jenny when . . . things get better . . .'

'Take care, Steven. I'll give her your love.'

Steven gave silent thanks for having a sister-in-law like Sue and reflected on how often he'd had to call on her in the past when the job became just too incompatible with normal life. This, in turn, forced him to acknowledge that Tally had been right. His attempts to minimise the dangers of the job had been ridiculous. Danger and death were always lurking on the horizon. That being the case, he couldn't expect any woman to share anything more than a fleeting romance with him. That conclusion was just about all he needed to make an awful day even worse.

It was now a little after nine in the evening and Steven sat in the car, pondering how he was going to tell Mary Lyons. He had a number for her at the university but she wouldn't be there at this time and she probably wouldn't be there in the morning because it was Saturday. He knew that many people these days chose to be ex-directory but he decided to check out directory enquiries anyway, asking for Professor Mary Lyons in the Newcastle area.

'37 Belvedere Road?' asked the operator.

'Yes,' said Steven, hearing no other option.

'Would you like me to put you through?'

Mary Lyons answered, giving her phone number in a clear voice, which struck Steven as being charmingly old-fashioned but infinitely preferable to 'Yeah?'

'Professor Lyons, it's Steven Dunbar. I'm afraid I've got some very bad news for you.'

'Oh, dear,' sighed Mary Lyons. 'I've been dreading this. It has to be about Louise, hasn't it?'

'She's had an accident . . . a fatal one. She fell from a cliff-top in Leeford earlier today.'

There was a slight choking sound and a long silence before Mary Lyons replied, 'I don't think for one moment you're telling me the whole story, Dr Dunbar. This is all tied up with the man who came to the department yesterday, isn't it?'

Steven found himself on the spot. 'He is part of the story,' he confessed, 'but it's complicated . . .'

'If only I hadn't been so stupid . . .'

'No, professor, none of this is your doing.' Steven did his best to sound reassuring, but as he knew exactly how she felt he wasn't sure he was helping. 'It was just an unfortunate series of events that no one could have foreseen.'

'I take it the police will be investigating this "accident"?'

'The authorities will leave no stone unturned in uncovering the truth,' said Steven, fearing he sounded like a government minister under interview. 'I promise you, justice will be done.'

'I just can't believe this has happened . . . Louise's poor parents . . .'

'The police are informing them. Professor . . . I know you've had a terrible shock but there's something I must ask you . . . You said that Louise found something strange or unusual in the results of the tests she was carrying out and pointed this out to the man who came to your department?'

'Yes, but they both agreed it had no significance for the proposed transplant.'

'I know you said you didn't see what the oddity was but I just wondered if there might have been something said about it that you can remember? Anything at all? I'm clutching at straws here.'

'No, I'm afraid not. It was just something mentioned in passing.'

'No matter,' said Steven, acutely aware of the woman's grief and now her discomfort at not being able to help.

'But you could look for yourself,' said Mary Lyons suddenly.

'I'm sorry?'

'I've just remembered something. When you asked Louise to analyse these samples and she asked me for permission, I told her that a record would have to be kept of the whole thing for the benefit of the university authorities – they're very strict about contracting for outside work, or rather the university's insurers are. A file was opened for her on the departmental server so she could list everything she did and cost everything she used in the analysis. The last thing she would enter would be her final report, which would remain on the file until the client was billed and the account settled.'

'And you think she might have done that before handing over the written copy?'

'There's a good chance she did.'

'How many people know about this?'

'Just myself and the lab manager.'

'Wonderful. I take it this wasn't mentioned at the meeting you and Louise had with the impostor?'

'It wasn't relevant,' said Mary Lyons. 'Although when he thanked us before leaving, I did remind him he would be getting a bill.'

Steven considered for a moment but didn't see how that could have raised any suspicion. 'It's absolutely vital that I see that report,' said Steven. 'And it goes without saying that no one else hears about it, professor.'

'Understood. When would you like to come?'

'First thing tomorrow?'

'Fine. It's Saturday. Not many people will be around, certainly not in the accounts department.'

Steven drove into Dumfries and booked himself into the County Hotel where he had a late bar supper and several gin and tonics before going upstairs to spend a restless night, waves of guilt over Louise Avery's death lapping on shores of surreal dreams in which broken bodies lay on red beaches under black cliffs and dark skies. They doused any immediate enthusiasm he might have felt for an investigation that was promising to take a turn for the better. He was up and gone by six a.m.

THIRTY-FIVE

Steven felt his pulse quicken in anticipation as he sat in Mary Lyons' office watching her use the computer keyboard on her desk to log on to the departmental server and summon up Louise Avery's file. The movement of her fingers was slow and deliberate; her eyes seemed to flick more than necessary between the keyboard and the screen. It made Steven reflect that this was an age thing. Regardless of intellectual capacity, people over a certain age often behaved as if they didn't quite belong in the company of computers.

'Here we are,' she said, followed by another silence. 'And . . . yes . . . she did file it.'

Steven closed his eyes and gave silent thanks as a tremendous weight seemed to be lifted from them both: they exchanged a rare smile. The head of department punched a few more buttons on her keyboard, the last with a final flourish, before getting up to walk across the room to her printer where she waited for it to grind into action. She returned with a copy of the report and gave it to Steven, saying, 'I hope this brings justice for Louise.'

Steven nodded and made a hesitant start on his next request, perhaps too hesitant, because Mary Lyons got in first. 'You are about to ask me to say nothing about any of this to anyone . . . including the police?'

'I know it's asking a lot, but I promise you there will be no cover-up over Louise's death. Justice will be done, perhaps in a roundabout way, but it will happen.'

They shook hands and Steven left for the drive back to London. He called ahead to the duty officer at Sci-Med and asked him to make contact with John Macmillan and relay his request that they should meet as soon as possible. He knew that Sir John and his wife often went away for the weekend but Macmillan always left a contact number at Sci-Med for emergencies. 'I'm driving down from Newcastle,' he told the duty man. 'Leaving now.'

'Anything else?'

'We're going to need scientific advice.'

'What sort?'

'Good question,' said Steven. 'An expert in transplant surgery and the science behind it.'

'I'll see who we've got on the list,' said the duty man. Sci-Med kept a list of consultants who could be called upon to offer advice. They were invariably experts in their fields who were paid a retainer but, more importantly, had the kudos of being classed as consultants to the government. 'D'you want me to call in the expert or wait until you've seen Sir John?'

'Speak to Sir John first and tell him I've requested it. See what he says and take it from there.'

'Will do.'

Steven had reached the southern end of the M1 when his phone rang and the Bluetooth car-phone speaker gave out the news that a meeting had been set up for four p.m. at the Home Office. Could he make it?

'No problem.'

*   *   *

Macmillan was already at the Home Office when Steven arrived ten minutes early. He was struggling with the coffee machine in Jean Roberts' office. Steven took over. 'Do we have an expert coming?' he asked.

'A transplant surgeon,' replied Macmillan. 'Jonathan Porter-Brown. Why do we need him?'

'We need him to spot what Louise would think was unusual in her findings. If he can do that, we might well have found why Monk killed her.'

'So why didn't our lab find it?'

'Let's hope our expert can tell us that too. We haven't compared the reports yet. There could be a difference.'

The coffee machine finally delivered the goods as Jonathan Porter-Brown arrived and was shown into the room. Steven broke off cleaning out the coffee holder to shake hands with the tall, tanned man in front of him. He was surprised to find his handshake limp and wet. 'Coffee?' he asked. 'I'm just honing my skills as a barista.'

Porter-Brown smiled. 'I'm impressed. Espresso, please.'

The three men walked through to Macmillan's office with their coffee and Macmillan thanked Porter-Brown for coming at such short notice.

'I'm a Sci-Med virgin,' the surgeon joked. 'I knew I was on your list, of course, but I haven't been called upon before. What can I do for you?'

'You're a transplant surgeon, Mr Porter-Brown, a top man in your field. We'd like your opinion on the participants in a bone marrow transplant we've become interested in. We need you to examine lab reports prepared on samples taken from the patient and the donor and to tell us if you see anything unusual about them.'

'Seems straightforward enough,' said Porter-Brown. He was

smiling but Steven couldn't help feeling that the man was nervous. There was something about his body language that suggested discomfort about being in his current surroundings. Steven found this an unusual trait in a surgeon: in his experience self-confidence – sometimes over-weening – seemed to be a prerequisite for the job. Maybe it was just the fact that the man had been summoned to the Home Office at short notice. After all, he'd just admitted that this was his first Sci-Med call-out.

Macmillan handed him the lab report on Patient X. 'This is the report on the recipient.'

'Fine,' said Porter-Brown. He read through the details and said, 'Nothing too unusual about the patient.'

'And this is the report on the donor,' said Macmillan, handing over the more detailed report prepared by the Sci-Med lab.'

'Gosh,' said Porter-Brown, leafing through the file. 'It's comprehensive, I'll say that for it . . . Was the lab being paid by the test? All that's missing is his inside leg measurement.'

Macmillan smiled but Steven was still seeing signs of nervousness in Porter-Brown as he read through the report. There was a slight line of moisture appearing above his top lip.

'I would say that the donor is as near a perfect match for the patient as you could possibly hope for,' he announced at last, putting down the file.

'Nothing unusual at all?' Macmillan probed.

'The only unusual thing I can see is the comprehensive detail in the analysis of the donor samples. Frankly, I'm not sure I know what half these things are.'

'We did request a thorough analysis,' said Macmillan.

'Well, you certainly got one, but as a transplant surgeon, all

I would be interested in is the blood and tissue type matches and they're perfect.'

Steven handed over the copy of Louise's report. 'Would you take a look at this report too?'

Porter-Brown took the file. 'Patient or donor?'

'Donor,' said Steven.

Porter-Brown started reading, but then stopped to pick up the Sci-Med donor file and began comparing them. He seemed puzzled. 'They're the same person,' he said. 'They have to be. It must be the same donor. As far as I can see, they're identical.'

'They are,' agreed Steven. 'Just different labs.'

'Oh, I see,' said Porter-Brown, his features relaxing into a knowing smile. 'You were checking up on the labs.' Steven and Macmillan smiled but didn't comment. 'Well, gentlemen, I can only say again that the donor is a perfect match for the patient. Both labs agree.'

'Nothing unusual at all?' Macmillan persisted.

Steven noticed the nervousness return to Porter-Brown, but in the end he shrugged and said, 'From my point of view, nothing at all. As for all these extra – and I have to say, prob-ably unnecessary – tests, I'm perhaps not the best person to comment. I'm only a simple surgeon, gentlemen.'

'Thank you, Mr Porter-Brown.' Macmillan smiled. 'We're indebted to you. Please accept our apologies for disturbing your weekend.'

'Glad to have been of assistance,' said Porter-Brown, getting up to go. The men shook hands again. Still moist, Steven noticed.

Macmillan accompanied Porter-Brown downstairs. When he got back, he said, 'Well, it seems we're no further forward.'

'There's something dreadfully wrong,' said Steven. 'As my old granny used to say, I can feel it in my water.'

'Can you or your granny be a little more specific?'

'I think we've just screwed up big time, asking Porter-Brown along as our expert.'

'His credentials are impeccable. He's a top man in his field,' protested Macmillan.

'I don't doubt it, but so was John Motram,' said Steven. 'That's why he was chosen in the first place. According to Cassie Motram, everyone involved in that damned transplant was a top player.'

Macmillan's eyes opened wide when he realised the full extent of what Steven was suggesting. 'Don't tell me you think Porter-Brown was actually involved in the operation?'

'It would explain why he was as nervous as a kitten throughout,' said Steven. 'That's not like a surgeon. He really didn't want to be here and I got the distinct impression he was hiding something every time you pressed him on whether or not he noticed anything unusual in the reports.'

'Bloody hell,' murmured Macmillan. 'If Porter-Brown actually carried out the transplant, where do we go from here? Talk about leaving your cards face up on the table . . .' He went to the drinks cabinet and poured sherry as if needing a distraction while he assessed the full implications. 'Alcohol can be such a blessing in times of stress, don't you think?'

Steven accepted the glass. 'They know everything,' he said.

'Only if you're right about Porter-Brown,' Macmillan reminded him.

'He would have been on the phone to the puppetmasters as soon as we called him in. They know we got our hands on Louise Avery's report after all . . .'

'But it's the same as the bloody one we already had,' protested Macmillan, starting to lose his cool.

'According to our *simple surgeon*, they are,' said Steven. 'But they can't be. I keep saying this but we're missing something.'

He picked up the two donor reports and looked at Macmillan. 'Let's go through these with a fine-tooth comb, even if it takes us all night.'

Macmillan only took a moment to concede. 'Why don't we use the audio visual equipment in one of the seminar rooms?' he suggested. 'If we see the test results side by side up on a screen, one of us might spot a difference more easily. It'll be better than sifting through masses of meaningless letters and numbers at a desk all night.'

'Good idea,' agreed Steven. 'But we don't have the reports on disk, only hard copy.'

'Then let's do things the old-fashioned way,' said Macmillan. 'There's an overhead projector in S12.'

THIRTY-SIX

The two men made their way to seminar room S12, an 'inside' room with no windows and a semicircular tier of seats facing a flat front wall, fronted by a desk, a few chairs and a lectern. Steven set up the overhead projector while Macmillan moved the lectern to one side and pulled down a projection screen from its ceiling mounting. Steven placed the first page from each of the reports side by side on the projector's glass platen and adjusted the focus until the text became sharp.

The reports had been prepared using different formats so it wasn't possible to match up all the pages, but the first page of each showed the major compatibility tests and it didn't take long for Steven and Macmillan to agree that there were no discrepancies. After that, it became progressively more difficult when the order of the tests started to vary. An hour and twenty minutes had passed before Steven murmured, 'Hang on . . .'

'Spotted something?'

'Fourth line from the top in the section headed "Co-receptors", it says CCR5 -/- in Louise's analysis, but in the other one I'm pretty sure it said . . .' Steven paused to change one of the sheets on the platen. 'Yes. Look there, in the Sci-Med lab report it says CCR5 +/+.'

'It is,' agreed Macmillan. He stared at the screen for fully thirty seconds before asking, 'Any idea what it means?'

'None at all, but it is a difference.'

'It is,' sighed Macmillan, rubbing his eyes. 'And, right now, it could be our needle in the haystack. I suggest we complete the comparison to see if we can find any others before we call in the boffins.'

Thirty minutes later both men were in agreement that there was only the one difference in the lab reports. The sound of the projector fan faded and Steven brought up the room lights.

Macmillan said doubtfully, 'Can that really be what this is all about?'

Steven felt inclined to share his doubts but said, 'I guess we won't know that until we understand what it means.'

'Let's talk to our own lab now,' said Macmillan. 'See what they have to say about the difference.'

'It's Saturday evening,' Steven pointed out.

'If what you suspect about Porter-Brown is true, time's not on our side. Get the duty man to call out Lukas Neubauer. I want him here tonight. Tell him to try for eight o'clock.'

Dr Lukas Neubauer, head of the biological section of Lundborg Analytical, seemed unfazed at being called out on a Saturday evening. When Steven mentioned this, he replied, 'Arsenal lost today; what more is there to live for?'

'There's always next season,' said Steven with a sympathetic smile, knowing that Arsenal's hopes for the Premier League title had all but gone. 'With the amount of money Sci-Med are putting your way at the moment you can probably buy them a new striker.'

The banter stopped when Macmillan entered the room and thanked Lukas for coming, apologising for the timing. He explained what the problem was and handed Lukas the two reports.

'The discrepancy seems to be in something called CCR5,'

said Steven. 'You give it a double plus while the other lab says double minus.'

Lukas, a tall, Slavic-looking man in his mid-forties, pushed his glasses up on to his forehead while he compared the two documents, holding them both up close to his face and alternating between the two. Steven, who had always got on well with him, thought he looked like an eagle contemplating his dinner as his eyes moved sharply to and fro. He knew that nothing much got past Lukas Neubauer: he was a born scientist who had to know how everything worked and how everything related to everything else.

'Interesting.'

'First, can you tell us what CCR5 is?' asked Macmillan.

'It's a co-receptor on the surface of human T4 cells,' replied Lukas, continuing to read the reports.

'Uh-huh,' said Macmillan, implying that he was still waiting for an answer to his question – one he could understand.

'The important thing from a human point of view is that viruses use it to gain entrance to human T4 cells,' said Lukas.

'What would its relevance be in a bone marrow transplant being carried out to help a leukaemia patient?'

'None at all.'

Steven felt encouraged. That would fit with what Mary Lyons had told him about Louise noticing something but she and Monk agreeing that it wasn't relevant. But he'd still gone on to kill her because she'd noticed it.

'I take it the plus signs mean that your lab found CCR5 to be present while the other lab didn't?' said Macmillan. 'A mistake on someone's part?'

'I don't think so,' said Lukas after a few moments of deep thought. 'I don't think so at all . . . You see the two plus signs? It means that we found the donor to have inherited the CCR5 factor from both mother and father. The other lab, however, has reported a double minus, which means that the donor would have no CCR5 at all. They had inherited a lack of this receptor from both their mother and father, not a common occurrence. Homozygous, we call it. There's actually a name for this negative mutation, by the way. It's called Delta 32.'

'Does this lack of CCR5 have drawbacks?' asked Macmillan.

'Not as far as we know, but it does have distinct advantages. Delta 32 individuals are immune to certain viruses – the viruses can't get inside their cells. I don't suppose it has any relevance here, but there's also a connection with research into Black Death.'

'Of course,' said Steven, suddenly remembering the précis of John Motram's research he had read in the file Jean Robert had prepared for him at the start of the investigation. 'It was the Delta 32 mutation that changed in frequency in the European population after Black Death struck.'

Lukas nodded. 'It seems it was a huge advantage to be Delta 32 at the time.'

'This was the basis of John Motram's research,' said Steven. 'The fact that Delta 32 made you immune to Black Death suggests that it was caused by a virus and not bubonic plague. He's an expert on Delta 32.'

'Which may be why he was invited on to the transplant team in the first place, if what we're seeing here is anything to go by,' said Macmillan, seeing another piece fit the puzzle.

'So', said Steven, turning to Lukas, 'if Louise says the donor was Delta 32 and you say he wasn't . . . which one of you is right?'

'Both of us,' said Lukas.

Steven and Macmillan looked at each other as if struggling to keep up. 'You can't both be right,' said Steven.

'Yes we can . . . if the samples came from different people,' said Lukas. 'That's my guess.'

'Just when I thought we were making progress . . .' said Macmillan.

'But I saw the samples divided up myself,' said Steven. 'I watched Louise Avery do it. She kept one set; I brought the other set back for you.'

'The airport,' said Macmillan suddenly. 'The samples were taken from you at Heathrow Airport. They were out of your possession for several hours.'

Steven rubbed his forehead as he thought about that. 'But if you're suggesting the samples were swapped before they gave us them back for analysis, it implies they already had samples from someone else . . . who was also a perfect donor for Patient X . . .'

'But didn't have the Delta 32 mutation,' said Macmillan.

'All ready and waiting,' said Lukas.

The implausibility of the scenario brought about a silence that lasted until Steven's face broke into a broad grin and he exclaimed, 'No, they didn't. They swapped them for samples taken from the *patient*. That wouldn't have been a problem: they already had those. The samples they gave us back came from Patient X. The only difference between him and Michael Kelly was the fact that Kelly was Delta 32 and that's what they were trying to hide. Louise had analysed the correct donor samples and noticed the difference so she had to go.'

'Well, we got there in the end,' sighed Macmillan. 'Now all we need is for Lukas to tell us why. Can you?'

Lukas smiled. 'Actually, I can. The Delta 32 mutation is the answer to a scientific riddle,' he said. 'For some years scientists have known that certain people were immune to the HIV virus. It didn't seem to matter how often they were exposed to the

214

virus or what lifestyle they led, they never become HIV positive and as a consequence never developed AIDS. This, of course, is hugely interesting to medical science because there's no cure on the horizon and not much hope of a vaccine either. It turns out that the HIV virus uses the CCR5 receptor to gain entrance to its victims' T4 cells and set up the infection. If you don't have CCR5, the HIV virus can't get in. It's as simple as that. If you get Delta 32 from one parent but not the other, you'll have a reduced risk of infection. If you get Delta 32 from both, you'll be totally immune.'

'So Michael Kelly was totally immune to the HIV virus,' said Macmillan. 'Why should that matter to a leukaemia patient?'

'Because the recipient wasn't a leukaemia patient,' said Steven, shaking his head as he suddenly realised what the whole affair had been about. Lukas nodded his agreement. He'd seen it too. 'They were trying to change the HIV status of someone who was HIV positive . . . someone who was very important . . . someone who was worth killing several people for.'

Macmillan appeared shocked. 'Can you do that?' he asked. 'Is such a thing possible?'

'It is just possible,' said Lukas. 'A German doctor carried out the procedure in Berlin a couple of years ago. His patient was an HIV positive man, dying from leukaemia: he desperately needed a bone marrow transplant. As an experiment, he was given a transplant from a donor who happened to be Delta 32 from both parents. The patient's HIV status changed to negative. As far as I know, it has remained that way. There wasn't too much press coverage about it because the medical establishment made it clear that this kind of procedure could never become the norm.'

'That would explain the wide search for a donor,' said Steven. 'That's why they had to cast the net so widely, hunt through all the civilian and military records. They weren't just looking for a perfect match for a marrow transplant: they were looking for a perfect match who was also Delta 32 from both parents.'

'So now we know,' murmured Macmillan.

'It's still a very risky thing to do,' said Steven. 'For this kind of marrow transplant, the patient's own immune system has to be destroyed by whole body irradiation over many hours.'

'So it would be a dangerous thing to do to a patient who didn't have otherwise terminal leukaemia?' asked Macmillan.

'Incredibly so,' agreed Steven.

'But evidently someone – or some people – thought the risk was justified to do just that to Patient X?'

'Apparently.'

'So they brought in the best brains that money could buy, found the best donor and took over the best facilities to carry out the procedure. Well,' announced Macmillan, 'they're not getting away with it. They've left a trail of destruction across the country and by God, they're going to pay for it. Of all the arrogant . . .' Words failed him.

THIRTY-SEVEN

'So what's our first move?' asked Steven.

'Now that we know what's behind it all, we use the proof we have that Michael Kelly was infected in St Raphael's and that his lack of aftercare contributed significantly to his death to call in the Met and force the hospital to reveal the name of Patient X and the names of those responsible for his care – if you can call it that.'

'We shouldn't underestimate the strength of the opposition,' said Steven. 'They may not be "official" but they've shown they have enormous power and influence.'

'I don't give a damn,' said Macmillan. 'I want them outed, every single last one of them.'

'If Patient X turns out to be a foreign potentate they may invoke diplomatic immunity or even the Official Secrets Act to neutralise any police inquiry.'

'My line will be that defence of the realm involves defending its citizens, not maiming and killing them,' said Macmillan. 'Wouldn't you agree?'

'Absolutely,' said Steven. He enjoyed seeing his boss on his high horse. 'I just think we should both be aware of what we could be up against when things turn really nasty. It's not just those who've been calling in favours who'll be after our blood, it'll be those who granted them too. The guys at Rorke's Drift probably faced better odds than us.'

'Doing the right thing is never easy, Steven,' said Macmillan. He let out a long sigh. 'It's been a long day. Can I offer you gentlemen a drink at my club?'

'Make mine a large one,' said Steven.

'My mother-in-law is staying with us at the moment,' said Lukas. Steven and Macmillan looked at him to see what this piece of information would translate into. 'A drink sounds good.'

The three men left the Home Office and started the ten-minute walk over to Macmillan's club. 'Have you heard if Dr Motram's making any improvement?' he asked Steven.

'I phoned his wife a couple of nights ago,' said Steven. 'The hospital is being very conservative with its prognosis but Cassie thinks he may have recognised her the last time she visited. The problem is that no one's certain about the long-term effects of the toxin. It could still prove to be a false dawn. Even if it isn't, it's going to be a long process.'

'Poor woman,' said Macmillan. 'One day you're married to one of the brightest scientists in the country, next you're wondering how you're going to teach him to read and write.'

As they entered the park, Steven stepped in front of the other two so that they wouldn't be walking three abreast and taking up too much room on the path while there were joggers about. Many seemed to be more concerned with looking at some instrument on their wrists than looking where they were going.

'At least they're not on bloody bicycles,' growled Macmillan, who seldom missed an opportunity to have a go at what he saw as a particularly self-righteous section of society, hell-bent on impeding his progress through the city.

One jogger, coming towards them, threw his empty plastic water bottle into the bushes in front of them and let out a great, hacking cough as he passed.

'Typical,' snapped Macmillan. 'Whatever happened to . . .'

He didn't finish the sentence. Instead, he collapsed to the ground and was unconscious by the time Steven got down on his knees beside him, frantically seeking a pulse. 'Call an ambulance, Lukas, would you? He must be having a heart attack.'

The ambulance was there within three minutes and two green-clad paramedics took over from Steven, who answered Lukas Neubauer's question as he got up with a simple, 'I'm afraid I don't know. There were no warning signs: he didn't complain of any chest pain or even feeling unwell. He just seemed to go out like a light. The sooner they get him to hospital the better.'

Macmillan's unconscious body was loaded gently into the back of the vehicle and the driver held the door while Steven got in. Lukas seemed hesitant and had just started to say that he didn't think he would come along when the other paramedic jumped down from the vehicle. 'It may be swine flu, sir,' he said by way of explanation. 'You'll need to come along and be given protection.' He more or less pushed Lukas inside and slammed the doors shut.

This strange behaviour, followed by the realisation that neither of the paramedics was in the back of the vehicle as it took off from the kerb, filled Steven with alarm. Something was wrong. Other signs came thick and fast. He saw that the front and rear sections of the ambulance had been strengthened with steel tubing and wire mesh: there were no internal door handles. They were effectively being held in a steel cage. The fact that the vehicle was not using its siren also registered when he heard another ambulance in the distance – the one they'd actually called for.

'It's a set-up,' he growled as he started tending to Macmillan – no easy task in the fast-moving vehicle. It was obvious now that the two men in the front had been lying in wait for them, all set to ensure their 'ambulance' arrived before the real one. Macmillan's collapse had been induced by something other than natural causes. Something had happened to him in the park and Steven needed to find out what.

The answer proved to be a small dart. Steven found it in the back of Macmillan's thigh. He removed it carefully. It wasn't big like the sort vets used to tranquillise animals; this one was much smaller. He hadn't seen anyone with a blowpipe in the park so he guessed it had been fired from a small air weapon, maybe a .177 calibre pistol. The dart had been modified to deliver a small volume of liquid – one millilitre at most, thought Steven. He thought back to the jogger who had distracted them in the park by throwing away a plastic bottle in front of them and then given a loud cough as he passed . . . it would have covered the sound of an air pistol being discharged. Too late, it was all too obvious, but Steven didn't have long to contemplate it. A gas canister was leaking its contents into the back of the vehicle.

When Steven came round, he immediately wished he hadn't: his head felt as if he'd head-butted a train and the state of his throat suggested he'd vacuumed up a small desert with it. Looking on the bright side – not easy in his present state – he reasoned that, if he felt this bad, he must at least be alive. He tried rolling over on to his side but had to postpone the operation for the time being at his head's insistence.

The last thing he remembered before passing out was thinking that his life was over. There was no way to avoid breathing in the gas that was filling the back of the ambulance and the smell hadn't given him any clue as to what it was or how dangerous it might be. It had robbed him of his senses but it had been quite a slow process, and now he felt pleased that he had not lost his dignity and given in to beseeching some non-existent deity to save him. How he faced death was important to him. Macmillan had been unconscious throughout and Lukas had used his final conscious moments to bang his fists on the insides of the vehicle demanding release, but he had curled up on the floor to think about Lisa and Jenny and Tally . . . and the good times.

He opened one eye and tried to focus on what was above him. He was indoors; he could make out a strip light on the ceiling above him. Its diffuse, bright light made him turn his head slightly to one side where he saw . . . furniture? White furniture? Maybe kitchen cupboards? It didn't smell like a kitchen though, he thought as he closed his eyes again for a moment, unless they had been using a particularly strong chemical cleaner. A groan came from somewhere in the room and concentrated Steven's mind. 'Who's there?' He was unpleasantly surprised at the gravelly sound of his voice.

'Is that you, Steven?' came the equally throaty reply.

'Lukas?'

'Yes. What the hell are we doing here?'

Steven, found that a strange reply. 'Where's here?' he asked, and swallowed, trying to clear his throat.

'My lab.'

'Your lab?' exclaimed Steven. 'They've brought us to your lab?' He had now managed to roll over on to his side and prop himself up on one elbow. He could see he was lying on the floor between two laboratory benches. 'Are you tied up?' he asked, slightly puzzled at his freedom of movement after having been kidnapped.

'No,' came the reply from the other side of the bench to his left. 'You?'

'No. Is Sir John with you?'

'Can't see him. Hang on, I'll have a look around . . . on my knees. Jesus, what was that stuff . . .'

Steven didn't reply. He was concentrating on pulling himself upright. He found that he still had to keep the palms of both hands on the bench to support his weight when he finally achieved it.

'He's up here,' said Lukas's voice from the top of the lab. 'He's coming round.'

Steven joined them. He suggested that they might all benefit from a drink of water and asked if the supply in the lab was safe to drink.

'It's mains,' replied Lukas. 'I'll get some beakers.' He rose to his feet slowly and supported himself with one hand on the bench while he slid back the glass door of a wall cupboard to take out three small, sterile glass beakers. Steven managed to prop Macmillan up in a sitting position with his back against a floor cupboard, and got up to take one of the filled beakers from Lukas and give it to him before taking one for himself. Water had never tasted so good. He could see that the others agreed.

'It's like that scene from *Ice Cold in Alex*,' said Macmillan, managing a half smile. 'Where are we?'

'The Lundborg labs,' replied Lukas, his expression a mixture of embarrassment and bemusement.

'Your labs?' exclaimed Macmillan. 'Ye gods, someone's going to have to fill me in on what's been happening.'

Steven filled in the blanks for him, ending with, 'And when we came round, we were here in Lukas's place.'

'They brought us here?' exclaimed Macmillan. 'How would they get in?'

'They must have used my electronic key,' said Lukas. 'It was in my wallet.' He searched through his pockets and was surprised to find his wallet there. He pulled out his key and said with amazement, 'They put it back.' After another check, he added, 'But they took my phone.'

'Mine too,' said Steven after a similar search.

Macmillan confirmed that his phone had gone too. 'This is crazy,' he said. 'Why bring us here and then just walk away and leave us? They take our phones but nothing else . . .'

'Maybe we've been mugged for our phones,' suggested Steven, tongue in cheek. The fact that they were alive and apparently free to go was making all three of them feel a whole lot better about life.

'Did you see them, whoever they were?' asked Macmillan.

'No. We came round just before you,' said Steven. 'We saw the two fake paramedics at the park but didn't pay them too much attention; we thought you were dying at the time. There's been no sign of anyone since we came round and it's beginning to spook me out. Monk has to be behind this and he was holding all the aces. With us three out of the way, there'd be no one left to ask awkward questions . . .'

'So why just abandon us? Why let us go?' asked Macmillan.

'What do you use this particular room for, Lukas?' asked Steven, who had recovered enough to be taking an interest in his surroundings.

'This is our biohazard lab,' replied Lukas. 'We have three labs but this is the one we'd use for handling dangerous things.'

'What's special about it?'

'It has two isolation chambers,' said Lukas, pointing to two glass-fronted boxes with stools in front of them. 'We don't have to handle many pathogenic organisms, but when we do we use these. The worker is protected by a glass screen and uses the armholes in the side to carry out manipulation of what's inside the chamber. Apart from that, the whole room is constantly under negative pressure so that air comes in but doesn't flow out. In addition to that, there's an airlock system on the door. We also have UV irradiation lamps to sterilise the room when no one's in it.

'Are we locked in?' asked Macmillan.

'We can't be,' said Lukas. 'They didn't keep my card. It's a master key.' He took it from his wallet and started to go towards the door.

'Stop!' yelled Steven.

THIRTY-EIGHT

'Don't touch the door,' said Steven. 'You said the room was under constant negative pressure but listen . . . the ventilation system isn't running at all.'

'We turn it off at the weekend,' said Lukas, and then had immediate second thoughts. 'But on the other hand, it should have started up automatically when someone came in here . . .'

Steven, who had been wandering round the lab, inspecting the benches, held up two glass petri dishes, one in either hand, and asked Lukas what they were.

Lukas looked puzzled as he walked over to join Steven. 'We don't leave cultures of micro-organisms lying around ever,' he said. He took one from Steven and examined it closely. 'It's like some kind of fungus,' he said. 'I don't understand it. This has nothing to do with us.' He looked at the other paraphernalia on the bench, more petri dishes, racks of test tubes, flasks. 'We haven't been working on anything like this. I've no idea how any of this got here . . .'

'I have,' said Steven. 'Monk's been setting the scene for one of his "accidents".'

Macmillan, who had now joined the other two at the bench, surveyed the scene and could take little comfort from the look on Steven's face. 'Go on,' he said.

'I don't think this is just any fungal culture,' said Steven. 'It's the organism they used on John Motram. The cultures have been left here to make it look as if we were investigating the organism when we had our accident. At least, that's what the authorities are supposed to think when they find us with our brains turned to mush.'

'But how?' asked Macmillan. 'We're not going to contaminate ourselves with these.' He eyed the cultures on the bench. 'Are we?'

'No,' said Steven thoughtfully. 'They're window dressing. We were supposed to come round, thank our lucky stars we were still alive and then walk out of here . . . and that's when it'll happen.'

The other two followed him over to the airlock exit where he stopped and turned round to look up at the ceiling, in particular the rectangular wire grating above them.

'That's for the positive pressure airflow into the room,' said Lukas, following Steven's line of sight. 'Air leaving the lab has to go through the filter system over there, maintaining a pressure differential.' He pointed to a series of extractor units on the other side of the room.

'It's my bet the system's been loaded with toxic spores of this organism,' said Steven. 'As soon we trigger the door release, the fans will spring into life, flooding the room with fungal spores instead of the fresh air they're supposed to pump in. Monk will have jammed the door on the other side of the airlock so we can't get out.'

'So we're trapped,' said Macmillan, reaching a conclusion no one felt inclined to argue with.

'Unless we can come up with a way of getting out of here without triggering the ventilation system,' said Steven, looking at Lukas, who shook his head.

'There are half a dozen safety systems in place to make sure that it does turn on whenever it looks as if the lab is going to be open to the outside world,' he said. 'There's even an auxilliary back-up if mains electricity should fail.'

'Shit.'

'What happens if we just sit tight and wait?' asked Macmillan. 'I mean, I know it could be a long weekend for us, but when one of Lukas's people arrives on Monday morning . . .'

'They'd trigger the fans; we'd be dead by the time they figured out how to open the door and it would still look like an accident. Besides, Monk isn't going to let that happen. He's going to come back to check on things and unjam the door mechanism so his "accident" looks perfect.'

'If you're right about all this and we should breathe in these spores, how long have we got?' asked Lukas.

'Depends how long it takes us to kill each other,' said Steven, to the horrified looks of the other two. 'I've thought a lot about what happened to John Motram. I'm sure the Public Health and hospital people up in Scotland identified the fungus correctly, but they weren't to know that it had been genetically modified. John Motram's symptoms had Porton Down written all over them . . . the madness, the aggression. This bug', he held up one of the dishes, 'has been designed as a bio-weapon. The clever thing to do these days is not to design weapons that kill but to come up with ones that will cause maximum disruption and create a huge drain on your enemies' resources. Something that drives your victim mad and turns him into a homicidal maniac, intent on killing his comrades, would be seen as the perfect weapon. The fact that the victim doesn't die himself but develops breathing problems and liver disease, demanding expensive and intensive medical care as well as restraint, would be seen as the icing on the cake.'

Macmillan shook his head. 'How would Monk get his hands on something like that?'

Steven shrugged. 'The old pals act again?' he suggested. 'A friend of a friend at Porton thought they might like to see how their latest project worked in practice? The tomb opening at Dryburgh would have been seen as the perfect scenario for a test run.'

Macmillan looked ashen and Steven knew why. Sir John was of the old school and, despite plenty of evidence to the contrary over the years, couldn't bring himself to believe that the UK would involve itself in such things. He'd never quite embraced the concept that you had to be as bad as the bad guys in order to survive. 'This is still all supposition,' he said, without much conviction.

'Then let's hope I'm wrong.'

'What d'you think Monk will do when he comes back and finds us still alive?' asked Lukas.

'Trigger the fans,' said Steven.

'Stupid question,' Lukas conceded.

'As I see it,' said Macmillan, 'we've no evidence that what Steven is suggesting is right but we can't take the risk of putting it to the test. We have to find a way of getting out of here without triggering the ventilation system.'

'Easier said than done,' said Steven, who was becoming edgy. He was very conscious of the fact that time was ticking by and Monk would be coming back.

'Surely we could afford to trigger the system as long as we could get out quickly enough afterwards?'

'We'd have to hold our breath for as long as it took.'

'What I was thinking of was an explosion,' said Macmillan. 'If we could blow a hole in the wall, we could escape to the outside. Do you have the wherewithal to do that, Lukas?'

Lukas looked doubtful. 'It's a biology lab, Sir John,' he said. 'We don't have much call for things that go bang . . .' He looked to the glass-fronted chemical cupboards without much conviction.

'What's in the red cylinder?'

'Hydrogen. We use it for creating anaerobic conditions for bacteria that don't like oxygen.'

'I seem to remember you can get a pretty fair bang with hydrogen gas, can't you?'

'You certainly can,' interrupted Steven, who was losing patience. 'There's no doubt we have the ability to blow ourselves to kingdom come, which might be quicker than the fungal route, but as for blowing a hole in the wall, forget it. Unless Lukas can come up with something like nitro-glycerine – or anything else that we could create a *controlled, localised* explosion with – we can forget the big bang theory.'

'Sorry,' said Lukas. 'No can do.'

'So where do we go from here?' said Macmillan.

Steven looked at his watch. 'We came round about twenty minutes ago. Monk would expect us to have walked into the trap and be fighting each other to the death by now. He'll probably be back here some time within the next hour to . . . tidy up loose ends.'

'Christ,' said Lukas. Macmillan said nothing.

'As I see it, there's no possibility of disabling the ventilation system for the reasons Lukas gave earlier – too many safety mechanisms – so that just leaves one option. We've got to remove the spores from the system. Monk and his pals couldn't have had that much time to set this up so it's my guess it will be something fairly simple inserted in the trunking above us. I've got to get up there to see if I can find it. What d'you think, Lukas? Is there room?'

Lukas looked unsure, glancing first at Steven and then at the grating above them. 'Could be a tight fit. You certainly won't be turning round much once you're in there.'

'Let's do it,' said Steven with an air of finality that spurred them into action, collecting lab furniture to make a platform below the grating. 'I'll need a screwdriver, a torch, maybe some wet cloths, wire cutters if possible but scissors or a knife at a pinch.'

'We've got a torch,' said Lukas, breaking off from platform building to open a series of drawers, one after the other, making them bang on their stops and remind everyone of the urgency of their situation. 'And a screwdriver . . . no wirecutters, I'm afraid . . . shit, where are the scissors? . . . plenty of scalpels . . . no cloths; we use disposable towels, but I can rip up a lab coat . . .'

Steven acknowledged the growing inventory with grunts as he undid the screws holding the grating on the ceiling.

'What happens if the grating's wired to the ventilation system?' asked Macmillan, holding the platform steady while looking up at Steven.

'We're fucked,' replied Steven without stopping.

Macmillan looked away. 'Can't complain about a nice clear answer, I suppose,' he murmured.

Steven removed the grating and lowered it to Lukas, who had returned to the platform with the bits and pieces he'd collected. In exchange, he took the things Lukas handed up to him and put them inside the open hatch. There was no point in putting anything in his pockets because there wouldn't be room to move his arms behind him once he was inside the trunking. He did, however, slip a couple of the scalpels between his wrist and his watch strap. He'd have to nudge everything else along in front of him. Finally, he took off his sweater and shirt and dropped them to the ground. With a last look below, he gripped the edges of the hatch, bent his knees and muttered, 'Up we go.'

THIRTY-NINE

There was a moment, after heaving himself up through the opening, that Steven thought it was not going to be possible. There had been just enough room for him to launch himself headfirst into the trunking, but he was left with his arms pinned behind him and no means of propelling himself forwards or backwards. He felt trapped like a cork in a bottle.

He had to fight off panic. Panic only ever made things worse. Uncoordinated wriggling was getting him nowhere. He focused only on his right arm, harnessing every bit of movement he could manage into bringing it underneath him and then wriggling it up past the side of his face until he could push it out freely in front of him. This instantly gave him confidence and more room to repeat the procedure with his left arm. With both arms in front of him, he found he could get some purchase. He was on the move.

He switched on the torch and looked at what lay ahead: a stretch of trunking running straight for about six metres but then meeting a T-junction, which would call for his first decision. He turned off the torch to save the batteries while he covered the six metres, something he did painfully slowly, his throat becoming dry and sweat running down his face in the hellish heat of the confined space.

He discovered there was no decision to make at the junction at all. The spur to the right led only to a blank plate about a metre away with bolts protruding through it, suggesting it might be some kind of inspection hatch. Steven's spirits soared momentarily when he thought that this might actually be a way out for all of them if the hatch led to a different room in the building, but further examination brought him back to reality. He could only see long threaded shafts of the bolts: the heads were on the outside of the plate. There was no way of turning them from the inside.

He turned his attention to what lay to the left and saw the large, motionless fan. It filled the trunking about eight metres back from the junction. The torch he was using wasn't powerful. It picked out the blades of the fan well enough and he could see its supporting framework, but he couldn't see what he wanted to see, the mechanism to inject fungal spores into the airflow. Did it exist? Steven felt his confidence wobble.

If the mechanism did exist, it would have to be located on this side of the fan for him to do anything about it. Should it turn out to be on the far side, he would have no way of reaching it. He'd be left looking at it through the mocking blades of the fan. He started wriggling forwards again.

By now he was blinking constantly to clear away the sweat that was running freely into his eyes, but at least the perspiration from his body was reducing friction and allowing him to move more easily through the metal trunking. He stopped after three metres to turn on the torch again but still couldn't see anything rigged in front of the fan. He turned off the torch and rested his head on his arms. Despair was threatening and was only being kept in its place by thoughts of a training sergeant of long ago, shouting at him in the mountains of North Wales when sleet was falling and winter winds were howling. 'When you think you've got nothing left to give, Mr Dunbar . . . you fucking well have, so get off your arse and let's do that all over again, shall we?'

Steven stopped about two metres from the fan and clicked on the torch. There it was, the most beautiful sight in the world, the protruding top of a round, pressurised container, by the look of it. It had been inserted in front of the fan from the room below. The trigger mechanism appeared primitively simple, a wire from the container attached to one of the fan blades. When the fan started turning, a valve would be ripped out of the top of the container and the contents would spray out into the airflow.

Steven moved closer and examined everything thoroughly to make sure he wasn't missing anything, but as far as he could see he wasn't. He slipped the plastic guard off one of the scalpels he'd brought with him and cut through the wire leading to the fan.

'And that's all there is to it,' he murmured, letting his head fall forward on to his outstretched arms. He lay there motionless for fully a minute, waiting for his breathing to subside until it became as shallow as a sleeper's. The sweat continued to trickle down his face but it didn't bother him any longer, he even took childish pleasure in charting the path of each drop as it sought the easiest contour of his face to follow. It was over; he'd done it; they were safe. In a few moments he would start the long wriggle backwards and return to the lab. Once down there, they could press the door release with impunity, enter the airlock space and batter their way through the jammed outer door.

Feeling physically exhausted but filled with enormous relief, Steven summoned up the energy to start the retreat. As he'd feared, wriggling backwards proved to be even more difficult than going forwards: a different undulating motion was called for, a more unnatural movement that had him gasping for breath by the time he'd backed up to the junction. He started to lose his temper when he encountered difficulty in trying to make the ninety-degree turn backwards: his legs seemed too long.

He had exhausted his entire vocabulary of swear words, used in every combination he could think of, when he finally succeeded in making it round the corner. He had to rest for a few moments to recover his equilibrium, the merest suggestion of a cool breeze caressing his cheek . . .

The breeze became a hurricane; the fan had been switched on. Steven yelled out but had to bow his head against the blast as the implications hit home like stab wounds. Monk had returned; he was down there. Christ, he'd been in sight of the finishing line and this had to happen . . . Monk was going to win: he would still be able to set up his accident and get away with it.

For the second time in a few hours, Steven found himself facing the prospect of death without any hope of a reprieve. As she grew up, Jenny would tell her friends that her daddy had died in an accident when she was young, but at least Tally wouldn't have to tell people she was a widow. 'I'm so sorry, love,' he murmured. 'You were right, I was wrong.'

Bizarrely, his old training sergeant popped up inside his head again. 'It ain't over till it's over, Mr Dunbar.'

Steven had to admit that what the maxim lacked in literary merit it had more than made up for as a mindset in the past. He would not face death with calm acceptance and dignity, as he had been prepared to do in the ambulance, but as a warrior who had served his country well and was looking for any opportunity to go down fighting right to the bitter end.

He'd left the torch and the other various bits and pieces up by the fan when he'd thought his task was over, but he still had one of the scalpels. he'd tucked into his watch strap on the inside of his wrist. This would be his only weapon, should he get a chance to use it, a slim steel handle with a painfully

234

thin three-centimetre blade that would shatter on the slightest impact but had an edge so sharp it would cut flesh to the bone before anything was felt.

Steven knew that he was in no physical condition to take on Monk. Apart from the lingering after-effects of the earlier gassing, his escapade in the trunking had used up just about all the stamina he had. Monk was a borderline psychopath with MI5 training behind him and probably armed, although he wouldn't want to use bullets if an 'accident' was still the plan.

'Come along, Dunbar, don't take all day,' came the shout from below as Steven moved closer to the hatch and felt his feet slide into the gap. The voice sounded upper class and amused. Steven felt his throat tighten with apprehension as he started to rotate, pushing himself up on to his elbows and letting his feet dangle above the improvised platform while he looked down for a footing.

'Easy now, we don't want you falling and hurting yourself.'

Steven took in that Macmillan and Lukas were sitting on adjacent lab stools, their hands secured behind them, although he couldn't make out how. He couldn't see Monk and that was an important factor so he held himself in the gap, using his arms to keep himself suspended while he waited for him to speak again. He needed to know where Monk was so that he could obscure the presence of the scalpel on his descent.

'No use delaying the inevitable, Dunbar,' came the languid voice from below.

The sound came from his left.

Using up what he feared might be perilously close to the last of his remaining strength, Steven moved round the lip of the gap so that the outer aspect of his left arm would be facing Monk as he lowered himself. His feet made contact with the platform of lab furniture and it shook slightly as he steadied himself. Monk was standing some four metres away, looking relaxed and holding a gun in his right hand. Steven, exhausted, naked to the waist, bathed in sweat and covered in grime from the trunking, felt close to capitulation, but that sergeant was still in his ear. *It ain't over . . .*

He hung his head, appearing totally exhausted but in reality looking for the most secure part of the platform, the bit that would give him most purchase to spring from if he got the chance to play his last gambit.

Monk took a step closer. 'They told me you were SAS, Dunbar. Maybe it was the Girl Guides . . .'

The step closer was what Steven had been hoping for. Monk had moved into range and it was now or never. In one last, adrenalin-fuelled surge, Steven whipped out the scalpel from the inside of his left wrist, dropped down to the secure part of the platform he'd identified and launched himself headlong at Monk.

Monk didn't see it coming. He'd been so completely in charge of events that the remote possibility of the exhausted wreck of the man in front of him turning into fourteen stone of flying avenger had not even appeared on his horizons. He had no time to contemplate his mistake. Steven brought the scalpel blade across his throat and brought his life to a very messy end as they both crashed to the ground.

Steven had intended nothing else. There had been no question of trying to overpower Monk and turn him over to the machinery of justice. That was for schoolboys' comics and story books. His one chance of survival had been to kill Monk with one blow and he'd done it, a success that now had him leaning over a lab sink being very sick. When he'd recovered enough, he freed Macmillan and Lukas. He'd no sooner done so than he had to return to the sink.

He felt an encouraging squeeze on his shoulder and half turned to see Macmillan, who said, 'I'm glad you can still feel that way,' and then left him alone with his thoughts and a very empty stomach.

Macmillan took control of the situation. He busied himself making phone calls and invoking Home Office authority to see that a clean-up operation avoiding the usual channels was put in motion while Steven and Lukas, now out of the lab and sitting in the Lundborg staffroom, sought a return to normality.

Lukas was in a state of shock. He'd scarcely said anything in the past ten minutes, choosing instead to stare down at the floor, apparently deep in thought but in truth transfixed by what he'd witnessed. Steven sought temporary escape through noting the trappings of everyday life around him, the *What Car* magazines, postcards from sunny places pinned on the wall, a row of coffee mugs with names of cartoon characters on them, the cash box for extra cups of tea and coffee. These were the things normal people had in their lives, people who didn't do what he'd just done . . . *had to do*, he reminded himself, *had to do*. But he feared that that judgement was destined to be questioned again and again, probably in the wee small hours of those nights when self-doubt came to call.

FORTY

Macmillan joined them. 'They'll be here soon and then we can all go home and get some rest. Steven, I've asked for a bio-hazard team as well as the cleaners. Perhaps you can fill them in about the location of the spores and how best to remove them?'

Steven nodded.

'You did well,' said Macmillan. 'I know you're not feeling at your best right now but you did what you had to do. If it weren't for you, none of us would be alive right now. It sounds very inadequate, but thank you.'

'Yes, thank you, Steven,' added Lukas, managing the semblance of a smile. 'On behalf of my wife and children, thank you very much. I never thought lab work could be so . . .' He failed to find the word.

Steven acknowledged their thanks with a nod but really didn't want to hear any more about it. The horror of what he'd done – *had to do* – was still too fresh in his mind. 'Did Monk tell you any more about what's been going on?' he asked.

'Nothing,' replied Macmillan. 'Arrogant, cold as ice and far too clever to engage in gloating or boasting. I've come across his type before. He would have killed us all without batting an eyelid. When he discovered you'd disabled his set-up in the ventilation system, there was no display of temper: he just took it in his stride and moved on to Plan B. Nothing was going to stop him achieving his objective.'

Steven closed his eyes and saw Monk pushing Louise Avery over a Solway cliff to her death. 'And that objective was to keep us all quiet about an operation to change some rich bastard's HIV status,' he said.

'I agree,' said Macmillan, picking up on the nuance in Steven's voice. 'It's beyond belief.'

Two black, unlettered vans arrived in the car park outside and two teams of technicians, eight in all, clad in white cover-all suits, began the business of cleaning up the aftermath of Dunbar vs Monk, after being briefed by Macmillan. The first thing they did was to zip Monk's body into a body bag and remove it. There would be no police involvement, no forensic examination, no photographs, no bagging of samples and ultimately no need to call on the Crown Prosecution Service because there would be no court case. Monk had lived outside the law: that's where he would stay.

Two of the technicians were seconded to Steven to receive instructions for the removal of the spores. One of them insisted on calling him 'guv'. Their first question was whether or not they'd need full bio-hazard gear. Steven assured them that that wouldn't be necessary: the container hadn't been breached. One of them already had a plan of the building ventilation system so Steven was able to pinpoint the location for them. 'It was inserted from below so it should come out the same way,' he said. 'It's pressurised, so be careful.'

'Right, guv.'

'Immerse it in disinfectant fluid as soon as it comes out.'

It was shortly after one a.m. when the vans finally drove off. The lab had been restored to its former pristine state – no mean feat considering the amount of blood that had been around – and the canister containing the spores had been neutralised as instructed. After a short hiatus, the cars that Macmillan had requested to take the three of them home turned up outside. Lukas locked the front doors of the lab and, in an attempt at humour, said, 'I'm not sure what I'm going to tell my mother-in-law.'

'I wouldn't go for the truth,' said Steven.

Steven knew he wouldn't sleep so didn't bother trying. He stayed up, sitting in his seat by the window, looking up at the sky, listening to Miles Davis, drinking gin. He found it hard to analyse his feelings now that he'd had time to consider. The only thing he was sure of was that he didn't feel good. On the odd occasion he did manage to drift off into shallow sleep, it was to a world full of bad dreams, no place to be; he was glad to be jarred into wakefulness again.

When the first grey light of dawn challenged the orange glow of the city's street lights, he forced himself to get up and face a new day, starting with a long shower – although he had the feeling of trying to rinse something away that wasn't going to go – and following that with toast and coffee. He'd been told by Macmillan to be at the Home Office by nine a.m.

'I've asked the commissioner of the Met to join us,' said Macmillan. 'We're going to tell him everything and make it clear that Sci-Med will not be party to any kind of cover-up. We want this whole sorry, misconceived business out in the open regardless of the identity of Patient X.'

'Good,' said Steven. He didn't doubt Macmillan's sincerity but did wonder about the practicality of what he intended. There had been occasions in the past when Sci-Med had been forced to back off in the 'public interest', but to be fair to Macmillan those instances had been few and far between and more than eclipsed by the times the man had stood his ground against some pretty serious pressure from the corridors of power.

In his time, Macmillan had presided over the demise of some very influential people who'd imagined themselves above the law. It was common knowledge that this alone had delayed his knighthood for many years.

Steven listened while Macmillan related all that had happened to the police commissioner, adding details when requested, particularly about the treatment of Michael Kelly and the 'accident' that had killed Louise Avery. When Macmillan had finished, the commissioner remained silent for a few moments, tapping his pen end over end on the table before finally saying, 'I knew something was going on. It's impossible to be in my job and not realise that. Rumours were rife but none of my people could quite get a handle on it. This usually means there's intelligence service involvement, but that didn't appear to be the case . . . at least not officially.'

Steven empathised with the commissioner. He was voicing the sort of frustration that he and Macmillan had felt over the past few weeks.

'Strikes me the whole thing has been orchestrated by a parcel of rogues,' said Sir John.

'But powerful ones,' said the commissioner.

'Be that as it may . . .' began Macmillan. He launched into a second insistence that there should be no cover-up. When he had finished, the commissioner got up from his chair.

'I think I should confer with some people and get back to you, say, in two hours, time? Better make that three, as it's Sunday.'

'Well, the game's afoot, Watson,' murmured Macmillan as he returned from seeing the commissioner out, but there was little humour in it. 'A drink?'

Steven had no desire to be anywhere near alcohol. 'Maybe a walk in the park?' he suggested. 'Or by the river?' he said quickly when he realised that seeing joggers in the park was only going to invoke memories of the previous evening. 'The river,' said Macmillan, who'd seen the same thing.

They had scarcely started to enjoy the sense of stability that Sunday morning by the Thames was giving them when Macmillan's phone rang. Steven couldn't deduce much from his monosyllabic replies. Occasionally, Sir John asked questions but didn't seem happy with the replies he was getting.

'That was the commissioner. A meeting's been called,' he said, ending the call.

'Where?'

'At an MI5 safe house in Kent,' he said, taking care to enunciate every syllable.

FORTY-ONE

'What?' exclaimed Steven. 'Why on earth . . .'

'He told me not to ask any questions. He promised all will be revealed later. The meeting's been called for eight p.m.'

'So you don't know who's going to be there?' said Steven, making it more of a statement than a question.

'No idea,' said Macmillan. 'But I do know I don't like it. I get the feeling HMG are about to ask us to keep our mouths shut. Wouldn't surprise me if the Foreign Secretary and Minister of Defence show up in person to plead the case for secrecy on behalf of their man.'

'And if they do?'

'No deal. You know my feelings.'

'Bit of an odd venue, though,' Steven remarked.

Sensing that there was more to Steven's comment than just a passing remark, Macmillan asked what was on his mind.

'I just wondered if we'd be coming back from this meeting.'

'That was the Metropolitan Police Commissioner on the phone,' protested Macmillan. 'Not some mafia don.'

'Who has been speaking to MI5 if we're going to be using one of their places?' Steven reminded him. 'But maybe I'm just too sensitive about accidents happening these days.'

'Maybe you're right. We don't know who we can trust. I'll put everything we know on an "insurance" disk this afternoon and post it to Jean's home address with instructions as to what to do if anything should happen to us tonight. There would be no point in harming us with that in the wild.'

'I take it we'll be going down together in one of the pool cars?'

'Actually, no,' said Macmillan, sounding slightly embarrassed in the light of what they'd just been talking about. 'The idea is to keep the meeting as discreet as possible, no official cars, no official drivers.'

'Just us . . . in a remote country house,' said Steven, without expression.

This reservations were becoming infectious. 'Do you think we should call off and suggest an alternative venue?' Macmillan asked.

'No, I was just playing devil's advocate. I can't wait to see which politicians are wriggling on the end of this particular hook.

Steven picked up Macmillan at the Home Office just before six p.m. and they drove down to Kent, first to Canterbury and then on to the village of Patrixbourne where they started following more detailed directions to Lancing Farmhouse, a converted oasthouse on its outskirts.

'Peaceful,' said Steven as they crunched slowly up the drive to park in front of the old red-bricked house beside several other vehicles; two Range Rovers, a Volvo estate and a dark saloon which Steven noted had the Maserati symbol on its grille as he passed. It was eight minutes to eight and they were the last to arrive, the commissioner informed them. 'No one's going to be fashionably late then,' said Steven, sounding surprised.

'You're about to see why,' said the commissioner, leading the way through to an inner room where he paused to usher them inside. 'None of us here do "fashionably late".'

Steven had to admit he had a point. The people sitting there were the head of MI5, the head of MI6 and the head of Special Branch.

Macmillan seemed immediately on edge. He looked round the room, acknowledging each man in turn before saying, 'Well, gentlemen, we make a formidable array of monkeys. Might one ask where our political organ-grinders are?'

'No politicians will be coming, John,' said the commissioner. 'Believe it or not, no politician knows anything at all about this business.'

Macmillan looked doubtful but restricted himself to saying only, 'Do go on.'

The commissioner addressed the heads of the intelligence services. 'All of us have been aware that something's been going on over the past few weeks but none of us has been able to nail it down. We knew bits of it but not the whole story. When I spoke to John and Steven this morning, it became apparent that Sci-Med had filled in most of the blanks and well done to them, but after conferring with the rest of you I can now fill in one of the blanks for them, the most important blank of all.' He turned to Macmillan. 'John, Steven's investigations have led Sci-Med to conclude that the operation carried out at St Raphael's was to reverse the HIV status of a patient and was done as a high-level political favour for a big player in either oil or Middle Eastern politics. You came here this evening to demand that the whole affair be made public.'

Macmillan remained impassive.

'You're right about one thing, wrong about the other. George can tell us more.'

George Meacher, the head of MI5, cleared his throat. 'When the commissioner called me earlier and told me what Sci-Med had come up with, something we'd been working on suddenly started to make sense. Just over a week ago, Sir Malcolm Shand, one of our ex-ambassadors to the USSR that was, had a nervous breakdown and was taken into hospital. Our interest was aroused when it came to our ears that he was insisting his life was in danger and that someone called Monk had been detailed to kill him. Monk's name has been cropping up quite a lot recently and we, of course, knew well enough who he was. Martin here became involved because of Shand's past connections in the old Soviet bloc. We both wanted to know what Shand had been up to.'

Martin Cessford, the head of MI6, nodded and said, 'We went to have a chat with him.'

Meacher continued. 'As I said earlier, he'd had a breakdown and was in a blue funk about what he thought was going to happen to him so a lot of what he said didn't make that much sense, but he kept insisting "the others" had decided he couldn't keep a secret so Monk was going to kill him. We managed to get out of him that the secret in question had something to do with a medical operation but not much more than that. After hearing what you chaps had come up with, we went back to see Shand. We were able to assure him that he was no longer in danger: Monk's killing days were well and truly over. We let him calm down for a bit and then told him what else we knew . . . perhaps mentioning that his former friends might actively be seeking a replacement for Monk. He caved in and spilled the lot.'

The commissioner took a photograph from an A4 size envelope and held it up for all to see. 'This, gentlemen, is Patient X.'

'Christ almighty,' exclaimed Macmillan. Steven was too stunned to say anything.

Their reactions seemed to please the commissioner.

'Gentlemen,' he said, 'an hour ago I was feeling very alone, standing in front of a fan the shit had just hit. Nice of you to join me.'

Steven and Macmillan were still having trouble coming to terms with the revelation.

'His father thought they could avoid a monumental scandal by repeating the Berlin experiment so he called on his friends for help. We all know about friends in high places. Well, they don't come much higher than that. Their mistake was in bringing James Monk on board. They obviously thought that Monk could make sure everything remained a secret, but as we all know it's not the act that brings you down, it's the cover-up.'

'They entrusted a psychopathic killer with making sure no one talked . . .' said Macmillan with a shake of the head as if he couldn't believe it. 'What did they imagine would happen?'

Heads nodded in agreement.

'But he had plenty of help,' said Steven.

'People would be anxious to please without asking too many questions,' said the commissioner. 'Blind eyes would be turned, requests nodded through. You know how it goes.'

'So, if no politicians were involved, no politicians know about any of this. Is that right?' asked Macmillan.

'As far as we can determine,' said the commissioner, looking to the others for confirmatory nods and getting them. 'Which brings us all to the big question of the evening. What do we do . . . just what the fuck do we do?'

The resulting facial expressions spoke of a general reluctance to say anything, which was eventually overcome by Macmillan. 'I think we can all work out what would happen if that domino were to fall,' he said.

'Couldn't have come at a worse time. Country's in enough of a mess as it is,' said the MI5 man, getting nods of agreement.

Steven couldn't disagree with what he was hearing but he felt a mixture of anger and impotence. The cover-up had left a trail of dead and damaged people. Were they to be regarded as expendable? He couldn't hold his tongue. 'It just shows what happens when the upper classes get together with a *plan*,' he said. 'Sounds like sports day in Fuckwit City.' Macmillan shot him a disapproving glance but the others chose not to voice any dissent. 'If no politicians can be held to account, how can the families affected be compensated?'

'Difficult,' said the commissioner.

'No proper channels,' echoed one of the others.

'But thanks to Shand, we know the names of all those involved,' said the head of Special Branch. 'It's going to be difficult to prove they had any direct involvement in what Monk did but it wouldn't be that difficult to let it be known that we know what they did. Perhaps their "better nature" could be appealed to . . .'

Steven couldn't help himself. 'And that of their "friend",' he added.

'Steven . . .' began Macmillan uncertainly on the drive back to London. He was very conscious of his colleague's simmering anger. 'I think we both need some time to calm down and think things over.'

'Nope,' replied Steven. 'You'll get my resignation in the morning.'

Macmillan could only sigh. It had been a very long day. 'Take time, please.'

Steven dialled Tally's number when he got in.

'Hello?'

The sleepy sound of her voice tied his tongue in knots.

'Hello, who is this?'

'It's an unemployed double-glazing salesman wondering if you still remember him.'

'Steven? Is that really you?'

'Yup.'

'What are you talking about?'

'No more Sci-Med. I've resigned.'

'Oh, God,' exclaimed Tally, now fully awake. 'Do you really mean that?'

'Yes. Does it make a difference?'

'Your name has been the last thing on my lips every night before I went to sleep. I always wished you well but I never really thought I'd see you again . . .'

'Let's make sure that never happens?'

'Deal.'

AUTHOR'S NOTE

Although *Dust to Dust* is a work of fiction, it is based on scientific fact. A study of the CCR5 protein – a chemokine receptor on the surface of T4 cells – has shown its absence (the delta 32 mutation) to be responsible for immunity to infection by certain viruses including HIV. A sudden huge increase in the numbers of people carrying the delta 32 mutation in Europe in the fourteenth century, just after the time of the Black Death, has given rise to the suspicion that Black Death was not caused by the bubonic plague bacterium as is popularly believed but by an as yet unidentified virus.

In November 2008, a German haematologist, Dr Gero Huetter, announced that he had reversed the HIV+ve status of a patient he was treating for leukaemia by giving his patient a bone marrow transplant with material obtained from a donor who carried the delta 32 mutation from both parents. At the time of the report, the patient had been HIV-ve for two years and had not been given any anti-retroviral drugs, the standard treatment for AIDS.